Beauty

Raphael Selbourne

Tindal Street Press

Reprinted in December 2009
First published in September 2009
by Tindal Street Press Ltd
217 The Custard Factory, Gibb Street, Birmingham, B9 4AA
www.tindalstreet.co.uk

A CIP catalogue reference for this book is available
from the British Library

ISBN: 978 0 955647 67 3

Printed in Great Britain by CPI Cox & Wyman, Reading, RG1 8EX

Birmingham City Council

To my mother, father and DB

Beauty

I

Some time before dawn in Wolverhampton, Beauty Begum got up from the sofa. She stood in the middle of the living room and scratched her scalp through short hair.

'*Feshab,*' she muttered, and went to the bathroom.

She used the *budna* to clean herself and flushed the toilet. At the sink, she washed both hands and wrists three times – *Bismillah hir Rahmaanir Raheem* – rinsed her mouth with water, and cleaned her nostrils, face and ears three times. After wiping her wet hands over her hair and shaking them off, she passed her forearms under the tap, and washed her feet in the bath.

Beauty put on a clean salwar from the cupboard and looked in the mirror at the mess she had made, two months ago, of her once waist-length black hair. She'd loved her hair and would brush it for hours, alone at night, after she'd finished cleaning her uncle Mukhtar's house in Bangladesh.

He and his wife would tell her how dark-skinned she was and that no man other than Habib would marry her. She'd overeaten, starved and drunk dirty water to make herself ill, and cut all her hair off when it had started to fall out. Let everyone in the village think she was mad, too. Her uncle Mukhtar had phoned Beauty's father in England; the girl was *faggol*, crazy, and was still refusing to be a proper wife to Habib Choudhury, the forty-five-year-old mullah of the village.

It had been a good match. He was a Choudhury, high *zat*, and they were *hom zat*. Low.

Beauty put her blanket and pillow in the cupboard under the stairs, and went back to the living room. After praying, she stood and looked down at the Parkfields estate from the third-floor window of the 'Dene' – a long, squat block of two-storey flats on a grassy mound. In the darkness outside, street lamps caught the drizzle and lit up the other blocks and the paths that led from black stairwells to half-empty car parks. Her eyes ran absently along the doorways, looking for signs of life. Between the flats, a taxi slipped past the row of shops on the road into town.

Al-lāh, where are we?

And what kind of a name was *Woolverhamtun*?

She'd been sent to Bangladesh to marry mullah Choudhury when she was fourteen, and since that first night five years ago when he'd come to her room and tried to lie on top of her and she'd screamed so loudly that he'd given up, she had managed to keep him away from her. She was still too young, his family had said, give it time. But Habib Choudhury was desperate to marry someone with a British passport and join his brother in the UK. He'd waited and waited, until finally Beauty had acted loony and her father – the old man – had come to fetch her. Convincing them she was mad had been her only way out. With her passport hidden from her and no money, where would she have run?

When they arrived in England the old man told her that he'd moved the family from London to Wolverhampton to be nearer her mum's relatives. By now Beauty no longer cared that they didn't tell her anything. They hadn't told her about the mullah.

4

Beauty had been outside twice since she'd been back; the first time to the shop and the Chick King – Southern Fried Chicken 'n' Kebabs – with her little brother, Faisal. The shop, a newsagent and off-licence, rented Bollywood films, sold overpriced tins and stuff in fridges to the white people who ate that kind of thing, and was the only place in the area that did top-ups. The old white lady in front of her in the queue had put a pound on her electricity card.

At Chick King the kebabs were quite good, not as good as in London where she had grown up, but not bad. Faisal had thought he saw her returning the Sikh guy's smile, so she hadn't been allowed to go there again. He'd poked her in the back all the way up to the flat and called her a *magi*. That night she'd thought about the Sikh's silver bangle and the dark hair of his forearms, and hated herself for it. Maybe Faisal was right; she was like a prostitute.

Beauty watched the lights come on in the windows of a flat in the block opposite. A door opened and a man hurried along the walkway to the stairwell, pulling his coat on as he walked.

What a place this was! Full of white tramps and Sikhs. There were lots of *hallahol* as well, which was good. Black girls weren't as scary as whites.

There were masses of Somalis in this part of town. She liked the way the girls did their headscarves. All the other kids were Somali at the mosque where Faisal and Sharifa, her little sister, went after school. They were the only two Asian kids there. That was one good thing.

If you go near Asians, that's it: 'Oh, did you hear your daughter's going out with this one? Did you hear your son's doing this?'

She went through to the kitchen to drink some tea on her own before the day started. She'd have to make sure the little ones got up to pray and were ready for school. Only they weren't so little any more. Faisal was thirteen now, and Sharifa nine. Her mother would be up at midday. Her older brother, Dulal – she always called him *Bhai-sahb*, brother – worked nights in a chicken processing factory; she would have time to cook for him and get his clothes ready when she got back home at four o'clock.

If she hadn't had to go into town to the Jobcentre course, she'd have spent the rest of the day making lunch.

Whatever they wanna eat, so you've got to cook.

She washed their clothes or cleaned the bathrooms, made dinner, did the ironing and made supper; then tea, tea, tea as they watched Bangla TV or twenty-four hour news into the night. When the old man went to bed she could take the blanket out of the cupboard, lie on the sofa and talk herself to sleep. She played out fights with her family, or scenes with boys whose faces she couldn't see. Mostly, she talked to herself.

The old man came into the kitchen dressed in his *longhi*. The darkness under his eyes almost reached the top of his white beard.

'Sa'haytay'ne?' she offered.

'O'eh,' he grunted, and sat at the table.

She put the tea before him, returned to the sink so she wouldn't have to look at his wet lips, and kept the tap running to cover the noise of him blowing and sucking his tea. She'd never liked the way his eyes followed her, but she'd stay in the kitchen until he'd finished. After that, he would smoke a cigarette in the living room while she went upstairs to wake the little ones.

*

If he prayed that would be something. But he's a monster.
If anyone tells him to pray he's gonna fight. He used to
beat Mum if she told him to pray, and if the big one did,
he threatened to kick us out.

At least he goes to the Mox on Fridays – that's one
thing he never misses. Not to the main one, though. He
doesn't know the town. No one teaches him. If anyone
does teach him, thassit, he's gonna blab about his family:
'Oh, my daughter done this! My son done that!'

Anyway, he's not them type of people that goes to the
Mox to talk to other Asians. If someone comes to the
house he thinks they're poisoning his wife or kids. So.
He's that type.

It was still too early to get the little ones up. Beauty crept
into her sister's room and slipped into the warm bed
beside her, laying her head on the thick, long hair that
covered the pillow. Sharifa grumbled sleepily at the
intrusion and turned away to face the wall. Beauty
ignored her protests and pressed up against her. Years
ago she'd changed her sister's nappies and fed her in the
night as if she'd been her own baby.

An alarm clock rang in Faisal's room next door and
was quickly switched off. Beauty listened to her younger
brother heading to the bathroom. Silence fell again.

He must have gone back to bed.

The door opened and his face appeared, looking
irritable.

'Get up, Sharifa, it's time for *namaz*.'

He pushed open the door and light from the landing fell
on Beauty's face on the pillow next to his little sister.

'What the fuck are you doing in here, tramp?' he demanded.

'Get lost, asshole. And stop playing with yourself
through there. You won't be able to pray.'

He came into the room and advanced towards the bed.

7

Sharifa had woken up and was stroking her older sister's arm under the duvet.

'Get out of her room or I'll go and wake *Bhai-sahb*.'

'Leave her alone, *Suto-Bhai*,' said Sharifa.

Beauty shrugged her hand off – she didn't need her baby sister's help. Her younger brother was getting nasty, swearing at everyone. Even at their mum. And her older brother had been distant towards her since she'd got back from Bangladesh.

'Fucking tramp – get out!' he shouted.

Beauty got up from the bed and shoved past him at the door. The punch landed between her shoulder blades and hurt, but she didn't cry out.

Later, after the little ones had prayed, they sat round the breakfast table in silence. No one wanted to talk to the old man. Early in the morning his *bud-bud-ding-ding* accent irritated everyone. Faisal slurped cornflakes while Sharifa picked at a piece of toast, her head resting on one hand.

It was nice back home in Bangladesh when people ate *murri* rice and *handesh*, if they had enough money for garlic and ginger. The little ones had suffered without English food. But Beauty had been born there. She hadn't come to England until she was five and, despite everything that had happened when she was sent back at fourteen, Bangladesh – *back home* – was in her blood. She'd missed pizza at first. But she'd cooked for her uncle and his family for five years, and had almost forgotten what it tasted like. The little ones had come over with the old man to bring her back to England, without the mullah. Faisal had spent most of the time crying and swearing at his cousins.

He looked up from his bowl and wiped the milk from the fluff on his top lip.

'What time you coming back from that course?' he demanded.

'You know it finishes at four o'clock, so why arx?'

'Just make sure you're back by twenty-past four. Take the spare mobile from the drawer – I'm gonna call you at four o'clock. There's no credit on it, so you can't phone anyone. And wear a salwar,' he said.

'Who am I going to phone?' she answered. 'And by the way, *doonsla*, you're not *Bhai-sahb* so don't tell me what to wear.'

'I'm not a bastard! Tell her, Abu!' he said to his father.

'Cry baby as well.'

'*Bas!*' the old man commanded.

But his words no longer carried much authority, nor could he meet his elder daughter's eye. Faisal didn't often call him Abu any more; the boy had even called him a paki . . . The old man knew they blamed him for everything. His sons didn't consult him any more on money matters and wouldn't tell him anything – not even where the centre of town was. Beauty stole from the housekeeping to keep him in cigarettes; she felt sorry for him, despite what had happened to her.

She looked at him now. His eyes glazed over as he stared at the box of cornflakes. His nose had become large and fleshy, the nostrils thick with black hairs.

He's still your flesh and blood.

She turned her back on him to wash the plates and wind up Faisal a bit more. 'You gotta go to the Mox after school, so you can't phone me.'

'Don't worry, I'll tell the messab. He'll let me out to phone.'

She knew that the imam probably would. Faisal was a clever kid. He had a *balla mogoz* – a good brain.

God knows what he's gonna do, or what he's gonna get involved with – nobody knows.

'They ain't gonna teach a dumb tramp like you to read anyway,' he said.

After her brother and sister had left for school, Beauty went to Sharifa's room where her own clothes were kept. She would rather have worn jeans, but there might be a row if she did. She didn't mind wearing a salwar.

I'm Asian, aynt I?

But the idea of walking through a new town was scary.

She picked out her pink muslin salwar, a denim jacket and her black headscarf, and spent some time getting the scarf right – tight over the ears and twisted to a ball at the back like Somali girls. Her makeup she applied sparingly – lipliner to show off her Cupid's bow, and black eyeliner drawn to a point at the corners of her eyes; a red nose stud, and the small earrings with the paper-thin gold leaves.

Perfect.

She ignored her father, smoking and watching TV in the living room, and went to the kitchen to take a ten-pound note from her mother's purse.

What's she got a purse for? They never let her go anywhere alone and Bhai-sahb does all the shopping.

And I'm just another sad sitting-in-the-corner girl, aynit.

She took two pounds for the old man's cigarettes, and put the coins on the arm of his chair on her way past. His dark face looked away. Neither spoke as she pulled on her jacket, took a key from the hook near the front door and left the flat.

A white boy stared as he passed her in the concrete stairwell. Beauty tugged at the edge of her scarf so that her hand covered her face.

'Oright?'

She didn't answer.

Friendly people here, though. As long as they aynt nosy.

It was too early for the *halla* she'd seen every day, hanging around, from the living-room window. Whatever the weather he wore a long padded coat, a scarf that covered his face and a large hat with ear flaps. He drank *modh* from a can, and talked to people he knew as they passed.

At the bus stop there was only a fat white man. His belly stretched his shirt between the buttons, showing white flesh and curling hairs. Beauty wondered why his nose was so large and red, and how he found his *mossoi* when he went to make *feshab*. The man lifted a massive hand to light the stub of a roll-up between his lips.

Beauty took a cigarette from the pocket of her jacket and looked around before lighting it. She could smoke here unseen from the flat, but if the old man came to the shops and saw her he'd tell *Bhai-sahb*, who would swear and call her a *ganjuri*. She risked it anyway, leaning against the window of the shelter as cars hissed past on the wet road. The smoke felt good as it caught the back of her throat.

Across the street an old Sikh woman came out of the shop and stood at the light, waiting to cross. Beauty had time for a few more puffs before she would have to put the cigarette out. Muslim girls weren't tramps.

She threw the long butt away as the woman got to the halfway island, and tugged at her scarf again as the *buddhi* came up to peer at the timetable through thick glasses.

A bus sped past while the woman's back was turned. She looked around in alarm, saw Beauty and squinted at her before smiling.

'*Betti, tu janti'hay bus kaha jari'ay?*'

'*Ha* bus town *jai'ga.*' Beauty didn't know if all the buses went into town.

'*Tussi mu-je decca sa'ti hoo?*' the old lady asked.

'Aunty,' Beauty said, 'I'm not from this place. *Me yaha se nehi hoo*, but *me' decca sa'ti hoo*. I'll show you.'

The old lady thanked her. God had sent her to help an old woman, she said. She asked her where she was from and what she was doing here.

'*Aunty, me' London se ai ee.* I don't really speak Sikh.'

When the bus came she let the woman get on first. The driver had a black beard and perfectly rounded turban. He smiled at Beauty as she gave him the money.

Just give me the ticket, egghead.

She was sick of Asian men perving at her.

The bus pulled off with a lurch that flung her onto an empty bench. She kissed her teeth in irritation, like the Jamaican girls in London used to do, and slid along the seat to the window. She wiped away the condensation with the sleeve of her jacket and looked out.

The only other time she'd been out of the house since she'd got back from Bangladesh was to the Jobcentre the week before, to sign on. They'd given her a reading and writing test. She'd told them she had a problem with her reading, but they still made her do it. If she had a reading problem, they said, she'd have to go on a course if she wanted to carry on claiming Jobseekers' Allowance. She'd managed to fill in her name, so they set her a date to turn up somewhere in town two weeks later. *Bhai-sahb* hadn't liked it, but they needed the forty-four pounds a week and the housing benefit; and if they wanted her to bring the mullah into the country she'd have to show the Home Office that she had a job and could support him. If she went on the course, it would mean letting her out every day from half-past eight to half-past four for six months, or until she got a job. They didn't like that either. They'd think she was flirting with boys, bringing shame on the family, and they'd soon start talking again about bringing

Habib Choudhury into the country. The old man didn't speak of these things in front of her any more, but she knew he still had a hold over *Bhai-sahb*. If her brother Dulal wanted to get married himself, he'd need the old man to arrange it.

Houses and flats slipped past the window. White people and schoolchildren got on and off the bus, but nobody sat next to her. She dreaded someone speaking. Apart from at the Jobcentre she hadn't spoken English to a white or black person since her first year of secondary school in London. There she'd only had black girls as friends. Not black boys. They were thieves.

Perverts too. Arx anyone.

When she first came from Bangladesh, the Asian children in the primary school in Bethnal Green used to laugh at her accent. The boys liked her, she knew, but the girls locked her in the toilets and pinched her in class. She was often sent home for slapping her tormentors. Her cousins, too, laughed at the way she spoke. Typical freshie from back home. The bullying was worse at the comprehensive, so she bunked off and spent her days catching the bus to Hackney and wandering the streets with older black girls. Her parents couldn't read English, and they ignored the letters from the headteacher. When inspectors came to the house, the old man told them that she'd gone back to Bangladesh; and she didn't go to school again. The mullah's pervert brother, who lived near-by, offered to teach her to read English and Arabic, and her father trusted his future son-in-law's brother. When the man started touching her – *down there* – she acted dumb and refused to learn any more. She was twelve years old and he told her mum that he'd seen her with boys in the street, that she flirted with grown men in Commercial Road. She'd become *hobiss* he said, bad like a white slapper, a *sinnal-fourri*. The best thing to do would be to send her back home to get married, before she did it with anyone – if she was still *anamo'ot* or *ful*, a flower untouched – and he offered to take her.

They'd be expecting her back from the course at half-past four. Beauty got off the bus in the town centre and followed the simple map, which the lady at the Jobcentre had given her, to the doors of the RiteSkills building.

2

Mark Aston woke up and turned over in bed to look at the light coming through the ragged curtain. He got up and stepped over to the window to tug the material back along the wire he had nailed to the frame; the sky was grey over the roofs of the terraced houses opposite, the dark slates polished by the rain.

He sat on the edge of the bed and stared blankly at his thin, pale legs against the mauve pile carpet, his head still heavy. A black Nissan Sunny Pulsar GTI-R accelerated past the house, its dump valve sneezing loudly at each gear change.

The nigger from down the road. Must be eightish.

Mark had to be up town for nine. What was the place called? Skillssomething . . . SkillsRite? He stretched and looked around the room for something to put on his feet. Half-filled bin-liners and broken video recorders, cigarette ends, crumpled socks and empty beer cans lay scattered about the floor, but he couldn't see any shoes.

He took care on the landing. The bulb had gone and the door to the kitchen at the bottom of the stairs was open.

Basstud dogs might've come up in the night and shit.

He peered down at the floor to make sure of the few steps to the bathroom and shoved against the door to force back the pile of dirty clothes behind it. The brown smears in the toilet bowl hadn't moved in a week; he'd used the bleach to clean the backyard, and the brush, clogged with dried paper, had gone brown and lay buried under the clothes behind the toilet. Mark gave up trying to remove the stains and let his stream hit the water, until the noise reached the dogs in the yard and they barked into life.

'PACKIDDIN!' His voice carried through the open window; the dogs caught the menace in it and fell silent.

As he bent over the sink to splash water on his face he could just make out his newly shaven dark hair in the piece of broken mirror propped up behind the taps. With the palm of his large hand, he stroked his skull from crown to brow. Stubble was beginning to show along his jaw and chin, but not enough to bother shaving until he went up town that night. He made a triumphant face in the mirror at the thought of getting laid later, sticking out a tongue pierced with a Union Jack barbell. Any slag would do.

Mark pulled on a pair of shorts and thundered down the steep, dark staircase. He stopped in the doorway of the kitchen.

'WODD'VE YOU FOOKIN' DONE TO ME KITCHIN, YOU LITTLE BASSTUDS?!'

Titan, a brindle Staffordshire bull terrier, edged along the wall towards the back door. A week's supply of dog meat had been pulled from the freezer and eaten, or left to thaw amid the rubbish dragged from the bin. The air was thick with the smell of dog shit and ammonia.

'LOOK AT THE STATE OF ME FOOKIN' CARPET! I'LL BUST YER FOOKIN' HEAD!' he promised the dog.

Mark picked his way through the debris to the front room to look for his trainers. His old Staffy bitch, Bess, thumped her tail on the sofa, ears back and head lowered.

'IT WAAR HIM OUT THERE, IT WERE YOU!

AND GERROFF THE FOOKIN' FURNITURE YOU BASSTUD!'

Bess slipped reluctantly from the sofa, circled near the front door several times and slumped to the floor. Mark stamped his feet into a pair of once-white trainers.

They've trashed me fookin' house again.

But his rage was directed against his stud, Titan, who was staying out of harm's way in the kitchen.

He went through to the kitchen to kick the dog into the yard. As he opened the back door the creature suddenly forgot its crime and jumped up, scratching claws down Mark's bare legs. He roared in pain and anger, whirled round and grabbed the beast by the thick skin of its neck, raising a huge and terrible fist. The dog dropped to the ground and struggled for the gap in the door, yelping as the fist smashed down, catching it behind an ear. Out in the safety of the yard it shook off the grazing blow, looking back at Mark warily.

But Mark wasn't going out there. He hadn't done the yard for a few days and the rain had turned the shit to mud. Another two Staffy bitches and his English bull terrier, Poppy, scratched at the doors inside their breeze-block homes. Satan was quiet in the end kennel.

Mark resentfully eyed the work that needed doing, but stopped when he saw pieces of chewed wood.

'AAAWWW! WHO'S BIN AT THE FOOKIN' BROOM HANDLE AGAIN?'

He turned away and slammed the door. The dog looked at the silent house, bent its head and sniffed at the shitty paving.

In the kitchen, Mark gagged as he picked up the turds in a plastic bag. Using a bucket of dark brown water, he mopped at the pools of piss and scraped up the rubbish with his foot. He'd have to go to the Poundshop on the way back from town and get another broom. If they had them. Otherwise it'd have to be Dinesh's, which might cost him two quid, two quid fifty. Without a broom, doing the backyard would be impossible.

He found a cup and a sponge under a pile of plates in the sink, made coffee and went into the front room. He switched on the computer he'd bought for a tenner from the recycling centre. He'd never had one before but had mastered it quickly. He'd added new hardware and downloaded the software for encoding DVDs and unlocking mobile phones, before the internet bill went unpaid and they cut the line. His film collection was looking good, though. Once his dole money came through he'd be able to get tons more music as well.

Ye'man. Nice one.

But that wasn't till Thursday. For now, he had enough for 'bacca and a bag of dog biscuits, if he used the twos and ones from the jar on top of the telly. Baz, up Graiseley, would do him fifty grams of Golden Virginia for a fiver, but there'd only be pasta to eat later, with nothing on it. Unless he gave that to the dogs, mixed with a three-quid bag of biscuits. Now that the dole had sent him on that fucking course to look for a job – *full-time for six months!* – he'd have to give up the cash-in-hand jobs to make sure the housing benefit still got paid. He could stop at Bob's and see if the back-box on his Karen's Mondeo wanted fixing. That might be a fiver and a couple of drinks at the club. The only thing he had left to take to Cash Converters was his mobile phone, which he'd have to sell if nothing else came up by tomorrow.

They're basstuds 'n' all. A quid fifty they give me for that gold bracelet I found.

Mark finished his coffee and rolled a cigarette from the scutters in the ashtray, pinching the end to stop the dusty remains from falling out. He considered the room and his possessions with satisfaction. Alan and Jean had given him the sofa three weeks before – he'd been walking past their house on his way to the shops as they were dumping it on the pavement; his PC was wired up to the stereo, the TV, amplifier and bass speakers – and the tunes he'd downloaded sounded good on it. Poppy's rosettes and photos on the wall were looking damn good, too – another six months and he'd be able to breed off her – and even though Bess had managed to get into the house overnight, the smell of dog had basically gone. It was tidier, too, now that Titan was banished from the front room and didn't come in and chew everything.

May as well tek him with me to fetch 'bacca.

The roach in the roll-up was beginning to burn his lip. He dropped it in the saucer at his feet, and got up to open the back door. At the sight of a lead in Mark's hand, the dog bounded in from the filth and rain, ran through the kitchen and leapt onto the sofa, squirming and banging its tail expectantly.

'GERROFF ME FOOKIN' SOFA! IT'S *NEW*!' He raised his fist again, grabbed the animal by the back of the neck, dragged it to the floor and, pinning it down under his knee, hooked the lead onto the collar.

He put on his luminous hi-vis jacket over his red England top and tugged a blue baseball cap down low over his eyes. As he opened the door, the dog burst past at the sight of the outside world, pulling Mark out of the house.

'WILL YOU FOOKIN' PACKIDDIN?'

Across the street two Kyrgyzstani peasants looked up from the open bonnet of their car. A third sat at the wheel, turning the engine over.

Aware of the audience, Mark commanded Titan to sit in a firm voice, like the trainer had told him. The dog sat. He took his time locking the door, pretending to shift some of the junk filling the front patch of garden. The dog remained sitting.

Betcher they ay got dogs like you in China. They'd probably eat you out there.

He stood for a second longer to zip up his coat and enjoy showing off his control and Titan's obedience. But the men were already peering into their car.

As he passed the covered passageway that ran down the side of his house, Mark noticed the smell coming from his backyard. He'd have to clean it before the neighbours got back tonight. It wasn't fair on them. Even if they were black. At least they were English, or spoke it. And they'd never said anything about the noise or smell.

They'm all right.

He had to watch out, too, for the old cunt across the road who'd grassed on him once for the smell. When the bloke from the RSPCA knocked on the door he'd just finished cleaning the kennels and yard. Everything had washed down the passage into the street, but at least the yard and kennels were clean. *Couldn't say fook all.* Some white guy had moved in two doors down, but Mark hadn't spoken to him yet. The Iraqis in-between didn't count.

Still, he had to be careful. *What with breeding 'n' that.*

He let the dog pull off towards the shops. Further up the street, an Indian woman in salwar-kameez and scarf recognized the dog and type of cap coming towards her, and took up her grandson's hand. Mark liked it that people were scared of his dogs. Old Pakis always crossed the road.

At the end of the street he turned away from Dunstall Park towards Graiseley and its row of shops. Up ahead, a white-robed figure was putting up a sandwich board on the pavement. PHONES: NEW, USED, MOST MAKES UNLOCKED.

The Somali looked up, recognized Mark and disappeared into his shop. Mark considered turning back to avoid him, but realized it wouldn't make much difference. The bloke – *some sort of Paki* – had given him a customer's mobile and promised Mark a fiver if he could unlock it. He'd taken the phone straight round to the indoor market and sold it to Dinesh for thirty quid. Since the dole had stopped his money, just for missing an appointment, he'd had nothing coming in – the money he'd got for the phone had mostly gone on dog biscuits. He'd avoided the shops for the last week, but had forgotten about it this morning.

Fook 'im.

As he passed the Somali's open doorway, he heard a foreign voice.

'Where my fuckin' phone, man?'

The dog turned and sprang for the shopkeeper's legs. Mark held on as the man leaped back, but let himself be pulled to the entrance so Titan could terrorize him into his shop. He dragged the reluctant animal away towards the mini-mart further along, where Baj Dev 'Baz' Singh had come out to see what was going on.

Baz liked it round here. The chippy, the bookies, his shop, the car stereo place, the park – *good area, man*. He nodded to Mark.

'Oright, geez?'

'Sowund.' Mark grinned and nodded to Titan. 'E's gerrin' nasty.' He'd had Titan off his foster brother and the dog had been brought up mean.

Baz didn't like the way the animal was looking at him, its head tilted to one side. 'Nah, he's a good dog, man.'

Mark asked him if he had any tobacco left. 'You couldn't fetch it for us, could you? I do' wanna leave him out here.'

Baz came back out of the shop with the tobacco, and Mark gave him a handful of copper and silver change.

'Five-fifty, yeah? It's right. I counted it jooss. I'll catch you later.'

Outside the bookies two black blokes stood talking loudly with a third who was leaning against the red doorway. There was enough space to pass, but he'd have to keep the lead tight in case Titan went for them. They didn't look like they were going to move, so Mark let the lead slacken a little. The dog shot forward, but kept its nose running along the pavement as they passed. The man in the doorway kissed his teeth at Mark's back.

He hated that noise. *Fookin' nigger shit*. He'd heard it too many times in jail, and he wanted to say something, but it wasn't a good idea round here. These days they had guns. He'd heard the shots of an evening coming from over Sweetman Street way. Besides, he liked the Newhampton area. He'd lived here a year and a half, knew the shopkeepers and a few other people, and it was near to town.

Too many Kosovans, though. Like them pair up ahead getting into that G-reg 405. Talking Iraqi – the ignorant basstuds. I've sin them lot at the car auction in Walsall driving off wi' no tax or MOT.

Mark hadn't Taken a car Without its Owner's Consent for two and a half years now; hadn't been in jail for eighteen months. Foreigners coming over here and doing what they wanted in cars pissed him off.

Tay right.

Service industry and admin workers passed by on their way into town, but Mark kept Titan close and ordered him to heel whenever people were in earshot. It sounded proper.

Outside his house, the Chinese were still listening to the downpipe on their Ford Escort blowing. Mark let Titan into the backyard, thought briefly about putting on some cleaner clothes, and left the house to retrace his steps into town.

As he reached the end of Newhampton Road he quickened his pace. He couldn't afford to be late. The dole would give him another ten quid a week for going on the course today, and if he missed the sign-up at nine o'clock they'd restart him the following week and he'd lose a tenner. He'd been up the town the night before with his ex and she'd insisted on drinking the last of his money, before letting him shag her on the way home. But at least he'd left some money at home for 'bacca. He remembered the first time he'd fucked her, in the bushes down by the supermarket, and what a right dirty bitch she was. She'd been a dirty bitch with others, though, when he'd been in jail for twocking that Renault, and they'd split up when he got out. His mate Nige had started seeing her a few months ago.

Dick'ead give 'er a car jooss to fook 'er and the big end went three weeks later.

Outside the RiteSkills building on School Street, a small huddle of New Deal claimants was waiting in silence on the pavement. Mark hung back until the doors opened. He pinched out his roll-up, put it in his pocket and walked up the steps into the building.

3

Twelve Jobcentre clients stood in the RiteSkills reception area, waiting for whatever was supposed to happen. The older men carried their lunch in plastic bags. Black-trousered women brought forms from their desks to the clients in the open-plan office, while multicultural men and women in various work poses smiled down from posters bearing the company slogan: 'Training People's Skills'. The staff approached the clients in turn and asked each one to confirm their name and address, and to sign a DH15 form. The clients gave their details quietly. No one wanted to be there.

Beauty Begum pressed herself against the wall, stuck between an old white guy with a walking stick and a youngish black bloke who'd smiled at her when she walked in scowling. She'd managed a quick glance at the other people waiting before she chose a spot to stand. A mix. White, black, young, old, a half-caste girl, a middle-aged Sikh woman, and a tall Somali woman with a big *hombol*. One of the young women working there was a Sikh.

A flirt, showing her stomach and flicking her hair. I bet her family'd chop her head off with a sword if she did anything wrong. Sikhs, man. Worser than anyone.

Beauty watched the Sikh girl approach.

Why's she coming to me first? Cuz I'm Asian?

'Hi there,' said the girl, smiling. 'I'm Bal – Baljinder. I

just need to get you to sign this form. Can I have your name, please?'

'Begum,' Beauty answered, not looking up. She didn't like to say her first name out loud. *Is that your real name?* She hated the question, but someone always asked it. Faisal taunted her with it like the white kids had done at primary school.

'And your address?' Bal asked.

'Three-oh-two Pendeford Dene.'

'Is that Wolverhampton?'

'Er . . .' Beauty was thrown by the question. 'Yeah. No . . . I don't know,' she faltered.

The room was silent.

'That's Parkfields,' said the black man standing next to her.

'Thanks,' said Bal. 'Can you just sign here for me, please?' She offered the pen and held the clipboard for Beauty to sign the DH15 in the box marked with a cross. *Don't look at me while I'm doing it.*

But the eyes watched as Beauty laboured to produce her signature.

There.

She gave the pen back.

'Thanks,' said Bal and took the form away to return with another for the next person.

'Have you just moved here?' said the black man.

'No,' said Beauty. 'I forgot if it was that place you said, or Woolverhamtun.' She didn't want to talk so much.

The man looked down at her. She was a pretty girl. Too skinny for him. Too pissed off as well. He preferred them big like the white girl working here, or the Somali woman. That was something to keep you warm on a winter's night. Besides, Indian birds – no chance there.

When it came to Mark's turn to fill in the form he wished he'd put cleaner clothes on. The place was close and warm and he could smell himself. The big-arsed bird with the little titties was walking over to him.

'Hiya, I'm Michaela,' she said. Her smile was cold. She didn't like the clients any more, not now the Jobcentre sent everyone with basic skills or employability issues here, and especially not this type. They always caused trouble, one way or another.

Mark straightened up. 'Hi,' he said, smiling for longer than she had.

'Who are you?' she asked.

'Mark. Aston.'

He craned his neck to look at the list in her hand, and at the shadow of cleavage between her small breasts.

'What's your address?' She leaned away from him. This one stank and was standing too close.

'Eleven Prole Street,' he said.

'Is that P-R-O-double L?'

'Nah. P-R-O-L-E.'

'Thanks. If you hang on here a sec until everyone's signed in, someone will be along to take you upstairs,' she said.

Mark leaned back against the wall and watched her arse from under the peak of his cap as she took his form back to her desk.

The door beside him opened and a tall man with red cheeks and white hair appeared. He was dressed in a black suit and shirt and wore a red tie. He nodded a count of the clients and called out over their heads, 'Michaela, how many are we missing?'

'Just two. If they're not here by half-past, we'll exit them and restart them next week.'

He addressed the group. 'If everyone would like to come with me up to the induction room – there's a lot to get through today.'

Following the trail of people upstairs, Beauty tried to

slip in front of a young white girl so that the black man wouldn't walk up the stairs behind her, but she wasn't quick enough. The salwar didn't reveal her figure, but she held her hands behind her anyway, palms out, covering her *hombol* in case he was looking. She knew from school how black kids looked at her bum. It was wrong, but at night, when the house was quiet, she'd lie awake and think about the rude things they'd said to her.

Beauty followed the others into a large classroom, where a horseshoe of tables faced a whiteboard and a single teacher's desk beneath it. She tried to leave an empty chair between her and the racist type with the baseball cap and football shirt, but the black bloke urged her on and she had to sit down next to him. He might not speak to her, but still, it was scary sitting next to people like that. The black guy smiled as he sat down on the other side of her. At least he was dressed nice. Clean. Not like the white people.

Tramps, man.

Chair legs clanged. The man in the black suit sat at the desk at the front, and busied himself with forms. The noise died down. He took off his glasses and slid them into his breast pocket, tugged at the knees of his trousers, cleared his throat and addressed the group in the deep voice of a heavy smoker.

'Good morning,' he said. 'My name is Colin Bushell and I'm the Employability and Training Skills Co-ordinator for RiteSkills, Wolverhampton.'

He paused to let the effect sink in on this new bunch of unemployed scroungers in front of him.

'Now, you've all been referred to us by the Jobcentre, because it has been identified that there are barriers to your employability, barriers that you need support with. In most cases that will mean help with yer reading, writing and numbers, and some of you with yer Wider Key Skills: Improving Yer Own Learning, Problem-Solving and Working With Others. And everyone will do their Jobsearching, CVs, and Best Practice for Successful Interview Techniques. At the end of the day that's what we do here at RiteSkills, as well as helping you to actually find a job.'

'I do' want a fookin' job!' a voice rang out.

Laughter erupted and Beauty looked up to see who had spoken. A white boy sat leaning back on his chair, swinging his legs and grinning at the room. His face was tanned, or unwashed; his clothes and trainers shapeless and dirty. He caught Beauty's eye and smiled, his uneven teeth discoloured by nicotine and lack of brushing. She looked down quickly.

The Employability Co-ordinator laughed with them. It was too early to lose them. Especially not to this gypsy half-breed.

'Stewart and I go a long way back, don't we?' Colin said.

Stewart ignored him.

'Well, sit properly and don't use that kind of language or I'll be speaking to yer adviser. You may get sanctioned and lose yer benefits.'

'Nah man, my adviser fookin' loovs me,' he said. 'She'd get it 'n' all, trooss me.'

Beauty looked in his direction again and he winked at her. She lowered her glance, covered her brow with her hand and touched her cheeks three times alternately with the tip of a finger so that God would forgive her for hearing sinful words.

Toba, toba astaghfirullah.

Colin stood up and handed out forms and pens.

'I'll explain some of the new sanctions procedures in a moment. Firstly, I need everybody to fill in this DH21 New Client Start-Up Notification.'

Some of the people in the room showed alarm at the prospect. Colin enjoyed their discomfort.

Beauty picked at the corners of the green and white form on her desk, her forearms shielding it from the men sitting next to her. She was sure of the first two questions, and wrote her name carefully. The nine little boxes on the line underneath she guessed were for her National Insurance number, which she knew by heart. She sounded out D-A-T-E from the next question to herself, but together the letters made no sense. The rest of the form, too, was a mystery, but she kept her pen over the page anyway. She glanced sideways at the black guy's form. He'd filled in one box more than she had, but had stopped and seemed to be thinking about his next answer. She put down her pen in irritation and folded her arms.

One by one the others stopped writing. Colin walked slowly round the room collecting the forms, scanning each in turn and asking its author a detail here and there. Beauty kept her head down but could feel him drawing closer.

As he stopped at the black guy next to her she tugged her scarf down and left her hand there to cover her face. But she sensed Colin in front of her and saw his liver-spotted hand pick up the form from the desk.

'Beauty? *Is that your real name?*'

There was silence and his question hung there, waiting for an answer.

She looked him up and down. 'You never heard the word before?' she said in a clear voice. Faces turned towards her.

'Sorry, it seemed like an unusual name . . .'

'For an Asian?' she interrupted. 'So, an Asian can't have a name like that?' She sucked her teeth. 'Thass a typical Bangladeshi name,' she added. Like Lucky, Fancy, Simple, Polly, Colly, Sweetie . . . She thought of her cousins back home and the girls in the village, and wished she'd been given a holy name instead.

If someone cusses your name you've gotta say something, aynit? Colin didn't reply. He didn't want another Equal Ops situation on his hands. He spent a few seconds pretending to read the rest of the empty form, before moving on. The noise started up again and Beauty could hear the others repeating her name.

Let them.

One of the older white ladies sitting a few seats away leaned towards her. 'Thass a loovly name, loov,' she said.

At eleven o'clock Colin let them out for their comfort break. Beauty followed the trail back downstairs, out of the building to the other side of the road, and stood apart from the small groups that formed on the pavement. The older men pulled out tins of tobacco with ready-rolled cigarettes inside. A large, round-faced white girl with a long denim skirt and a small nose approached.

'Oright? It's Beauty, ay it?' she asked.

'Uh-huh.' People spoke funny here. Her little sister had picked up the accent.

'Thass a really noice nayum. Suits you.'

'Thanks,' said Beauty, but didn't know what else to say.

'Have you gorra spare fag?' the girl asked.

'Sure.' She took the packet from her breast pocket and offered it. The girl's fat fingers struggled to remove a cigarette.

'Thanks, Beauty. I'm Nicola. Tonks. Have you got a light 'n' all?'

The rude, dirty boy spotted the cigarettes and left his group.

'Yo!' he called to Beauty, showing his stained teeth. 'You told 'im, all right! I berr'e waar expectin' that, fookin' 'ell!'

Stewart balanced in front of her on the edge of the pavement. 'He's a right tosser, that bloke.'

'Is he?' Beauty said, not looking up. 'I didn't know.'

He looked at the cigarette in her hand and nodded at it.

'Can I go twos on that fag wi' you?'

Share a cigarette with you? You gone crazy?

She gave him the whole cigarette and he swaggered back to the group, flaunting his trophy to the fagless.

'Got it off that Asian bird,' she heard him say.

'Her's gorra name you know!' Nicola shouted back at him. 'Dey you hear 'er jooss?' She turned to Beauty. 'Do' worry about him – he's a fookin' knob!'

'Oh right.' Beauty smiled to hide her embarrassment.

'See? You can smile!' Nicola said. 'Hey!' She turned and called out to the others. 'She can smile!'

'Sshh! Don't!' But no one looked over.

'Y'm not from rowund here, am y'?' Nicola asked. 'I can tell from yer accent.'

'No, I'm from London.' White people were nosy in this town.

'Oh, roight.' She sounded impressed. 'I ay never bin to London.'

Arwa type – innocent.

The two girls smoked in silence.

'Hey,' Nicola said. 'We'm giwin' to the pub at lunchtime. D'you wanna coom with us? You can meet me chap?'

'Er . . . Pub's not my thing,' Beauty said. She looked down at the pavement.

'Coom on, it wo' hurt.'

'Maybe next time.'

Beauty remained alone. She finished the cigarette and watched the half-caste girl from the group come towards her, hair stretched tight back against her head, a diamond beauty-spot jumping as she chewed.

'God, what a bunch of tramps!' she said. She stood next to Beauty and lit a cigarette. 'I'm Lesley. Where you from?'

'Hackney,' Beauty lied. A *halla* should know where it was.

'Oh really!' Lesley said. 'Christ, what you diwin' here?'

Beauty was glad not to have to answer as the girl carried on.

'I love Hackney. D'you ever go to the Empire?'

Beauty saw the girl glance at her salwar and headscarf.

Hackney Empire? The big white and brown building on Mayor Street?

'Yeah, I did,' she lied again.

Where they do concerts?

'Who did you go and see?'

'Uh . . . just some Bhangra singers.'

Al-lāh, amarray maff horrio ami missa mattissee. Would God forgive her for lying to this girl?

'What? All that Indian stuff?' Lesley said. She did a little dance on the pavement, Punjabi style at first, shrugging her shoulders up and down, hands up and palms out, then stuck out her arse and wiggled it.

Beauty laughed. She didn't mind the mocking dance. From a white person it would have been a different matter. She watched the girl's bum as she turned round in front of her, the tattoo arching up from the white pants sticking out from her low-cut hipsters.

'Have you seen any boys you like?' Lesley jumped round to face the pretty Indian girl again.

Beauty flushed. 'No, not really.'

'The black guy next to you's OK,' Lesley said. 'But I think he plucks his eyebrows.'

'You're joking!' said Beauty.

'I berr'e's got a nice one, though.'

A nice what?

32

'Y'm really pretty, d'you know that?' Lesley said. 'You got lovely eyes and such a sweet smile.'

Beauty saw her eyes flick critically over her salwar-kameez again. She'd wear a nicer one tomorrow, or maybe jeans and boots.

'You're pretty, too,' she said awkwardly.

'Thanks, Beauty. Here, d'you smell that white guy next to you? He fookin' stinks a dogs, man.'

Kutayn! Dogs were *haram*. Unclean.

'Come and sit next to me when we go back up,' Lesley invited. 'We can have a laugh at these tramps.'

She linked her arm through Beauty's and led her back across the street. Beauty was happy for the girl's friendliness and the cover it provided. Maybe she could still talk to people, after all. Some people. Talking to girls and looking them in the eyes wasn't too bad. Boys were another matter. In her night-time conversations with them it was easy. They said nice things to her, pleaded and argued with her parents and brothers, and often took her away in a warm car. She hadn't talked to a girl outside the family for five years. The old man and *Bhai-sahb* usually left her behind when they went to visit uncles, so she only saw her cousin-sisters when they came for Eid. She'd start cooking days in advance, *handesh* and *noon*, *feetta*, white rice with fried onion, different tandoori meats, boiled eggs and fried rice, samosas, *shamaai*, *kurma*, *parotha*, *fob* and salads. She served everyone, then ate alone in the kitchen when they'd finished. The old man told people she was mad, so her cousins avoided her.

Let them. They're all married now, so good luck to them.

She followed Lesley back up the stairs to the classroom, watching the girl's hips swinging from side to side in front of her.

Doesn't she feel no shame walking like that?

Why should she?

Beauty decided she liked the girl.

Mark sat down with a cup of tea he'd made in the clients' kitchen as the two girls came into the room laughing. The half-black bird was as fit as fuck, and the little Paki in the pyjamas that had been sitting next to him wasn't bad either; at least she didn't stink of curry. He pulled the peak of his cap lower and drank his tea. It was a pain in the arse coming to this place. If he'd got his business plan together sooner, the Jobcentre would never have sent him here. But time had slipped by and the forms were long since lost in the living room.

He'd spent all morning under his cap, the turned-up collars of his jacket hiding his face, paying little notice to what was said. He'd taken one look at the prick with the white hair and knew he was some sort of screw. Probation officer? Or Nacro? There were no fit birds to look at either, apart from the half-caste girl, and that sort only went for *nigg-ahs*. There were two or three slags, though. He'd seen the fat bird with the denim skirt at Flanagan's on pound-a-pint night. She might be up for it. If he could get a fiver together he could go up town later tonight and see if she was there. At least now he'd have an excuse to talk to her. Perhaps he should sell his mobile phone at Dinesh's on the way back home and buy a cheaper one when his dole came in. No one rang anyway, and there was never any credit on it. Any spare cash he had was always needed for something else.

Them basstud dogs must owe me a fookin' fortune by now.

His other Staffy bitch, Honey, was pregnant and her pups would pay him back. He might even be able to move somewhere better with the money if she had a good litter.

And maybe he'd have some more mates by then. The ones he'd made drinking up town weren't really mates. Small Paul had even tried to get Mark stealing cars again. And he had. Only once though, for the ride, dumping it and the run home, but he knew he shouldn't have done it. With six months left on a three-year ban he shouldn't be pissing about like that. Once he'd got his licence he'd be sorted. He'd show his mam he was doing all right. He'd go back to Burntwood and drive round the town till the cops recognized him. They'd be sure to blue-light him. Their faces when he pulled out his driving licence! Him! Mark Aston – aka 'South Staffs Car Crime'. It would be too sweet to risk pinching a car now.

A decent bird would be all right, too. Not like that fucking slag of an ex.

The rest of the afternoon passed slowly for Beauty. The boring old white guy banged on for hours and gave out pieces of paper she couldn't read. At half-past three she followed the other newly inducted clients out into the rapidly filling stairwell, merging with the Iraqis, Kosovans, Somalis, middle-aged Asian women and native black, white and Asian youth who poured from doorways above and below her. The noise of different languages was deafening and she kept close to the wall as bodies brushed past. Young Iraqi men, drawn by her looks and headscarf, stared and waited on the landings for her to pass, smiling and nudging one another.

Perverts, them Iraqis. B'dmaish number one.

On the pavement in front of the building, people stopped to light cigarettes and chat. Most weren't in a hurry to go anywhere. Beauty stood next to Lesley, but waited until the Indian *buddhis* had all gone before she lit one up. Nicola gave Beauty her phone number on a strip of paper torn from one of the forms they'd completed. Yes, she'd give her a ring some time and go out.

She told Lesley she had to go home and turned down the offer of a walk round town. Her mother wasn't well, Beauty said, she had to get back. Something wrong with her thingy. They'd see each other tomorrow.

As she tugged her scarf down and headed up the incline towards the church at the top of the road, the phone rang in her breast pocket. She pressed the green button and held the phone to her ear.

'Sis?' Faisal's voice said. She didn't answer. Her brother never called her *Afa*.

'Sis?' he said again. 'Is that you?'

Let him worry a bit more.

'Who did you think it was gonna be?' she said finally.

'*Why didn't you fucking answer?*' he demanded. 'And who was that black bitch you were talking to?'

Beauty hung up and looked around her. As she reached the corner a hand shot out and grabbed her by the wrist. Faisal pulled her towards him.

'Get your hands off me, you freak,' she shouted, wrenching her hand free and walking away from him.

'You were smoking!' he said, hurrying to catch up. 'I saw you. Wait till I tell *Bhai-sahb* and Dad.'

'Tell them whatever you want. Go to hell with yourself,' she said, quickening her pace.

'So who was that *halla* you were talking to?' he insisted, keeping up with her.

'Why? Did you like her arse?' she said. 'You gonna think about it later in bed?'

They rounded the corner and headed towards the centre of town.

'And keep your hands off me or I'll scream.' She spoke loudly enough for the people outside the Child Support

Agency and the yellow-fronted discount supermarket to hear.

Too many white people for you here, Faisal? What you gonna do, beat me up in the street?

Faisal hung back and let his sister walk ahead. She'd start limping soon enough. Her foot had never got better after *Bhai-sahb* kicked her that time.

4

Mark paused to light the rest of the roll-up he'd put out earlier. He watched from the other side of the street as a boy grabbed the Paki bird's wrist. He heard her shout and saw her pull away. Boyfriend maybe? Brother, more like.

It was Asian shit, none of his business.

On his way home he stopped at Dinesh's. He sold the mobile phone for twenty quid and bought a broom handle for two pound thirty. He walked to Pet Land on the Stafford Road to get a ten-kilo bag of dog biscuits and carried it home on his shoulder. He'd be all right for a few days. He could even fetch a five of weed and still have enough for five pints up town later. Four, if he bought one for that fat bird Nicola, if she was there. That wouldn't be until eleven o'clock.

Feeding the dogs, doing the backyard and having a bath would take up some time, but the rest would weigh heavily. Without the internet he couldn't get on MSN and talk to Julie – the woman from Newcastle he'd met in a chatroom after he'd seen her profile and photo online. They'd both leave microphones switched on in their living rooms all evening. Mark would spend his time hunched over the computer, downloading films, listening to music, smoking and drinking coffee or cans of beer if he had enough money. She was there, over the speaker, occasionally talking to her kids in the background, and chatting to him like they were in the room together. After three weeks she'd sent him a picture of herself topless holding up heavy breasts, and another, bent over a kitchen table in a thong and sagging stockings. She convinced him to play with himself while looking at the photos. Her fat didn't put him off, and at least she couldn't see him, although she must have heard him groan as he came. They'd talked about getting webcams, but that was before the line got cut. Since then they'd not spoken and the house had fallen silent of human voices. At least the dogs were there to welcome him when he opened the front door.

As long as they ay shit in the kitchen.

They hadn't, although one of them had pissed somewhere. Still, they'd been locked up all day, so fair play to them.

Mark went outside to do the yard while it was still light. The drizzle had stopped, and even though the shit hadn't hardened, some of it could be shovelled into the black bin-liners stacked up against the back fence. He'd have to find someone with a car soon to take him on a bin run to the tip. Who?

He grabbed Titan's face, showed him the new broom handle and raised his fist.

'Goddit?' he asked. 'Touch this and I'll lob a fookin' brick at yer head.'

Mark scattered a bottle of bleach over the yard and hosed the filth under the fence. It would run down the passageway and collect on the pavement between his house and the neighbours'.

So what? Iss clean out here, ay it?

He did the kennels, scraping three days of shit from each stinking hole, and replaced the newspaper on the floor. He left the dogs to run around the yard, went to the kitchen and filled five bowls with biscuits, putting one in each kennel. He shoved Titan into the kitchen to eat alone and shut the excited English bull terrier in the backyard. He'd have to let Satan out later. That damn dog would kill the others. *And 'e ay no Staffy like Bob said.*

Mark washed his hands over the plates in the sink, wiped them on his trousers and flicked on the kettle, emptying his pockets of the loose tea bags he'd taken earlier that day from the clients' beverages facility. He made a cup and went through to the front room, sat down, and slurped at the steaming liquid in satisfaction. The tea tasted better for having been pinched from that place. He put on some music and switched on the TV with the sound turned down. It filled part of the emptiness, but the urge to talk to someone grew. Flanagan's closed at midnight and if he went too early his money wouldn't last. He could go to the club to see Bob, but he'd have to buy a drink, and if he was going to pull that fat bird later, if she was there, he'd need the time it'd take to drink four pints. An hour should do it.

A knocking at the door brought him to his feet. The dogs barked in the backyard. He remembered who it would be as he opened the door – the man from Tenant Loans come for the repayments on the fifty quid he'd borrowed. He had to pay back seventy-five pounds at a fiver a week, and they came to the door to get it.

The Ghanaian gave him a receipt, closed his folder and left without saying a word.

Cheeky basstud. I'm payin' his fookin' wages.

As he closed the front door, he spotted the new neighbour from two doors down standing by the side of his Fiat Punto, its bonnet open. The man had a neat haircut and was wearing expensive-looking clothes, a clean shirt and proper shoes. Mark watched through the rip in the grey net curtains as the man looked from the engine to a manual in his hand. They'd nodded to each other a couple of times in the street, but the bloke had seemed scared of his dogs. *I told him they dey bite.* Not recently at any rate.

Mark went out into the street, pretended to look in his bin and let the lid fall shut. Now was a good opportunity to be neighbourly and kill some time until he went out, even if the bloke did look a bit posh. Besides, he was white, and not one of them new lot of foreigners coming here. *Poles 'n' that.*

'Y'oright, mate?' he called out when the man turned at the noise.

Peter James Hemmings saw the neighbour with the dangerous dogs standing outside number eleven. *What were they . . . pit bulls?* He'd returned the nodded greetings thrown his way on the few occasions he'd encountered the thug, and had jumped back in alarm from the squat beasts straining at their lead and clawing at the pavement to reach him.

'Do' *worry, they do' bite.*'

Peter hadn't been convinced.

'Er . . . hi,' he said and turned back to the diagram in the manual.

Christ! How had he ended up in a place like this? Just to get away from *her?*

'Are me dogs bothering you, what with the noise 'n' that?'

Peter caught the smell of long-unwashed clothes and dogs. He risked a sideways glance at the man next to him: his closely shaven dark hair and sideburns; sharp jaw and cheekbones; cap tipped to the back of his head; large fists hooked to the pockets of filthy jeans; battered trainers.

'I hadn't really noticed,' he said. It was better to lie. Safer. You never knew with types like this. Not that he'd ever known any types like this.

The thug was grinning at him with yellow teeth.

'Thass oright then, cuz they can be a bit noisy at times. D'you know woddamean?'

Peter had heard the thug shouting at them, and he worried that the stench coming over the intervening fences would penetrate his shirts drying on the washing line.

Mark nodded to the car. 'Woss wrong?'

The bloke didn't have a clue.

'Jump in and turn the engine over. I bet I can geddit giwin'.'

His neighbour didn't move.

'Do' worry, I know wodd'm diwin'.'

Peter got into the car and turned the key in the ignition. Nothing.

Mark checked the HT leads and the dizzy cap. 'Try it again,' he called after a few moments.

The engine caught. He stepped away from the car and told his neighbour to leave it running.

'Told you I could diw it,' he said. 'You wanna get them plugs looked at, though. Y'm on three cylinders.'

Peter got out of the car and peered at the engine, unsure where the plugs were or how many cylinders he should be on.

'Thanks,' he said. Was that enough? 'I, erm . . . owe you,' he added.

Mark eyed his neighbour's brown loafers and ironed shirt.

'I'll have a cup of coffee if y'm offrin',' he said.

Mark followed his neighbour into the house and took in the front room at a glance.

Shit TV and stereo.

A sofa and a couple of armchairs, a coffee table and a lamp.

Eh? Books?

Not much.

The lucky basstud's got central heating, though.

Mark had spent a fortune on the electric. If he hadn't rewired the meter in November he would never have made it through the winter. The debt on the display stood at seventy-six quid, but so far no one had come round to check up.

He spotted the closed laptop and the cables going to the internet box on the wall. Nice one. He might be able to get his updates.

'I'm Mark, by the way,' he said, offering his hand.

'Peter. Hi,' said Peter, taking it. 'Nice to meet you.'

Mark was disappointed by the limpness of his neighbour's handshake.

'Do you take milk and sugar?'

Mark followed him into the kitchen. Fridge-freezer, microwave, washing machine. Nice.

'Yeah, one. Cheers.'

He leaned against the worksurface and watched Peter take clean cups and some fancy coffee pot thing from a well-stocked cupboard.

'Fookin' 'ell! I wish my kitchen looked like this,' he said. 'Me fookin' dogs've trashed the place!'

Peter was aware of the thug's eyes on him and the mocha, and wished he'd bought some instant coffee.

'Everything was here when I rented it,' he explained.

'I bet yer landlord ay a Paki!'

Peter flinched at the harshness of the word and looked at the yob leaning against the worksurface.

'Mine's a Paki and the house is a shit'ole,' Mark said.

'I think mine's Sikh.'

'Same difference, ay it?'

Mark took the cup and went into the living room.

'How long you bin 'ere then?' he asked. 'Few months?'

'Three,' Peter said.

That was about right, Mark thought. He'd clocked the new car in the street just before Christmas. Taxed till July. About forty seconds he reckoned it would take him to pinch it. Not that he was going to.

Said he sells books. A proper job like.

Mark looked around the room again. The armchairs were comfy. Clean, too.

The coffee tasted like shit though.

He spotted the torn packet of cigarette papers poking out from underneath a book on the coffee table.

'Have you got any *boodha* on you?' Mark asked, nodding at the cigarette papers and grinning. A white neighbour who lived alone and liked a smoke! He might want company from time to time, too. Might even want to go up the town on the pull. Mark hated walking into pubs and clubs alone.

A mobile phone rang on the coffee table. Peter picked it up and felt the familiar crushing weight of guilt at the name flashing on the display.

Kate . . . Kate . . . Kate.

'Ay you gonna answer that?'

Peter let it ring out, putting the phone back face down to avoid seeing the reproachful: 'Missed call'.

'It's my ex. She'll ring later.'

The phone rang again.

'Sorry, I'll have to answer it.'

'Yeah, I know what it's like,' Mark said. 'You go ahead, mate. Do' mind me.' He settled back in the armchair.

The bloke's weed wasn't bad either.

Peter went into the kitchen to answer the call.

'Hello? It's me,' said Kate. 'Why didn't you answer?'

Peter tried to feign innocence. 'Sorry, I was in the kitchen. The kettle was on,' he explained. 'How are you?'

'I'm not very happy *atcherley*.'

Peter stifled a groan. 'Why?' he asked. 'What's happened?' He tried to make his voice sound concerned. Nothing had ever happened.

'I think we need to talk.'

Oh God!

'What about?'

'What do you mean, *what about*? Fucking *us*!' she shouted.

Stupid question.

'Look, please, can I call you back in five minutes? There's someone here.' She wouldn't like that.

'*Who?*'

'It's the guy from two doors down,' he said. 'He just fixed something on the car. It wouldn't start. We're having a cup of coffee.'

Did she believe him?

'Oh, that's right! Other people always come first with you. You're so selfish. When have you ever got time for me?'

'Please, can we talk about this later? I'll phone you straight back.' He kept his voice low so that the brute male in his living room wouldn't hear the pleading in his voice.

'*You fucking better!*'

Peter felt the needle of her voice in his ear as he returned to the front room, his throat tight and his stomach clenched. He sat down heavily in the armchair.

Mark looked at him and at the pained expression on his face.

'Why do' you jooss tell 'er to fook off?' he offered. 'Not that it's any of my business.'

Peter didn't mind the suggestion from this stranger. Yob. But the idea was too alien to entertain.

'I can't,' he said. 'It's not that simple. She's got – you know, she gets . . .'

Mark looked at him.

'She suffers from depression, or something,' Peter said. 'It's probably all rubbish. There's nothing wrong with her.'

'You never know wi' that,' said Mark. 'I had it once. I'm all right now. Had counselling and everything, man.'

'Oh right,' said Peter. Had he put his foot in it? 'I mean, I know there are genuine cases.'

'It's all right,' Mark said. 'Do' get me wrong, lots of people blag it.'

Mark finished his coffee, stood up to go and passed the crushed roach back.

Peter took it from Mark's suspiciously dirty fingertips and didn't want to put it in his mouth.

'There's still a draw left.' Mark waited for him to finish it. 'Come round for a smoke when you want. I'm giwin' to fetch some later if you need any,' he said.

'Erm . . .'

'Or I could pop round tomorrer if you want them spark plugs looking at. It'd cost you more than a tenner in a garage . . .'

Peter got the hint. 'Yes, thanks for looking at the car earlier.'

'No problems. Thass what neighbours are for, ay it?'

Peter shut the door behind his guest and rubbed his lips clean. Wasn't there some disease from dog shit that made you blind?

He sat down in the armchair and closed his eyes. Five minutes, and he'd have to ring Kate back. He couldn't face another ear-burning conversation thrashing over their differences, listening to her sobbing, the accusations and but-I-love-yous. How long would it go on for tonight? Half an hour? An hour?

Why couldn't he *jooss tell her to fook off* like that bloke said?

What was his name? Mark?

At least he might be able to buy weed from him, and wouldn't have to go back to London for it. But he didn't like the idea of someone fetching it for him. Someone like Mark would be bound to take a cut. But Peter knew he'd have to put up with it until he could get a dealer's number, which would mean getting friendlier with the thug. Christ! Wasn't it time to give up?

He sent Kate a text message saying he was going to have a quick shower. That should buy him an extra half-hour before the inevitable conversation. Perhaps if he said he had to take the car to a garage he could cut it short. Then he'd have the evening free to . . . to . . . what?

He looked round the room. A lived-in sofa, two armchairs and a coffee table left by the previous occupants. The small TV, the laptop and the old stereo he'd brought with him, along with his books and clothes. It wasn't much to show for a decent university education and nearly forty years of life. His job selling school books wasn't worth mentioning. He'd been able to move quickly when the transfer he'd asked for came up; he'd told Kate he'd be made redundant unless he relocated to the West Midlands and she'd believed him. It had seemed easier than having a breaking-up conversation, and he'd packed the car and fled. He knew she'd never come to live here. Surely now she'd get the message. But her constant threats to slide back into depression had paralysed him, made him reluctant to deliver the death blow to their 'relationship'. Maybe now that he had moved, things might just fizzle out.

Once he'd got away Peter had realized he had no other plan. He'd imagined that with his new-found freedom would come a rush of the joys of life. So far it hadn't. Nevertheless, the first month away from her had been sweet. He'd reread some of his favourite books, and had fallen asleep in front of made-for-TV films with no woman there to tell him otherwise. '*Are you coming to bed now?*' wasn't a question.

But his literary heroes were less consuming than he'd anticipated, and merely reminded him that he was doing nothing useful with his life. The television and internet had taken their place. They didn't challenge his inactivity in the same way. The realization that he wasn't going to have a career of any interest or reward had hit him since he'd reacquired his independence of thought away from *her*. His youth had passed him by in idle and unproductive contemplation of life around him. For the past five years he'd watched Kate's friends thrusting themselves ever further forward in various media environments, braying their ignorance and surface knowledge wherever they went. At social gatherings his own underachievement embarrassed him in front of his intellectual inferiors. Worst of all was the endless talk of property prices and DIY, in which he could only take part through association with Kate's loft conversion. The 'what-are-you-up-to-these-days?' questions had become harder to answer, and he knew her friends told her he was a useless freeloader. Balls to them. Who cared if they'd been to Iraq for the BBC?

But the idea that he might be jealous disturbed him. At one time he'd thought he'd do something creative. He'd even sat down to write, but had soon realized he was unable to follow Goethe's imperative that a writer should turn his attention to the real world and try to express it; to write one must have something to say. All that Peter had laboured to produce had been a list of grievances born of his despair at the dumbing-down and coarsening of the arts. How many acclaimed novels had he flung into the corner of the room, enraged, when he reached the inevitable 'he was sat' and 'they were stood'? And what was the moral purpose of these novels?

And after each failed attempt of his own to put his thoughts on to paper Peter was left with the nagging question:

What's the point?

To anything. Everything.

At least now he could look at pornography on the internet in peace.

5

Faisal Rahman caught up with his older sister as she passed the library. Beauty ignored him, and kept walking. When they reached the bus station she asked him if he had any money. He lied and said he hadn't. She didn't want to walk, but couldn't admit to having money herself. That would start a fight about where she'd got it. They'd have to walk the two miles home.

He'd start nagging once they were away from people and past the mess of roadworks, traffic lights and underpasses, and out onto Cannock Road. She could feel her foot beginning to hurt, but kept going and tried to hide the pain in her scowl. Cars crawled past them and Beauty slowed down.

'You OK, sis?'

'My foot's hurting,' she said.

'It's not far now. We're nearly there.'

Now he asks me if I'm OK. What does he want?

'Get Dad to take you to the doctor,' he suggested.

Right across the road from the flat and the old man has to come with me.

'Sis?'

'What?'

Girls. White probably.

'What's a good present for somebody?'

'How should I know? You lot never buy me nothing.'

No Eid clothes, birthday presents, nothing.

'It depends who it's for,' she added, grateful that he still asked her for advice.

'A girl,' he admitted.

'Well, if it was me, I'd get something expensive,' she said. 'Gold. Maybe a necklace. Or a mobile phone.'

That's gonna kill him. He won't spend money on anyone. Spoilt kid gets everything he wants.

Faisal was silent. 'I thought maybe a CD,' he said.

'What! For a tenner? You cheapcake! Anyway, what you doing buying presents for a white girl?'

'How do you know she's white?' he said.

'You've just told me.' At least she had something on him now, and maybe he wouldn't cause trouble when they got home.

'You ain't gonna say anything are you, sis?' he begged, and went quiet again as he realized how she'd outwitted him. '*Bhai-sahb* ain't gonna believe a lying tramp like you anyway.'

She'd pushed him too far. Now there would be a fight.

They walked on in silence, but he quickened his pace and told her to hurry up. At the shops by the crossing she waited as he went in to spend some of the money he'd said he didn't have. She stood by the shop door and pulled her jacket about her, grimacing with the cold and the pain in her foot. Faisal came out, his pockets stuffed with chocolate bars. They crossed the road and headed over the grassy mound to the concrete stairwell below their flat. Beauty winced as she climbed the stairs behind him, and stuck her tongue out at her younger brother's back in his new Adidas tracksuit. Preparing herself for what was to come, she followed him along the concourse, took a deep breath as he opened the front door, and went in after him.

*

The flat was quiet. *Bhai-sahb* would be asleep upstairs, and the old man was probably watching television in the sitting room. Her little sister would be lying on her bed reading. What else could Sharifa do? Faisal never let her go on the internet and she wasn't allowed a radio. Their mum would be asleep as well.

Beauty took off her shoes, went down the corridor and into the bathroom to wash her feet. She could stay in there for a while before the little one or the old man banged on the door and told her to come out.

The cold water made her gasp and she looked at the swelling lump on her left foot. If the old man had paid to put a curse on her, she didn't want him to know it might be working. He'd said that curses wouldn't work on a *shaitan*. At least that meant she wasn't a devil.

She'd found the *tabiz* in her pillowcase a month before, and had broken open the wax seal with shaking hands. The tiny roll of paper that she pulled from the small tube was full of Arabic words written backwards. At first she couldn't imagine where he'd got it from. Not in Wolverhampton; he hadn't been anywhere and they didn't have any money. Had he borrowed some, she wondered, or maybe got a Hindu to do it? They were cheaper.

But when she showed it to *Bhai-sahb*, he went crazy and forced the old man to admit he'd paid an *ulta-imam* in Birmingham five hundred pounds to curse her.

Back in Bangladesh he'd paid imams nearly a thousand *taka* to make her want to marry the mullah, and be good. When she got ill her brother had called a doctor, but the man didn't know what was wrong with her. *Bhai-sahb* thought the mullah's family might have cursed her for refusing to live with him, and he'd gone round the villages looking for the highest imam he could find to come and see her. The elderly man in the Punjabi suit, whom he brought back with him, had scared her. But he'd spoken kindly, looked about the house and the rough land around it, and eventually pointed to the fish ponds near-by. There was a fish with a *tabiz* tied round it, the imam had told them. Find the fish, take off the *tabiz* and the girl will get better.

Beauty had watched from the house as the men dragged nets across the ponds and inspected each fish. Finally they found it. *Bhai-sahb* broke open the *tabiz* and ran to the old man shouting, the fish in one hand and the roll of paper in the other. The old man shrugged and came into the house. He hadn't helped to look.

Beauty turned the tap off and thought about washing properly before going upstairs to pray.

What's the point?

'*Toba, toba,*' she said aloud, touching her cheeks three times protectively.

Al-lāh dhway, I didn't mean it like that.

If she went to pray they'd say she was only pretending, doing it to hide from them and make herself look holy.

I aynt never seen Bhai-sahb pray in my life. He read Siffara and Qur'an a bit, then gave up. He was into dodgy stuff so he gave up everything. Back home they thought he was a gundha till he got rid of his gangster clothes.

She touched the lump on her foot lightly.

Al-lāh, why they doing this to me? What did I do wrong?

I aynt going to marry no one to save the old man's face. I'd rather die. Especially not a mullah. For him I suffered.

Why didn't the mullah give up and marry someone else?

Cuz he wants to get married legal way and come to this country. He's balla zat and the old man wants to lift his own name back home.

Beauty rubbed her feet dry and put on some sandals,

opened the door and listened. She could just make out the noise from the television in the sitting room and the old man muttering. She walked quietly down the corridor and into the empty kitchen to start cooking. He'd want a lamb and chicken curry. The little ones couldn't eat anything too hot so she'd have to make another two, without *naga*, the chilli peppers the old man liked. Dulal, her older brother, would eat whatever she made, depending on his mood. But if there'd been a fight, he wouldn't touch anything she'd cooked. She might have poisoned it. If he ate after a fight, he'd get diarrhoea the next day. Of that she made sure. It had taken him years to realize what she did. Beauty laughed and pulled the sack of onions from the cupboard.

'What the fuck are you laughing at?' Faisal's voice startled her.

'Nothing. Can't I laugh?'

'To yourself? You're fucking crazy.'

Beauty chopped the onions. They'd always told her she was *faggol* and she'd believed them. The old man had told Miss McKenzie, her primary school teacher, that his daughter was mad. When she was eleven years old they heard her talking to herself and took her to see imams, so she started talking to herself in Turkish instead. Their neighbours in London at number 36 were Turkish and she'd learned how to say *bir*, *iki*, *uc*, *merhaba* and *hoscakal* from their six-year-old daughter. The old man had stopped them playing together, but Beauty remembered the sounds and rhythms of the child's prattle and talked her own gibberish version of it to herself whenever she thought anyone was listening at the door.

'Well, what were you laughing at?'

'Mind your own business.'

'Was it something the *halla* said?' he insisted.

'Why do you keep talking about her? Did you fancy her?'

Beauty knew she had to be careful. He was easy to wind up.

So what if I do? Fight's gonna come sooner or later anyway.

'And who were those blokes with you?'

'What blokes?' she said. 'I didn't see no blokes.'

'Liar. There was two blokes standing there, laughing and talking.'

'So what? It's a free country, aynit?'

What's free?

'You shouldn't have been with them.'

Why not?

But she couldn't argue with him. She knew she shouldn't have been standing with them.

'Anyway, *Bhai-sahb*'ll be up soon,' he said, and left her alone in the kitchen again.

I didn't want to go on that course. He forced me.

Since they'd got back from Bangladesh her older brother had been cold towards her. He hadn't wanted her to marry the mullah either, but he blamed her for the mess that had come of it, and he knew he wouldn't be able to get married until it was sorted out. Who else could he blame?

Beauty finished the onions and started on the garlic and ginger. She'd cooked for the family since she was ten years old, when her ama had gone into hospital. Tonight she would make the *hutki*, too, for her mum, just how she liked it. She stood at the cooker, measuring powders in a wooden spoon and stirring them into the onions, garlic and ginger. Above the frying she heard noises from her older brother's bedroom overhead. He'd be down soon. She made *sagu*, and set a place for him at the table. Maybe he'd be too tired to get angry before going to work. It would depend on how much trouble the little one managed to cause.

She listened to steps coming down the stairs and watched as a form approached the ribbed glass of the kitchen door. Maybe it was only Faisal – he was getting so big these days she couldn't be sure. The handle turned and her older brother, Dulal Miah, stood in the doorway, hair flattened and eyes dark with sleep. He was putting on weight – his neck had fattened out and his nose seemed thicker and flatter. He was starting to look like the old man.

He smiled at his sister.

'All right, sis?' he croaked, shuffling to the table and sitting down heavily. Beauty put the bowl of porridge in front of him.

'Do you want tea, *Bhai-sahb*?' she asked.

'Yeah,' he said. 'Thanks.'

Thanks!

She filled the kettle with water and threw in two handfuls of loose tea and a piece of cinnamon after it.

That's gonna be tasty.

'How was the course?' he asked.

'Dunno. It hasn't really started.' She wanted to say how embarrassing it was sitting next to white people, how the black blokes looked at her and how shocking the things that the white girls said were, but she knew he wanted her to go.

'Stick at it. They might find you a job.'

'Yeah, but I've got to do the reading first.'

'That ain't gonna work.' He sounded irritated. 'Didn't you tell them we tried everything? Can't they just find you a job?'

He must have really needed the money; and he was right about the reading. She knew the alphabet, but how letters became words remained a mystery. There was something wrong with her, she knew that now. They didn't need to tell her.

'They're gonna talk to us one by one tomorrow and see what we want to do.'

He grunted and spooned *sagu* into his mouth. She put the tea in front of him and went back to the cooker, asking about his work over her shoulder. Things were going OK, he said. They were going to make him a supervisor soon.

Beauty heard footsteps overhead again and hoped it was her mum.

Faisal came into the kitchen in another new tracksuit, carrying his new mobile phone. Dulal had had to buy it for him – as payment for doing well at school and staying out of trouble.

'Yo, blood,' he said to his older brother, slapping him on the shoulder.

'Don't talk like a fucking *halla*.'

'At least I don't hang around with them like I saw her doing today,' Faisal said.

'I wasn't hanging around with black people. I was saying goodbye to a girl I sat next to,' Beauty said.

'Faisal, stop shit-stirring or you'll get a kick. Get me the post.'

Dulal Miah carried on eating and drinking tea while he opened the letters addressed to his mother and sister from the Department for Work and Pensions. He grunted in satisfaction, put the letters down, leaned back in his chair and rubbed his stomach.

'Sis, don't bring no more shame on us.'

Shame? I didn't bring no shame on no one.

'I aynt shaming you,' she said.

'Good. Cuz that'll be the end if anything else happens.'

What are they gonna do now? Kill me? They already tried that.

'And make sure you help Mum with the washing.'

Help Mum? She doesn't do nothing. All right, I can't blame her for that, she's my mother.

'Yeah, sure,' she said.

She glanced at Faisal and could tell from his fidgeting that he was deciding whether to say more.

'She was smoking Dad's fags as well.'

Beauty saw her chance. 'Did you want them for your white girlfriend?'

'She's lying, *Bhai-sahb*,' he said. 'I ain't got no white girlfriend. She's lying like she always does.'

'I told you to stop shit-stirring,' Dulal said.

Beauty could feel her older brother looking at her and she waited for the shouting to start, but he didn't say anything. She turned to face him, but he remained silent. Faisal looked at his brother. What was wrong with *Bhai-sahb*? What he'd just heard was usually enough to send him into a rage.

Beauty turned back to the cooker. Dulal's calm, and the cold look in his eyes, worried her more than his shouting. It could mean only one thing.

Mullah Habib Choudhury.

Had she missed the signs? Had there been any? She hadn't heard the phone ringing more than usual, or the whispered conversations that stopped when she came into the room. She should have expected it, though. Dulal wanted to get married. He was twenty-five and needed a wife, but what family would let their daughter marry a man who couldn't control his own sister? Once they started asking around they'd soon find out about Beauty's failed marriage. And besides, he'd never find a decent wife, born here, unless the old man arranged it, and as long as she refused to bring the mullah into the country, the old man swore that he wouldn't. He had promised her to Habib Choudhury long ago, and so far he hadn't been able to make Beauty keep his word.

Maybe she was wrong. Perhaps *Bhai-sahb* was just tired of fighting. He knew she'd been through a lot. He still asked her advice on what job to take, how to put up with Paki comments at work, or how to ask a girl out – not that he ever did.

Dulal stood up and left the kitchen, shutting himself in the sitting room with the old man. Faisal went upstairs, not sure what his brother's silence meant. But Beauty understood. Was that why her mum was still in bed? The talk would come later that night, before *Bhai-sahb* went to work.

Beauty carried on stirring the meat with the melting onions and decided to make some dal. There was nowhere but the kitchen for her to go. Faisal would hear if she went to Sharifa's room and tell her to get out. They didn't want a *sinnal* like her influencing their little sister. Sharifa might turn into a slapper, too.

She finished cooking, laid out the dishes behind her on the sideboards, sat down at the kitchen table and waited for them to come in.

Why do they always call me a slapper? Sinnal this, slapper that. Magi, too. And tramp, tramp, tramp.

You went out with that Sikh boy.

I didn't even kiss him! What would they do if I wasn't a virgin like Fatima, or Lucy, Uncle Abdul's daughter? Her husband found out on her wedding night!

They'd tell you to use honey so he wouldn't know.

Beauty wasn't sure how the honey helped, but a cousin-sister had once told her your husband wouldn't know that you weren't a virgin if you used it.

It makes it small again, aynit. Down there.

The door to the sitting room opened and the old man appeared. He stared at her from the end of the corridor, before turning to go upstairs.

So what they gonna say this time?

The mullah's pervert brother's hassling the old man here and his family's hassling from back home. It's shaming him.

Beauty closed the kitchen door and sat down again. She put her foot on the chair, continued biting her fingernails and listened as the toilet flushed.

They went on at me night and day. Took me to imams, put curses on me – khalla zadu – to make me say yes. The old man said he'd kill himself.

What was I supposed to do? They told me to say yes – hobbul – and I could go back to England the next day. Thass how I got married, Muslim way, but I didn't let the mullah anywhere near me. They told him to wait, so he backed off.

And she had cooked, cleaned and looked after her uncle Mukhtar and his family for five years, washing their clothes by hand.

Seventeen people! Even his slave started bossing me, after he got her pregnant – Allah give him guna one day.

Then they thought she'd gone mad so they left her alone.

Aynt I?

Al-lāh, what am I gonna do now?

Get out!

The kitchen door opened.

'Crazy bitch is talking to herself again,' Dulal Miah said over his shoulder to the old man.

6

Somewhere in North London, Kate Morgan jerked awake in her Victorian end-of-terrace ground floor flat with original features, and reached for her mobile phone.

'Bastard,' she said. Seven o'clock in the evening and he hadn't even bothered to send her a text message. She must have nodded off waiting for him to ring back.

Kate yawned and stretched. Emotional and physical exhaustion were typical symptoms of depression, she'd read, and her therapist had confirmed it. She let the phone fall to the floor, propped herself up against the pillows and scrunched her dark, shoulder-length hair.

The bed felt empty.

Was another woman in his?

She'd stopped it from happening once before. Who was to prevent him from doing it again?

But Kate didn't think he would. Peter was sexually inactive. In the six months before he'd left he'd not come near her once. She was still attractive, had good boobs and hadn't put on much weight around her bum since her early twenties. Even her GP agreed that she was suffering from the sense of rejection and her uncertain relationship with him. Worse was the damage he'd done to her self-esteem.

Kate picked up the hand mirror and tweezers from the

bedside table, started to pluck her eyebrows and wondered whether Peter might be gay.

By half seven he still hadn't phoned. She'd have to take some St John's Wort and a cup of herbal tea to stay awake. She got out of bed, put on a heavy towelling dressing gown and, clutching it around her, shuffled to the door. The flat was *so* cold.

Halfway down the corridor she was struck by dizziness, and literally had to drag herself along the wall to the kitchen. She made it to the kettle without blacking out completely, then pulled herself along the worksurfaces to a chair. She sat down, wincing. The stabbing pains in her legs and back were coming on again. Actually she'd been feeling a lot worse recently, and was positive she was coming down with something. She shouldn't let Peter make her feel like this. Her low self-esteem was deepening her depression, making her more prone to whatever illness was going around.

'I'm an attractive and nice person,' her therapist had urged her to say aloud.

Perhaps she should take the initiative and confront Peter: demand to know if he still loved her and whether he was seeing someone else. Time was passing her by. How long could she afford to wait?

Peter paced between his reflection in the kitchen window and the mirror at the bottom of the stairs. He ruffled his short, fair hair to bring out the widow's peak of the maturing male and admired his straight nose and hazel eyes. He still felt very good-looking.

He picked up his phone from the coffee table and slumped onto the sofa. Should he call her? He'd have to. He had to be stronger and make a clean break. This was supposed to be his prime, when attractive women in pencil skirts and white blouses offered him their phone numbers. It was Kate's presence in his life, even if only at the end of the phone, which still held him back. And look where he'd ended up to escape her hooks and chains.

He pulled up her number and let his thumb hover above the call key. He'd tried to leave her before, but both times she'd had herself referred to a clinic by her counsellor – 'therapist', she liked to call him. He knew he should have left her then, but he'd felt sorry for her and guilty for a fling he'd tried to have with another woman. When she'd sobbed from the hospital bed that she loved him, what could he do?

Kate was still the attractive and sometimes interesting woman he'd met five years ago; still more or less rational for three weeks in a month. He'd tried to talk to her about PMS when the GP had prescribed antidepressants, but she'd hurled a book at his head. The pills had made her 'mood swings' worse; that much psychobabble he could accept. He soon noticed that she dropped the names of the drugs into conversation at the art gallery openings and shows for which she lived, as she did the names of famous people, familiarity with which rendered her acceptable to the self-obsessed in-crowd, sipping from glasses of bad white wine.

Peter put the phone down, sat back and shut his eyes. He'd wanted to leave without telling her the truth, without having to watch those unnerving scenes and sobbing fits which had weakened his resolve last time. This time he'd lied his way out. He was depressed, he'd told her – this surely she would understand – by his lack of success. If he sorted himself out financially, maybe even 'got on the property ladder' somewhere affordable, perhaps then he could think more clearly about the future.

He knew he hadn't dealt with it very well, and so far the physical distance between them hadn't helped either.

She phoned every day to describe at great length the day's torments and to tell him how much she missed him. He missed her, too, he said. At least he had managed to avoid going to see her. He was tired by driving all week. She said she understood, and hadn't shown any interest in coming to Wolverhampton.

The thug from two doors down had been right. Perhaps not 'fook off'. But Peter knew he had to deal with it properly.

His thumb pressed the call button and he waited. Kate answered at the second ring.

'Hu-llo?' She sounded more relaxed, friendly.

'Hi,' Peter said, tensely. He needed to keep some steel in his voice.

'I'm sorry about earlier. I've been feeling really low all day,' she explained.

'Don't worry about it.' He was pleased with his clipped tone and new determination.

'It's been hard for me, you know . . . since you went away,' she said.

Peter remained silent. Voices passed the window. Let her get it out. He'd wait for his opening.

'I'm not coping very well,' she went on. 'It's knocked my confidence. It's like I'm being rejected . . . like I was no good.'

Peter stifled a groan. Here came the disarming plea to his sense of pity. But he wouldn't let it work this time.

'Kate, it's not like that . . .'

'It hasn't made me feel very special,' she said. 'It's really undermined my self-esteem, you know?'

Peter winced at the familiar phrases. She must have been to see her counsellor. She always came back from her appointments belligerent and accusatory. Assertive, she called it.

'You know why I had to get out of London.' Peter

heard the pleading tone in his voice. This wasn't going how he'd intended.

There was the sound of a choked sob.

'So, if you had a better job here you'd still want to live with me?' she asked.

'Of course,' he lied. This was a disaster.

'You're not seeing someone else, are you?'

Peter clenched his fist. 'No!'

'Do you still love me?'

Here was his chance. But how could he tell her?

'Of course,' he said, cursing his weakness. 'It's just that . . . look, maybe we do need to talk.'

'About what?' Her voice was cold and suspicious.

'I mean . . . it's been hard for me too, these last couple of years,' he said, amazed that such words were coming from his mouth, finally.

'What do you mean "these last couple of years"? What's been hard?'

'Well. You know. I've tried to . . .'

'To what?'

'To be there for you.'

Silence.

Then, 'Oh, I see! You mean my illness has been hard for you? If you love someone, you help and support them. That's what people *do*, Peter.'

'That's what I've tried to do.'

'By leaving me without a support network?'

'You've got all your friends, and your mum and dad.'

'My parents are no fucking use. What have they ever done for me?'

'You're all right now, though, aren't you?'

'Depression's a mental *illness*. It doesn't just go away!'

Peter rubbed his temples, pain creasing his forehead. How long would she persist with this?

'You're not ill, Kate. It's all in your head.'

Silence again.

'Very fucking funny, Peter. *Don't you dare belittle my suffering!*'

He could imagine her rocking and hugging herself on the floor next to a radiator. He'd never been able to find out exactly what her suffering consisted of – something about being criticized by an overbearing mother and made to feel worthless. The counsellors she'd seen had convinced her of it, Peter was sure.

'Don't forget what you put me through two years ago,' she hissed.

Maxine, the blonde from Head Office. Maxine. The one with the fantastic figure. It wasn't as if anything had really *happened*. Not the way he'd planned it. Kate had found his phone and the messages arranging the rendezvous before he'd had chance to consummate the affair. And then there was the miscarriage Kate had had. She'd seen the relief on his face and had never forgiven him.

Guilt deflated him, as it always did.

'Look, I'm sorry.'

The phone began to burn. Peter switched it to the other ear. How much longer would he have to endure this?

'I just wish you could love me for who I am,' Kate said. 'But you obviously don't care what happens to me.'

'Oh, for fuck's sake. Of course I do!'

'Don't you raise your voice at me. *I deserve a bit of fucking happiness too, you know!*'

The line went dead.

Peter switched off the phone. He knew that wouldn't be the end of it, but he wasn't going to call her back. In defiant mood he got up from the armchair and turned on the laptop. Analsluts.com might help keep up his resolve. He sat at the shaky computer desk watching the egg timer on the screen, then decided to take his time over it and went to the kitchen to make more coffee. There was nothing to do until *EastEnders*. Perhaps he could have a smoke, too.

By the time he settled down in front of the screen the search engine was waiting for him. He went to a free listings page, an A to Z of sexual preferences, and started at the beginning, following the links to the thumbnail galleries.

'Anal fisting.' Too grim.

'Beads – Gorgeous Busty Blonde Inserts Beads.' He couldn't quite make it out, but it looked like long red fingernails poking a line of rosary beads up a woman's arse.

'Big boobs.' Too dull.

'Butt plugs.' He'd save that for later.

'Camel toe.' Too much up-skirt schoolgirl stuff. Tempting, but he didn't want it on the hard drive.

'CBT.' What the hell could that be? Surely not Kate's Cognitive Behaviour Therapy? Psychiatrists taking advantage of patients on couches?

Peter opened the link. Clothes pegs attached to men's genitals.

Cock and Ball Torture.

7

Mark Aston sat on his new sofa in the warmth of the halogen heater. The mess in his front room didn't look so bad in its glow. That bloke Pete seemed all right, and it was good to have a white neighbour you could borrow a smoke off of. Pete's house was much better, too. Clean and well-decorated. Mark's was shit. He'd laid the carpet himself, but after a few months the dogs had pissed on it that many times he'd had to take it up and stuff it in the cupboard under the stairs until the smell had dried out. He'd put it back down three weeks ago and it was all right. The rest of the house was fucked, though, apart from the back room, which he never went in. He was saving it for Honey and her pups. This time, he couldn't afford to lose any. Last time it had been that Paki landlord's fault. He'd given Mark a shit house. No central heating or double glazing either, and three of the puppies had died from the cold.

Still, at least he ay been round to pick up the top-up on me rent what the housing benefit do' cover.

Missing that appointment at the Crown House Jobcentre had been a real choker. The bastards had signed him off and cut all his money, without any warning. He'd gone straight up there as soon as he'd discovered he hadn't been paid. It looked like others had missed appointments, too. People were shouting at every desk, demanding their money immediately. The two feeble security guards couldn't cope and had called for back-up over their radios.

He'd had to reapply for his housing and council tax benefit, as well as his Jobseekers' Allowance, which they wouldn't pay until his new claim had gone through the system. In the meantime he'd had to make do with a hardship allowance of thirty-seven pounds a week until he'd served a six-week sanction period for missing the start of the course at RiteSkills. The housing benefit for the six weeks might not get paid either; they were deciding that at the minute. Just for missing an appointment!

Still, he'd started the course now. The JSA would get paid from next week, plus the extra tenner, and he had enough money from selling the phone to get a five of weed before he went up town that night.

He waited until it was darker before going to the phone box at the bottom of the street to call Paula. She'd been raided again recently and didn't like giving you the weed in daylight. The cops hadn't been able to do her though; she never kept anything in the house. She knew one of the neighbours had grassed her up, but not which one, so two nights after the raid she'd slashed all the tyres of every car on the street.

Fair play to 'er.

Mark hoped she wouldn't send her son Darren out to bring him the weed. You could always tell he'd pinched a bit by the way he never wrapped the clingfilm like she did. He was only twelve, so what could you expect? Mark had done worse by his age.

At the phone box some Kosovan was shouting down the line in a foreign language. Mark waited impatiently for less than a minute, wishing he'd brought Titan with him, then decided he didn't need the dog. He opened the door and asked the startled man if he was going to be long, mate, because he had an important call to make.

The Kurd hung up and made way for the white man.

'Ta,' said Mark.

Paula's number rang. She only lived up by the shops but didn't want people coming round to the house.

'Oright Paula? It's Mark.'

'Ullo bab! Am y'oright, am y'?'

'Ar, sowund.'

'What d'you want?'

'Can I come and fetch a five?'

'Where am you?'

'At the phone box on Dunstall Road.'

'Darren'll bring it. There's too many five-oh rowund 'ere.'

'Nice one, Paula. See you.'

'Ar, see you, bab. Tra.'

'Tra.'

Mark kept the phone pressed to his ear. He might as well stay out of the cold. The Kosovan could wait for a bit. Darren would be there soon anyway.

Two minutes later he hung up as he saw the boy's white cap rounding the corner at the end of Leicester Street. He left the phone box and walked towards him, stopping in the darkness between lamp posts.

'Oright Daz?' Mark said.

'Sowund.' *Prick*, the boy thought.

Mark gave him the five-pound note and the twelve-year-old took a small cellophane wrap from the pocket of a new Bench jacket. Mark held the weed in his fist. It felt all right.

'Say hello to yer mam for me,' he said.

'Yeah, sure,' the lad answered, wheeling away on his bike. He didn't like Mark. He was too friendly.

Back at home Mark inspected the clingfilm. It was untouched. He'd roll a fat one, get a can from the fridge and listen to some music in the bath. That would kill some time before he went out. He'd need to iron some clean clothes dry, too. He could do that in front of *EastEnders*.

By eight o'clock Peter had only got as far as P for Panties. The tightly stretched white cotton made his chest ache and he saved some of the images for a soft-to-hard full-screen slide-show of the evening's findings. He ignored Pantyhose – the word made him cringe – and left Peeing and Puffy Nipples for later.

EastEnders was dull. It had been ever since Sharon had died in a ball of flame on Tracey Fowler's bench in the park. Peter picked up the TV guide to see if there was anything else that would help draw out his internet research. He didn't want to have to do it twice just to fill up the evening. But there was nothing to watch, apart from DIY programmes, chat shows with special guests who were the presenters of other chat shows, repeats of unfunny sit-coms, opinion-as-fact on the news, or lurid documentaries with titles like *Half Ton Man, The Boy With A Tumour For A Face,* and *The Woman Who Lost Forty Stone And Put It Back On Again.* Or there was a two-part thriller that had started the day before.

Peter stood up and went back to the computer.

Mark found himself with nothing to do. If it had been Wednesday or Thursday *The Bill* would have been on. He brought the iron and board in from the kitchen and ran upstairs to fetch a discoloured and misshapen jumper from the cold spare bedroom. He sniffed at it but couldn't tell if it was mildewed. He'd know when he ironed it, and if he left it in front of the fire it should be ready for later. He thought about knocking on that bloke Pete's door to see if he wanted a smoke. Pay him back for earlier on.

The file was building up as Peter passed through Peeing Lesbian Secretaries (English sites mostly), Rope Bondage (alarming and Japanese), Shemale Blowjobs (Brazilians with perfect breasts, large hands and Adam's apples), and Weird Insertions (painful-looking German gynaecology and pictures of feet up men's arses). Ignoring some of the more disturbing elements, he reordered the pictures to build up to a finale. Satisfied with the arrangement, he settled back to watch the slide-show. He'd finish off at the second viewing. After two hours he was aching and the relief would be huge, heightened by the light-headedness from smoking.

The doorbell rang as he reached the last three slides and his final throes. He looked round as the release came, his enjoyment of the delicious relief wrecked by the interruption. He cleaned up hurriedly, slammed the laptop shut and went to the door, breathing heavily and stuffing himself back into his trousers.

He looked through the spyhole and recognized – Mark, was it? Jesus, what did he want?

'Oright Pete! Thought you said you were coomin' rowund.'

'Oh . . . sorry, I didn't realize.'

'I fetched some weed jooss. You skinned up earlier, so I thought I'd offer. If you want.'

'Actually . . . erm, I'm sort of falling asleep on the sofa. I've got to get up early in the morning.'

'Oh well, I won't stop for long in that case. I'm off up

the town soon anyway.' Mark looked at Peter, waiting for him to stand aside and let him in.

'Sure. Come in,' Peter said. He'd need the weed.

8

Beauty lay on the sofa, exhausted and aching. Her arms and wrists hurt where she'd been pulled and punched. They hadn't hit her as much as in the past, because now she had to go out every day. She'd got two hard slaps across the face, but the stinging would be gone by the morning. *Bhai-sahb* had done most of the shouting and hitting, while the old man stood at the door, his eyes shining as they always did when she got beaten. She'd have to go back to Bangladesh, Dulal said, marry the mullah legally and bring him back to this country. She only had to live with him for a year to make it look good for the Home Office. Once he was allowed to stay in Britain she could divorce him.

That's what they said, but would it be like that? And if she didn't want to marry him then they would send her to live with the old man's brother in Saudi Arabia. His sons were looking for wives, too.

The choice was hers.

Beauty had refused, and got the first slap across the face. The old man told his son not to hit her where it would be noticed. Like at primary school when Miss McKenzie had asked her about the bruises on her back. Beauty saw the anger in her brother's eyes. She tried not to flinch at the blow, but she knew they would probably hear her sobs that night when the fight had ended. And he did slap her face again, harder, catching her cheek with the ball of his open hand. The blow knocked her sideways, but the sideboard was there and she managed to stay on her feet.

Beauty's mother screamed from the open doorway for him to stop.

'*Ar ita horissna!*'

The old man cursed his wife and slammed the door in her face.

'Ama!' Beauty cried. But what could her mother do?

The old man stood at the door, trembling with rage.

'Which is it going to be?' Dulal Miah asked her.

She refused again. And so it went on. Eventually Dulal tried to reason with her.

'Who else is gonna marry you? You ain't gonna find anyone – you're ugly, dark and dumb – who's gonna look at you? Anyone marries you's gonna drag you by the hair and kick you out the kitchen door.'

She'd heard it before, but her brother's words always hurt more than his punches. And what if he was right? With a broken marriage behind her, who would look at her? And it was true, she was dark-skinned; darker than anyone else in the family.

The men left the room. Beauty's mother pushed past them to comfort her child, and persuade her to do what was right. It wouldn't be so bad, she said. Once she'd spent a couple of years with Habib Choudhury and divorced him she would be free to come back home and look after the family.

Later on, after they'd eaten the food Beauty had prepared, Dulal told her to stay downstairs and not go up to Sharifa's room where their mum would be explaining everything to the little girl. That her big sister would be going away again soon. Back home or to Saudi Arabia. Beauty would have liked to have gone upstairs to lie down with her mother and sister, and feel their warmth on either side of her, but *Bhai-sahb* and the old man rarely let her do that.

Beauty got up from the sofa and went to the window to look down on the estate. There was more life outside at this time of night. Scary black blokes in hooded tops and young Iraqis moved about in the darkness below her. She'd be on a flight back to Bangladesh, or Saudi Arabia, as soon as they'd fixed everything. How long? In two weeks? A month?

They were all tired of fighting now. Tonight had been the last time.

I'll go there, get married, and come straight back, aynit?
No, you won't. They'll keep you there until you do what everyone wants. You'll give in eventually.
Al-lāh, I gotta get out.
How? You got no money. Where you gonna sleep?
In the station.
You'll get raped by black blokes.
They got places for Asians in London.
They'll find you wandering about and stick you in a loony bin, the same way what happened to Fatima.
I am faggol like her. Crazy.

Outside, the rain fell through the glow of the street lamps. Beauty looked at the squat buildings below her in the darkness, and across the road to the tower block. What would it be like to live there, alone, and look down from its windows? Free.
To do what?

Stuff. Like walk to the shops on my own and talk to people. I won't have to stay in, looking out of the

window. I won't have to listen to the old man shouting at
my mum. I won't have to turn the TV over when they
kiss on EastEnders.

You can't watch people kissing on TV. Thass gross!

OK then, I won't have to cook and clean for them
again, ever.

But Mum can't do it; she's ill.

She aynt ill, she just says that to make me do
everything. Anyway, Sharifa can learn how to do them
stuff. She's old enough.

She's only nine.

So? I started when I was that age.

Thass a different story. You were born back home.
Nowadays-girls don't learn to cook.

So the old man can help out. Mum won't have to do it
all. Bhai-sahb's a good cook, too. And at Eid I won't
have to cook for everyone and sit alone.

You'll always be alone.

I'll meet people. Not everyone out there's a monster.

Who's gonna be friends with a dumb corner-girl?

Maybe I'll stop being dumb. I could try the reading
thing again.

That aynt gonna work. They tried everything.

Like what, the mullah's pervert brother?

What else you gonna do?

I'll be able to . . . to go out at night.

Thass for Sikhs. You're a Muslim girl.

Muslim girls don't go out? I saw what they were like in
Dhaka. I'll be able to wear what I want, too.

What about Mum?

She'll be OK. They can tell people I'm ill. Gone to hospital.
And the fighting's gonna stop if I go. It's gonna be better
for the kids too. Fa ranná. This aynt good for them.

*

It's a zinna though, aynit?

Sleeping with a bloke – thass a zinna.

Parents come first and Allah comes second – thass in the Qur'an.

I aynt never going back to Bangladesh. I aynt living with no mullah. And I aynt going to that other place . . . Saudi Arabia . . . neither. No one comes back from there.

9

Peter shut the front door and invited Mark to sit down. He glanced at the laptop. The green lights flickered on the side of the computer, the modem running. Inside, the last slide would still be up on the screen, but he couldn't exit it without raising the lid or switching the laptop off at the wall, which would look strange.

'Coffee?' he asked, going into the kitchen.

'Tea,' Mark said. 'Got any skins?'

'Somewhere,' Peter called, coming back into the sitting room to find them. Mark was standing by the computer, his thumb on the catch of the laptop. Peter took the single stride to the table and clicked the lid shut.

'That's private,' he said. 'Work stuff.'

'Sorry,' said Mark. 'Just seeing what make it is. Nice laptop.' He picked up the cigarette papers and went back to the armchair.

'Here, I waar interrupting anything, was I?'

Peter reappeared with two mugs.

'How long have you been living here?' he asked Mark.

Getting on for nearly two years now, Mark said. Came down from Burntwood to get away from old mates and bad influences, sort his head out and start afresh, did Peter know what he meant?

He did.

Wolvo was all right, man. Dunstall Park, too. There were too many foreigners around though.

London was the same.

Still, there were plenty of cheap pubs and birds. Well, slags. What more did he want?

Peter watched Mark's large fingers crumble the dried weed along the bed of tobacco on the cigarette paper, noticing the span of his knuckles and the blue dots of home-made tattoos on each one. Mark looked up at him.

'Do' worry, I ay front-loaded it,' he said. 'Here, you got any chunes?'

He hadn't. He'd left his stuff in London, at his sort-of ex's.

Couldn't he listen to something online?

The speakers didn't work very well, Peter said.

Mark had some computer speakers Peter could lend. Got them down the re-cyke. Or he could borrow him some CDs. Did he like dance music?

Er . . . yeah, it was OK, although he didn't get much chance to listen to music.

What about in the car?

The stereo was playing up.

Mark could fix it – anything like that. He was a damn good mechanic, too.

Really?

Ye'man. He could have a look at it this weekend, if Peter wanted.

Yeah – that would be great.

Mark passed Peter the spliff. The bloke seemed all right. A bit scared, like, and a pushover as well, but he might be a useful pulling partner that night. At least he wouldn't have to walk into the pub on his own.

Did Peter fancy coming up the town for a drink in a bit, Mark asked.

Peter was a little tired.

Mark, too, needed an early night. Had to be at the course for nine the next morning. But it was pound-a-pint night up Flanagan's and there'd be loads of birds there. It would do Peter good to take his mind off his ex. (Had Peter told her to fook off, by the way?) And when was the last time he'd been out on the town?

Peter hadn't been out in Wolverhampton.

Right, that was settled. He was coming out.

What was Flanagan's like?

Sowund. He needn't worry, the place wasn't rough. Mark didn't like trouble either, but there were so many fucking knobs around these days you had to be careful.

Peter passed the spliff back. He wasn't sure about going 'up the town'. Mark didn't seem the type who avoided trouble. Still, he looked as if he would be able to handle himself in a tight spot. And it was true, Peter hadn't been anywhere without Kate for a long time. It might do him good. He used to go to pubs and clubs looking for girls. Why not here? It would beat the hours he'd otherwise spend on the internet. Talking to real people might provide some mental stimulus, too. And if he was careful not to chat up some maniac's girlfriend or catch the wrong person's eye, he might get through the evening without a glass shoved in his face. Wasn't that what happened in pubs in towns like this? He didn't fancy walking there though.

'Shall we get a taxi?' he asked Mark.

'Am you fookin' mad?' It was only a ten-minute walk. The price of a cab would buy him four pints in Flanagan's.

They could get a taxi back though, couldn't they? Peter would pay.

Whatever. He just had to go home and iron some clothes and they could go straight away.

*

At ten o'clock Mark knocked on the door and they set off. Peter had put on a clean white shirt and a pair of straight navy blue trousers, and had patted his cheeks with aftershave. He felt good in his tan loafers. Mark, he noticed, had made an effort to smarten himself up with clean jeans, misshapen but polished Rockport shoes, and a saggy, grey acrylic jumper. He'd shaved to leave long, thin sideburns, and he smelled strongly of body spray. And he looked tough enough. Maybe people would stay away from them.

At the bottom of the road Peter nodded to the street sign.

'Do you know why it's called *Prole* Street?'

'I've got no idea, mate. Why?'

'It's a strange word. Prole, as in – well, you know . . . proletariat.'

'Prol-a-what?'

'Proletariat.'

'Never heard of it. What is it?'

'It means . . . er, working class.'

'Dunno what you're on about, mate, sorry.'

'I could be wrong. Maybe it's just a name. You'd have to go to the library to find out.'

'Why the fook would I wanna do that?'

At the row of shops in Graiseley, Peter kept his eyes lowered as he threaded through the people standing on the pavement outside the chip shop or leaning into the open windows of parked cars. A police car bumped over the speed humps and made him feel braver.

When they reached Asda and the Molineux, Mark cut through the badly lit, empty car park of the football stadium to the long subway under the ring road. The walls of the tunnel were covered with talentless graffiti, the floor stained every few paces with faded explosions of vomit and blackened trickles of piss.

'I kicked in some Baggies here six month back,' Mark said.

'What are Baggies?'

'Christ! You don't know shit! Baggies – West Brom fans. Small Paul phoned me – he's a mate a mine – said they'd got three of them surrounded, so I legged it up here. Course, I dey do things like that no more. Got too much to lose, what wi' me dogs 'n' that. Who's gonna look after them if anything happens to me?'

Peter looked sideways at him. Was Mark smiling wistfully at the memory of kicking a West Brom fan?

He had come out with a madman.

The rest of the journey passed without alarm. The subway brought them to the centre of town, to bright and deserted Monday night streets. Maybe it wouldn't be so life-threatening after all.

Flanagan's turned out to be a large pub full of yobs in sweatshirts, jeans and shoes like Mark's, heavy gold chains and sovereign rings. The air was thick with cigarette smoke and yelled conversations over loud music. As Peter followed Mark through the crowd of young men clutching pints to their chests, he scowled at the back of Mark's head to stop himself from catching anyone's eye and was surprised to notice that people moved to let them pass. Maybe everyone was conscious of the potential for sudden and explosive violence in others. Or was it just Mark's hardness? Whatever the reason, by the time they reached the bar Peter felt more confident than he had when they'd walked in.

'What do you want to drink?' he shouted to Mark.

'Get Carling. It's a quid a pint. The Carlsberg's two quid and Stella's two-forty. I'll get the next ones in.'

Peter would have preferred the stronger, more expensive beer, but felt he should avoid an ostentatious display of wealth. He'd already put a ten-pound note in his trouser pocket to avoid having to pull out his wallet.

As they waited for the beer Mark scanned the crowd for any birds he knew, especially the fat one from RiteSkills and her mate.

He spotted Nicola sitting in a far corner with two girlfriends, the table in front of them covered by empty pint glasses.

'Let's go and talk to them over there,' he shouted to Peter. 'I know two of 'em, and the other one looks all right 'n' all!'

Peter nodded and followed him through the crowd. Younger men moved out of the way of their brimming glasses.

'Oright? It's Nicola, ay it? D'you mind if we sit down wi' you? There ay nowhere else.'

Mark slid into the empty chair next to Nicola.

'Hi,' Peter said, smiling awkwardly as he sat down on the other side of the table. The girls smiled back.

'All right, mate?' said the blonde girl in the England top. 'I'm Louise and this is Kelly.'

'Hiya, mate!' Kelly's voice was deep and rasping. She had long dark hair and pale skin, thick-lensed glasses and a chest that swelled under a tight top.

The girls resumed their chat. Peter took off his jacket, made space for his drink on the crowded table, and unwrapped a packet of twenty Benson and Hedges.

'Fookin' 'ell, 'e muss be loaded! Giss one a them fags.' Kelly's outstretched hand got a slap from Louise.

'God, Kells, y'm awful! Give the poor bloke a chance to offer!' she said, and they both laughed.

'Do' mind her, her's fookin' rude!'

Peter noticed their cheap supermarket brands of ten

Superkings, mumbled something in reply, and offered the pack round the table. Everyone took one.

Kelly lit the cigarette and inhaled the smoke appreciatively.

'Thass a proper fag that, ay it? Not like them roll-ups. We only smoke straights when we'm in towun,' she told Peter. 'Just in case you thought we was posh all the time.'

Mark patted his pockets and said he'd have to nip out and get some fags in a minute. He didn't want to look skint. That Kelly was fit. He'd seen her in Flanagan's before and reckoned she'd be up for it. If he could get past the fat one.

'Pete's me neighbour,' he explained, leaning forward and shouting over the music. 'He asked me to fix his motor cuz he sin me working on loads of others, and he knows I'm pretty good wi' me hands. Ay that right, Pete?'

'Er . . . yeah. He's a really good mechanic.'

'An' he wants one of me pups when Honey gives birth. Reckons they're the best damn Staffies 'e's ever sin.'

He sat back and drew on his cigarette, satisfied that he had caught Kelly's interest. Birds loved dogs.

Peter watched and listened and snatched sideways glances at Louise. Kelly seemed to be asking Mark the right questions about the dogs: Kennel Club registrations, their back legs and mange. Why shouldn't Peter try chatting someone up? A little gentle flirting would help get him back into practice.

'Y'm not from rowund here, am y'?' Louise asked, turning to him.

From near London, he told her. He'd come here for work. What did she do for a living? He could think of nothing else to ask. But the girl took the cue and chatted freely about her job in a care home.

Was she boring him?

No, not at all.

Louise asked him about himself and he answered briefly, as he usually did, conscious of his dull answers. She seemed impressed, however. He had a proper job. He realized he looked successful and sophisticated in her eyes, and, for the first time in years, felt free of the need to exaggerate, or apologize for his failures in life. Kate had always told him he was threatened and challenged by what she called 'strong' women, presumably like herself. What she meant by a strong woman, he didn't know. And so what if he didn't want to be threatened?

He studied Louise between answers, sips of beer and puffs on his cigarette. She had the fresh complexion of a young woman, with blue eyes and thin red lips. Her eyebrows were slightly darker than the fair hair tied back in a ponytail. As she leaned across the table to reach the ashtray, her football shirt stretched across her chest, revealing the outline of her small breasts. But her finger-nails were bitten down, her hands chapped red, and the veins showed through the skin on her pale forearms, which were bruised by the pinching and punching of the service users with severe learning difficulties for whom she cared. Kids with mental problems, she said. She loved her job and the children, but couldn't survive on the wages and had had to take on some more hours in an old folks' home.

How old was she, if she didn't mind Peter asking?

Twenty. It was young to be married, waar it?

Maybe a little.

How old was he? she asked Peter.

Twice as old as her, basically.

Really? He didn't look it, she said. Honestly, blokes she knew of his age looked like old men.

As he inched towards her and leaned unnecessarily

close to catch her words, he caught glimpses of her slightly plump thighs in the charcoal grey tracksuit, and of the fabric creasing between her legs. She gave Peter a sense of womanly warmth. She'd had a rough life, he fantasized, and he would be the first sensitive man to caress her. The movement of her small breasts under the nylon of the football shirt was an inspiration. Like fresh apples.

He looked over at Mark and felt a beery warmth towards him, too. He was glad he'd come out.

When Nicola went to the bar, Mark moved next to Kelly. Pete looked well in there with that Louise bird and no one in the pub was staring at them either. You never knew at Flanagan's on pound-a-pint night. There was always the odd mouthy kid with something to prove. Mark would have to keep his eye on Pete. The bloke didn't know how to look after himself, and it wouldn't do to have him kicked in the first time they went out. He'd remind him it was his round again in a minute.

Kelly was gagging for it. Looked like a right dirty bitch. Small, with big tits. She seemed to like hearing about his dogs too, although she had allergies, she said. Mark assured her that cat hair was different to dog hair, and that his dogs never came in the house anyway. She moved her leg against his. Perhaps he could invite them all back to his house for a smoke – that would sound casual enough, and if they said no he wouldn't feel he'd been blown out. Better still if they went to Pete's. He had tea and coffee, and dog hair wouldn't be a problem. He couldn't expect to shag her in Pete's house though. A couple more pints, mind, and she'd be well away and it wouldn't matter where he took her. He worked out a plan to get rid of Nicola. If Pete offered to pay for a cab then Kelly and Louise'd be more likely to come, and there wouldn't be enough room for her.

Nice one.

Later, in the taxi, Peter pressed himself against Louise's thigh and rested his hand on his knee, hoping she might do the same, and by the time they had reached the Newhampton Road their fingers were brushing. A surge of desire filled him. But as the car pulled up in Prole Street she pressed his hand and said she would stay in the taxi and go home. She was on an early in the morning and her mum would be waiting up for her. She'd see him again if he went to Flanagan's next week. Peter wasn't disappointed. She'd given him enough to fill his thoughts later.

Peter and his neighbour exchanged a meaningful handshake while Kelly leaned through the window of the cab and kissed Louise goodnight.

She was just popping into Mark's for a bit, she said.

10

At six o'clock the next morning Beauty opened her eyes. The dawn was grey beyond the sitting-room windows. She wasn't sure how long she'd been lying on the sofa, or if she'd even been asleep. She went to the bathroom, washed quickly, and instead of returning to the sitting room to pray, crept upstairs to her sister's bedroom where her clothes were kept.

You can't use a bag, the old man will see it.

I can wear three pairs of knickers and a pair of jeans under two salwars. I'll wear the black kameez, the one that's too big. I can fit another two under it and a couple of T-shirts.

What about the old man? He's always staring. He'll notice.

Beauty's mother and sister were fast asleep, their faces lost in each other's hair on the single bed, her ama's breath catching in her throat.

I might not see them again.

She slid open her drawer as quietly as possible and picked out the clothes she wanted. Her mum would notice they were missing, but not until later. She'd be gone by then.

What if she tells Bhai-sahb when he gets back from work? They'll come looking for you at that place.

They aynt gonna go down there. There's too many
white people. They can't drag me off the street.
Can't they?

'Sis, what you doing?'

'Nothing. Go back to sleep.' Beauty moved quietly to
the bed, took Sharifa's face in her hands and kissed it.

'What's going on, sis?'

'Nothing – go back to sleep or you'll wake Mum.'

'You OK?'

'I'm fine. I've got to go out early. The old man will
make you breakfast. I'll see you later, after school.'

She picked up the small pile of clothes, took a last look
at the sleeping forms and closed the door behind her.

She held the door handle, reluctant to let go, and
listened to the sound of the old man's snoring coming
from his room opposite.

What about taking some jewellery?

They'll kill you. And stealing's a zinna.

That stuff's mine. They was wedding gifts. I can sell them.

The clothes were tight but she managed to put on three
pairs of knickers, three salwars, a pair of jeans, two
kameez and three T-shirts, and went to the kitchen to
take some money from her mother's purse.

How much money shall I take?

Enough for a few days in a hotel.

Fifty pounds?

Thass too much, aynit?

The old man shuffled into the kitchen in his slippers and
his crumpled *longhi* as Beauty was setting the table for
breakfast.

'I have to go into town early today. Can you wake the
little ones up and make the toast, please?'

It was the most she had spoken to him in weeks. He grunted, but didn't seem suspicious. She put some tea before him and went to the sitting room. It was too early to go. Faisal might get up and wonder where she was.

Money, phone, cashpoint card?

In my jacket.

They'll go mad when they find your passport's gone.

She returned to the kitchen and told the back of the old man's head that she would see him later. Wisps of grey hair stuck out from underneath his *tokhi* but he made no sign of having heard her. Beauty took her jacket, heavy with her belongings, from the hook in the passage and listened to the silent flat.

Go.

She tugged her scarf and hurried to the stairwell. Her boot heels echoed as she clumped down the steps.

From the bus stop she looked up at the bedroom windows of her family's home. The curtains were still closed.

Am I gonna see them again?

The bus crawled up Cannock Road in the early morning traffic, past red-brick factories with broken windows and dead chimneys.

11

Mark looked up at the fit little Paki bird as she came in late, carrying a bag. Everyone was drifting in whenever they liked. He was fucked if he was coming in on time tomorrow. It damn near killed him getting up in the morning. Kelly had left him drained at six o'clock.

Give 'er a right good seeing-to, dey I? I ay no two-stroke: two pumps an' a squirt.

But he knew it hadn't quite been like that, and he was glad when she'd gone; her visit had left him feeling uneasy. At first she'd seemed normal. She'd sucked him off in the armchair and done a little strip. Had even offered to play with herself in front of him. Later, as he was giving her the good seeing-to over the arm of the sofa, she had urged him to push harder. She'd sounded frustrated, and howled at him to stick it up her arse. The lights were on, and her arse, which he parted to oblige her, hadn't looked that inviting.

He'd done it anyway and it seemed to satisfy her. The noises she made excited him and within a few strokes he came.

'Ooh, it feels like I shit misself,' she'd said, laughing as he pulled out. She turned over on her back and joked about the spunk running out of her arse on to the sofa.

Later she'd talked about sex until he overcame his disgust and became hard again. This time she sat astride him and rubbed herself to screaming point. He'd scrubbed himself clean as soon as she'd gone and slept for two hours before getting up to go to town – on time. His balls ached as he walked.

Beauty stuffed the small rucksack she had bought in a camping shop under the table, and sat down next to a black-haired lady with no front teeth. The attendant had looked at her suspiciously when she'd come out of the changing room with the newly-purchased bag bulging with the layers of clothes she'd taken off, but he hadn't challenged her.

No one appeared to take much notice of her arriving late. Colin was talking, and the clients, fewer in number than the day before, looked tired and bored. Beauty was glad to be there. At least she had somewhere to go.

'. . . and we need to co-elate this information and cascade it back up to the Jobcentre so they can interpretate it.'

What the fuck was he on about? Mark closed his eyes and wondered if his other bitch might be pregnant. Titan had been in the kennel with her for three days. She should start showing soon if she was.

'. . . so if you'd all like to diarize your Jobsearch dates, that'll be that, all done and dusted.'

Colin Bushell sat back, satisfied he had got through this part of the morning without the usual whining interruptions.

'How are we supposed to look for work if we godder come yur every day?'

There were murmurs of support from around the room for the speaker: a pale, middle-aged, tracksuited man in a checked Burberry cap. Colin knew how to deal with this scrounging git of a Welshman.

'If you've been claiming benefits for more than six

months, and actively seeking work, which is part of your New Deal agreement, you're obviously having difficulty finding a job. Hence why you've been referred to us by the Jobcentre for training and support.'

He'd have to watch this one. Perhaps send a note to his facilitator. The man might be a troublemaker, try and whip up the others. Colin had seen his notes. Four or five kids, and he hadn't worked for six years. Well, Colin had him by the balls now. The rules were clear. If they didn't turn up they'd lose their dole money, housing benefit, council tax benefit and whatever else they were screwing out of him from the taxes he paid.

Colin shuffled his papers to show he was ready to continue with the morning's programme. He still had to get their CVs done, the Equal Ops quiz and the Learning Styles Initial Assessment and Diagnostic. He'd tell them about their permitted absences later. The scum didn't deserve twenty days' sick and holiday over six months. That was more than he got.

'It's not that there aren't any jobs. They just don't pay enough.'

The room agreed again. A Jamaican man in ironed jeans and a checked shirt pointed to the Welshman and addressed Colin.

'Dublin's right. Jobs don't pay enough in this town, gaffer.'

The black guy who had sat next to Beauty the day before began to laugh.

'Shut your nose, George. You never worked in your life!'

The forty-five-year-old George Taylor leapt to his feet in indignation and cursed his accuser in a stream of patois and teeth-kissing, *ya'ras*, *blood-clart* and *bumba-clart*. When he had finished he pulled a Guinness bar towel from his back pocket, wiped his brow and sat down. But the two men were friends and he wasn't angry. And it was true, he had never worked.

Beauty stopped listening and picked at the stitching of her jacket. Had her brother found out she'd gone yet? What would he do?

Her stomach turned and her throat hurt.

The woman with no front teeth asked her if she was coming to the pub at lunchtime.

'Thanks,' Beauty said. 'I've got to go and sort some stuff out.'

'Coom after. Where you giwin'?'

'I need to find a hotel or something. I left home.'

She hadn't meant to say it aloud. Beauty looked at the white *buddhi*, but she didn't seem shocked, or interested.

Don't never talk about your family to no one.

'There's a hotel at the bottom of the road. Why do' you try there?'

Colin Bushell waited for the talking to die down. They'd just have to lose their precious break if he couldn't get through the paperwork. Besides, he hated the way they helped themselves to the tea and coffee. It shouldn't have been free. And he was sure some of them filled their pockets with tea bags before going home.

'There *are* jobs out there, and we're here –' he began.

'I worked thirty years at Dunlop before they shut down,' said a large-bellied white man with short grey hair. 'I'm fifty-eight years old. Who's going to give me a job at my age? Round these parts the engineering work's all gone. What do you want me to do, stack bloody shelves in Asda for a hundred and fifty pound a week? You find me a decent job and I'll do it.'

'Exactly,' said the pale Welshman, whose own working

years numbered far fewer, at least as far as the DWP was concerned. 'How d'you expect me to live on that with five kids?'

Shouldn't have had so many children, Colin thought, but he knew he couldn't say it. This rat was the type to report him for 'discrimination' and he'd have to explain himself to the manager. Again. Would he himself find another job so easily at fifty-six?

'You'll be expected to provide evidence of having applied for a minimum of two jobs each week. Otherwise your Jobcentre adviser will be informed and you may lose your benefits.' That would shut them up. It usually did. He'd give them a few seconds to digest this latest piece of information.

But the clients' attention had been drawn to the door that had opened behind him.

Beauty looked, too, at the tall, slim black man standing in the doorway.

Al-lāh! What is this?

Delford Johnston's black combat trousers were tucked into his eighteen-hole black Dr Martens boots. A heavy gold chain hung round his neck and rested on a tight black jumper under a thigh-length black leather jacket. His freshly-shaven and polished brown skull shone. He came into the room, raised a hand heavy with gold sovereigns and pulled his sunglasses down his nose to look at the faces around the room. Those who knew him looked away.

His eyes widened as they came to Beauty and her headscarf at the end of the row of chairs. He held his palms out and greeted her with the *shahada* of the convert to Islam.

'*Ash-hadu anla elaha illa-Allah. Wa ash-hadu anna Mohammadan rasul-Allah. Asalaam alaikum.*'

'*Alaikum salaam.*' Beauty returned the greeting in a low voice.

'Let me go and sit next to my sister,' he said to Colin and his audience, and slipped into the empty seat beside her. 'Hello, my little beauty! And what have we got here?'

Beauty flinched at the insult. 'Have some fucking respect!'

George Taylor winced. You didn't cuss Delford Johnston and get away with it. The girl didn't know who he was.

Delford laughed off Beauty's reproach. '*Bismillah hir Rahmaanir Raheem,*' he said.

'Yeah, yeah. You're a good Muslim,' said Beauty and tugged her scarf down.

She remembered his sort from Hackney.

He's a gangster, aynit. A gundha, sharabi and a pervert ganjuri.

'Sorry, Colin. Do carry on,' Delford said, with exaggerated politeness. 'I won't be staying long anyway,' he added. He laughed and slapped the table. He'd like to see this bearded prick try and stop his benefits. He looked round at the younger men, used to hearing laughter when he said something funny.

Mark Aston stayed under the peak of his cap. He'd been padded up with niggers like this before.

Thinks 'e's ten men.

Fair play to the Paki bird though! Nice one!

'Good to have you back with us, Delford,' said Colin. We were just about to have a look at your *curriculum veetees.*'

'You ain't looking at my teepee!'

Delford nudged Beauty and laughed at his joke.

While the man explained what it was, Beauty returned to picking at her jacket, throwing quick glances at the others in the room.

What was it like to be one of these people?

If she stayed out, would she become like them?

At least they didn't have to worry about marriage stuff. They were free from that.

She studied the tall Somali woman. Her scarf was done in a bun at the back, and she wore a long beige skirt with flat-soled boots and a loose red polo neck jumper. She caught Beauty's eye and smiled.

Pretty lady.

Big, too.

That's how they are sometimes, hallahol.

At eleven o'clock Beauty hurried out of the building and headed along School Street to the hotel she'd been told about. As she walked across its carpeted lobby she felt the eyes of the uniformed receptionists on her. What would they think, seeing an Asian girl on her own?

Nothing. They're white. They aynt gonna think nothing.

'How can I help?' asked the older one, looking down from the raised platform behind the counter. The other woman disappeared through a side door.

'I need a room for a few days,' Beauty said.

'Certainly. Would that be a single, or a double?'

'Single or double what?'

'Room.'

'A single,' she said, and reddened. *I am dumb.*

The woman tapped computer keys.

'We have a single room free. That will be sixty pounds a night, payable in advance.'

'Sixty pounds? For one night?'

'Yes, that's correct.'

She didn't have enough, and the woman was waiting for an answer.

'I've only got fifty pounds,' said Beauty. 'Less now.' She blushed. Why did she keep saying things aloud? Was she going loony?

'Have you tried the George on Darlington Street?' The woman's voice was friendly. Beauty shook her head.

'Maggie, how much does the George cost a night?' the woman called to her colleague.

Beauty's cheeks burned. Did she have to shout?

'Forty-five pounds,' came the loud answer.

The woman looked at her sympathetically.

'Have you tried a B&B? They're usually cheaper. I can . . .'

'Thanks, I'll find one,' Beauty said and turned away.

As she shuffled through the revolving door and out into the street she felt light-headed. She didn't even have enough money to stay out for two nights. How could she go home after two days? Better to go now and avoid getting beaten up.

The noise of the traffic streaming round the island was too loud. She stood on the pavement, the wind fluttering her salwar around her legs.

When she got back to the first-floor room the only person there was Horace, an old Jamaican. She twitched the corners of her lips in greeting, kicked her bag under the chair and unwrapped the chips she had bought. The smell of vinegar rose with the steam and filled the room.

'Wh'appen, me girl?' Horace greeted her.

'Mm-huh,' she answered, through hot chips.

'Ya ahright now? Ya have somewhe' f' tahn?'

Beauty swallowed. 'Eh?'

'Somewhe' to live?' Horace repeated.

Al-lāh – how does he know?

That white lady must have told him.

'People aal tahk 'bout you,' he added.

Horace looked from Beauty to the food.

'I'll be fine,' she said.

She picked up a chip, and his eyes followed her hand. Was he hungry? She noticed his battered shoes and shiny trousers, and the sagging pockets of his old black jacket.

'Aren't you having lunch?' she asked.

'Me nah gat no money till me giro come tomorra.'

Beauty put the chip down. 'Take these, I can't eat any more.'

'Nah, yar ahright.'

'Go on.'

Horace got to his feet slowly.

'No sense makin' them go to waste,' he said, and took the food back to his chair.

Beauty watched as he raised a trembling hand to his mouth and began to eat.

She looked away, sorry for embarrassing him.

Al-lāh, how can people do that?

He's hungry and old.

Eating someone else's food! I'd rather die.

He aynt eaten.

I should have given him some money for chips.

He was smoking outside earlier. If he's got money for fags, he could eat.

He's Jamaican, though, aynit? Cigarettes and drink – that's what sharabi spend their money on.

Where'm I gonna stay tonight?

There was no one outside the building. Beauty walked up to the empty churchyard at the top of the street and sat down on one of the wooden benches. She looked around at the graves and wondered what the words said.

As the clock moved towards half-past twelve the other clients drifted back from surrounding streets and through the churchyard. Some nodded to her. The large Somali woman with the red jumper stopped at the bench.

'I hear you leave home,' she said.

Everybody knows.

The woman sat down next to her.

'That is very difficult. I leave my husband and boy and come to this country.' She gestured around the church-yard and the brown-brick council offices in the square beyond the railings.

'Have you got place to sleep?'

She asked Beauty if she had any money, and told her not to waste it on a hotel. She could stay with her for a few days, if she wanted.

'You don't go to hostel,' the woman continued. 'They are terrible place, full of drugs people. It's not safety.'

The woman told Beauty her name was Hana. She took out her purse and passed Beauty a photo of a small boy, sitting on his mother's lap.

'Sweet,' said Beauty.

'It's two years I don't see him. He seven now. So, you stay with me?'

Beauty looked at her, and the people passing, going somewhere. Home, maybe. Could she trust the lady?

'I take you to Civic Centre now. It's here.'

Hana pointed to the building across the plaza in front of them.

'You make appointment to see Housing Officer, and say you have no home.'

The woman walked slowly across the square and talked about how hard it was in Somalia for her husband and little boy, of the wars with countries Beauty had never heard of. But she felt safe with the lady, and it would only be for one night.

12

At three o'clock she was on the bus going back to Parkfields. Hana lived in the tall tower block across the road from Beauty's family. Perhaps it was a good thing she would be close to home. Her brothers wouldn't think to look so near. As long as she wasn't seen going in or out of the building, it might be all right for a few days.

Hana showed Beauty round her clean and simple flat, and took her to a bedroom so she could phone home. She closed the door and told Beauty not to worry. Things would be OK.

Beauty didn't want to ring yet, dreaded saying the words:

I aynt coming back.

She went to the window and looked out over the dual carriageway and the estates of Parkfields.

How high they were!

Was her ama really down there?

She don't deserve this.

And I didn't deserve that infection the mullah's brother gave me with his dirty fingers. Say it:

I aynt going back!

Beauty picked up the phone. Her heart pounded in her ears as she waited for someone to answer.

'Hello? Who's that?'

Faisal.

'*Ami*,' she said. 'It's me.'

'Where are you? And what are you doing with my phone? *Bhai-sahb*'s gonna go mad when he gets up. It's half-past four.'

'Just shut up and listen. Is he awake?'

'Where the fuck are you?'

'Go and wake him.'

'No fucking way! He'll kill me.'

'I aynt messin' about. Go and get him.'

'You better come back before he gets up or they'll be a fight.'

'I aynt coming back.'

Silence.

Then, 'They're gonna go mad! They'll fucking kill you. Wait there while I get *Bhai-sahb*. You better come back or Allah's gonna punish you big time. *Allah guna diba*.'

'Let Him. I aynt coming back. Go and wake *Bhai-sahb* up. I aynt talking to you.'

She hung up.

'*Al-lāh!*'

How long would it take to for Dulal to call back? Faisal would be running up the stairs two at a time, bursting into his brother's room.

The phone rang.

'Hello?'

'Sis, what's going on?' Dulal Miah's voice was heavy with sleep. Beauty struggled to speak.

'I can't do it.'

'You can't do what? What's happened?'

'I can't live with the mullah. Or go to that place.'

'Where the fuck are you?'

'At a friend's house.'

'What friend?'

'It's a girl's house. Somebody I met on that course. She's Muslim.'

'You with some other fucking prostitute?'

'Don't swear at me, Dulal.'

She'd never used his name before. She pictured him standing in the hall downstairs in his underpants and vest, which she had washed.

'Come back, sis. We can talk about this,' he said.

'I aynt coming back, *Bhai-sahb*. I can't take it no more. I'm getting out.'

She leaned against the window and looked down at the flats below, and thanked *Al-lāh* she wasn't at home.

'Be back here in an hour and we won't say any more about it. I know you been through a lot. I won't tell the old man.'

'*Bhai-sahb*, I aynt coming back. Don't you get it?'

She could never have spoken to him like this if she had been at home. He'd have punched her across the room.

'Be back in an hour or there'll be trouble!' he shouted. 'This is a fucking *zinna!*'

Beauty sat down on the bed and held her knees between her hands to stop them shaking. She'd told him! Her mouth felt dry and her chest still hurt.

He thinks I'm gonna go back.

I aynt!

I'm out!

But she knew it wasn't over. He'd phone again and then come looking for her.

She went to the bathroom to wash, returned to the bedroom and tried to recite the sunset *namaz*.

'*Alhamdo lillahi rabbil aalameen ar rahmaanir . . .*'

What was she supposed to do?

'*Maaliki yaomid deen iyya kana budoo wa iyya kanastaeen ihdinas siratual mustaqeem . . .*'

Was she turning her back on Him too?

'*Siratual lazeena an amta alaihim ghairil magh-doobe alaihim walad dualleen. Ameen.*'

Was He listening?

Beauty went back to the sitting room. It was better to be with someone, until her brother phoned back.

'What he say?' Hana asked. She'd changed into a knee-length denim skirt, white woollen tights and a white jumper.

'That I was doing a *zinna*.'

Hana laughed.

'Why is it *zinna*?'

Beauty didn't know. 'What happens if I do other bad stuff?' she asked.

'Like have a boyfriend?'

'I didn't mean *that*.'

The woman smiled at her. 'Why not? You can have a boyfriend.'

'Don't you get pregnant?' Beauty asked. Was it a stupid question?

'You don't have to be pregnant. You can use *condoms*.'

Beauty blushed. What little she knew had come from cousins, giggling about what a bride could expect on her wedding night, and from things the black girls used to say at primary school that she'd never understood. Her mum had warned her that just being near a man was enough to get pregnant.

What if I was pregnant? What would Bhai-sahb do then?

'Yeah, I know about that,' she said.

I am dumb.

She touched her cheeks. It wasn't good to be talking like this already.

Beauty looked round the sitting room. The flat was clean and warm. If Hana could live like this, why couldn't she?

How much did it cost?

Three or four hundred pounds for a deposit and the same every month for rent.

'Can you get it?' Hana asked. 'Have you got things to sell?'

'I might be able to get my sister to bring some of my jewellery.' It was wrapped up in a sock at the bottom of her bag, with her passport.

Beauty felt guilty for lying to someone who was helping her.

'You can sell all things in Wolverhampton,' said Hana. 'How much money you got now?'

She had about thirty pounds.

'OK, that is enough for five people to eat. I give you money back when the boys are coming.'

Beauty started. What boys?

'It's OK,' said Hana. 'It's my friend, and two his friends. They just coming for eat and after we go out maybe. You come too?'

Beauty didn't want to be in a house with men.

'Where are they from?'

'Dudley.'

Was that a country?

'What are they? Pakistanis? Somali?'

'They Muslims, Kurdish,' Hana said. 'You can stay here if we go out. Anyway, maybe you like one of them?'

'I don't think so.' Beauty looked down and felt her face flush.

What's Kurdish?

'Don't worry. They just friends,' said Hana. 'It's good to have friends. They can help you when you need.'

Maybe the woman was right. Why was it so bad? If she

didn't think it was wrong, why should Beauty? The lady was married with a kid. As long as the 'boys' weren't Iraqi.

But she wished she'd found a B&B instead.

Muslim women don't have men friends that visit at night.

13

Mark Aston sat with his feet on the dashboard of Bob's K-reg Transit pick-up on the way back from weighing in the metal they'd collected. A day spent scrapping with Bob never brought in less than forty quid. They'd just picked up nearly two tonne around the streets of Bilston and Bob had split the money evenly with him, fifty quid each, even though it was Bob's van, diesel, insurance and everything. Mind you, Mark had done most of the heavy lifting. It was good work when he could get it, which wasn't that often. Bob's nephews usually went with him, or Karen's brother Mick. Fair play to him though.

Mark had often heard more concern for his welfare in Bob's voice than in his own mother's – she never phoned him on his birthday or at Christmas. Bob was a sound bloke. He put work Mark's way whenever he could, either fence-building, looking for scrap metal or fixing cars for Bob's friends and relatives, which was near enough everyone in the city. Mark had met Bob through his ex-missus, and had immediately taken a liking to the short man, his pot belly and cheeriness. And he was still a hard bastard, despite his size, his greying hair and good nature. Mark had seen him sort out a couple of loan sharks in a pub toilet and knew he did unofficial evictions for Asian landlords with troublesome tenants, and he was forever dealing with the messes his extended family members made for themselves. He'd nearly taken a swing at Mark once with a crowbar for winding him up about something when they'd been laying paving outside a house in Codsall. He was one of ten brothers and sisters, and if you needed anything he was the best person to see. He worked hard to look after his ex-wife and kids and had a hand in all sorts, from greyhounds to scrapping metal, car boot sales and building. His house and garden were piled high with useful things. Most of what Mark possessed had come from Bob. He looked up to the older man, and wanted to become like him one day – a pillar of his family and community.

'Get yer fookin' feet off the dashboard will you,' Bob said as they reached Wolverhampton. 'D'you wan' us to get pulled, wi' that fookin' hat on as well?'

'Sorry, mate,' said Mark. 'The van's clean though, ay it?'

'I can do without the hassle. You coming down the club for a pint?'

The Transit bumped up onto the pavement outside the All Saints Working Men's Club on Earl Street. Mark slammed the ill-fitting door and followed Bob into the building: a low, red-brick square with two lounges and a function room at the back.

He tipped his cap back on his head and greeted Tony and the ageing and suited Gerald behind the bar. Mark liked walking in with Bob, filthy from scrapping metal. It showed others he was trusted enough to work with, and had become part of the clan.

They sat down on the fixed padded benches near the bar and sipped their pints. Mark rolled a cigarette and Bob eyed him.

'They'll kill you them things will, one day,' he said.

Mark raised his eyebrows as he licked the paper and nodded in agreement.

'You still giwin' up the towun wi' them lunatics of a night?' Bob asked him.

'What? Wi' me mates, you mean?'

'Them lot ain't mates. They'll drag you into all sorts a shit again, specially that little one.'

'What, Small Paul? He's all right. They're jooss drinking buddies.'

Mark thought of the Vauxhall Cavalier he'd crashed into the lamp post on Gorsebrook Lane a few nights before. Maybe Bob was right. Paul had egged him on to do it. It had been a piece of piss to rob (he'd taken out the hazard light switch, put it back upside down and it unlocked the ignition) and it had made him feel good to relive his youth and show off his knowledge of motors to someone. But he'd realized the next day it was a stupid thing to have done. He'd have got three years this time, for the drink-drive.

'You know what'll happen if you get caught,' Bob warned.

'I ay pinched a car since I got out a year and a half ago, Bob. I swear.'

'Keep yer voice dowun, for fook's sake, will y'? Fookin' 'ell.'

'I ay giwin' back inside,' Mark said, lowering his voice.

'Well you wanna watch it driving.'

'I know. Look, I drove that Omega for Alan the once, but you saw that car. It were mint. You ay gonna get pulled in that kinda motor during the day.'

'You will wi' that fookin' hat on!'

'Have you gone mad? You think I drive around like this?'

'Well, you wanna sort yerself out, smarten up and get yerself a good woman.'

'I'm all right as I am, Bob,' Mark said. He liked Bob's nagging.

'Bullshit am y'.'

'Why not? I got me dogs, and one of 'em's about to drop – which could give me a grand. I got me house. Yeah, it's in bad condition, but the rent's paid, I got work wi' you, I'm diwin' all right.'

'You need somewhere else to live with all them dogs.'

'Bob. You know I look after them dogs, tek 'em out, feed 'em.'

He didn't like the suggestion that his dogs suffered.

'OK, keep yer knickers on. I ay havin' a go. You need somewhere with a bigger yard if you want to breed properly. And a driving licence. When's yer ban up?'

'Six months.'

'Well, don't drive again.'

'I got too much to lose, Bob.'

'Anyway, I ain't yer old man. You do what you like.'

Mark came back from the bar with two more pints.

'What yer diwin' later?' Bob asked.

'Nothing. I do' fancy giwin' up the town again. I might bump into that Kelly bird from last night.'

'Oh ar, knacker you out did she?'

'Summing like that.'

'Come up here later. There's a do on out the back. Steve's coming with his missus and Karen and Hayley'll be here.'

Peter Hemmings sat in his car behind a lorry at the slow-changing traffic lights on the A5 in Brownhills, listening to Five Live Traffic and Weather. He adjusted the speed of the wipers and looked across at the driver of the car in the next lane, a young girl mouthing the words to a song and bouncing in her seat.

He couldn't remember the last time he had been moved by any music. Had he grown out of it? His loss of interest in the other passions of his youth had only become apparent to him recently. Once, everything he beheld contained some existential significance and he had marvelled at the world and human endeavour. But what had filled the gaps left by his waning philosophical wonder? Sex? Or, more accurately, internet porn?

Peter stared unseeing at the truck in front and thought again of Louise, the care worker he'd met the night before. He felt a wave of non-sexual longing for her. To lie down with her, fully clothed, and feel her warmth next to him, or her fingers touching his, would be enough.

Had he lost the desire to do lewd things with a woman? Years of a mutually disastrous and unsatisfactory sexual relationship with Kate had been largely his fault. Occasionally he blamed his poor performance on her *Cosmopolitan/Marie Claire* need for 'fulfilment', and her Anglo-Saxon lower-middle-class squeamishness about touching his erect member as lovingly and frequently as he did himself. Could he find pleasure only in front of the computer screen? And could he really regain his love of life?

Peter slipped the car into gear and pulled away from the traffic lights. The beige council flats of Brownhills slipped past. This was where you ended up if you drifted from one lousy job to another without doing a vocational post-grad course. The books Peter sold were imbecilic study guides to the woeful GCSE English curriculum. He'd read the entire *English Literary Heritage* in a lay-by on the A460 between Walsall and Burntwood in the time it took to eat the supermarket sandwiches he usually had for lunch. Apart from something by Shakespeare and Wordsworth tacked on at the end, he'd barely recognized his own cultural patrimony.

Peter dreaded becoming the man in the Rover 75 whom he saw in the car park outside the office in Rugby, where he went for his monthly area meetings. A crumpled and balding sales rep with a pot belly and a mac. Peter still felt young enough to turn his life around and to reach Zarathustra atop his mountain. Quite how, he didn't know. But he was aware of the danger of becoming a middle-aged onanist with an unfulfilling job and little money. Not much Will to Power in that.

The road became a dual carriageway. Peter flicked the indicator and accelerated past the lorry.

Maybe things weren't so bad.

At least he was free from Kate.

He could take part in life again and see what opportunities arose. A fling with a local girl like Louise might be an entertaining enough starting point. Wasn't she the modern version of a healthy, rosy-cheeked wench from a Thomas Hardy novel?

And it would be more romantic than the fruits of his internet searches.

14

Beauty lay on the bed in the spare room. It was six o'clock and Dulal hadn't rung back yet. What did that mean? That they expected her? Surely they'd noticed the missing money by now, and would know she had enough to stay somewhere for a night. Maybe they thought she'd go back when it ran out. Perhaps they hadn't decided what to say and were arguing about it. Her mum would be worried, wouldn't she?

Good they don't ring. I aynt gonna answer. They'll try and make me go back.

What they gonna say if the mullah's pervert brother phones them?

Nothing. They'll just tell him I'm still not well. They done that for years.

She sat up at the sound of the front door opening and the low voices of men in the corridor. She took some cotton wool and cream from her bag and began to wipe off her makeup. She didn't want any men to think she had put it on for them. Had they at least *salaam*'d each other? Beauty wouldn't have minded if they had been white. At least a white person wouldn't think she was doing anything bad.

Hana called her name from outside the bedroom. Beauty looked at herself in the mirror in the cupboard.

Her mother's pale face looked back at her, and was gone.
Bismillah hir Rahmaanir Raheem.
Al-lāh, Don't let them stay long!

She could see one of the men at the end of the corridor.
Iraqi!
The other two stood up and greeted her when she came in to the sitting room.
They were all Iraqi! Beauty didn't like Iraqis, or others who looked like them.
They were like *freshies*, straight from back home. They weren't used to seeing women alone, and perved in the streets.
The three men sat down. They were wearing flared faded two-tone jeans, tight ribbed jumpers and heavy jewellery. Cheap gold shone against the thick black hair poking out of their collars and sleeves.
Hana told her their names but Beauty didn't listen. She returned their greeting, eyes down. The place stank of their perfumes.
'*Alaikum salaam.*'
She sat down on one of the armchairs and looked at her hands on her knees. As long as no one spoke to her they would get on fine. On the coffee table were three neat piles of keys, foreign Marlboro Lights and mobile phones. Nothing fitted in the pockets of their trousers.
The broken chat continued around her. The youngest Kurd, Darav, or something like that, smoked and tapped his lighter on the table. He caught Beauty's glance and offered her a cigarette. She sneered at him and stood up.
Her phone was ringing, she told Hana.
Al-lāh! What am I doing with this magi and three Iraqis?

Beauty stayed in the bedroom until the Somali woman came and asked her for the money for the pizza. It was in her jacket pocket on top of her bag by the door, she told her.

When she went to the living room the food had been set out on the low table. She took a plate and the smallest slice of pizza and sat in an empty chair. She tore off pieces of the greasy dough with her fingers and covered her mouth with her hand as she chewed. A man shouldn't see a woman eat. She tried not to look at the others but was drawn to watch each in turn. They all ate like animals.

Hana's worser. Why doesn't she close her mouth?

Beauty waited until someone else had finished eating before returning to the bedroom. She knew she couldn't stay there another night. She'd go to the Jobcentre tomorrow and talk to her adviser. The lady there might help her find somewhere to live.

She lay on the bed, closed her eyes and imagined what it might be like to live on her own, unmarried and away from home. No one she knew, or had heard of, had ever done it. Not alone. They always had a boyfriend. What had happened to them? Sweetie went to Wales, and Safia . . . where was Safia now?

When she opened her eyes again Beauty could no longer hear voices or laughter. How long had she been asleep? Had everyone gone?

She got up and went to the living room.

The youngest Iraqi was sitting in an armchair, smoking.

'Where are the others?' she asked.

'Huh?'

'Where's Hana, and your mates, cousins, brothers, or whatever they are?'

'Ah . . . Telan he go to petrol station shop for to buy cigarettes,' he said, smiling.

'Where's Hana?'

'She go . . .' he pointed vaguely towards the door.

Beauty didn't wait for the answer. She couldn't sit in a room alone with him.

As she passed Hana's bedroom she heard the woman's voice cry out.

Beauty tapped on the door, pushed it open and stared at naked limbs twisting and writhing on the double bed, at a man's hairy *hombol* rising and falling, at a wrinkled sack of skin swinging beneath.

She fled to the spare bedroom, pressed herself against the door and shut her eyes.

Al-lāh, where am I? Why have You let this happen to me?

Let me go home.

You can't – they'll kill you.

She touched her cheeks nine times – *nahuz ub'illa min zalik* – but the image of what she had just seen remained. Her head spun and she felt sick. She wanted to lie down but didn't dare move away from the door. There was no lock on it. What if the other one in the sitting room had the same idea? She knew she couldn't stay there a moment longer, but where could she go? Hana had spent Beauty's money on the pizza. How could she ask for it back now?

She wanted to throw up the food she'd eaten. It was poisoned by the woman's sin and the Iraqi's naked body.

I should have phoned Nicola.

Maybe it's not too late. Call her.

What if the Iraqi attacks me?

15

Beauty opened the door slowly. Her jacket was eight or nine steps away. She held her breath and inched forward, straining her ears for sounds of movement from the living room, leapt to grab her jacket and bag and flew back along the corridor to the bedroom.

She blocked the door with her foot, panting and listening for approaching steps. If he came anywhere near her she'd scratch his face off. She tore open her bag, pulled out a pair of jeans and struggled into them, found the crumpled piece of paper and pressed in the numbers on Faisal's phone, praying that Nicola would be at home.

She was! *Shoban shukor alham dul'illa.*

Could Beauty come round? She was a bit stuck.

Yeah, *shooer.*

It wasn't too late?

Nah, man.

Thanks. She'd be round as soon as she could.

Raby Street in All Saints. R-A-B-Y, number 37. Where was she? Parkfields? A taxi wouldn't cost more than four quid from there. Did she have a number for a cab? Nicola would call one for her and text her the details. Tra-a-bit.

Beauty closed the phone and asked God to bring the white girl peace.

Al-lāh tairay shanti horrio.

*

A taxi would be there in five minutes, but she still had to get past the pervert in the sitting room. Maybe if she got Hana out of her room it would provide some protection. But she didn't want to see the woman again, or the man with the hairy *hombol*. She didn't even know which of the two he was. Did it matter to Hana?

Beauty put on her jacket and pulled the rucksack onto her back. She'd need both arms free to slap the Iraqi if he tried to stop her from leaving. She opened the door enough to peer through the gap. The bastard had moved to this side of the table. She couldn't see his face but she wouldn't be able to get very far before he saw her. There was nothing for it but to walk towards the front door. The key was in the lock. It would take her five seconds.

She got halfway before the Kurd saw her. Beauty stopped, but he didn't get up. She took another two steps before he spoke, and she froze again.

'You go now?' Darav said.

She kissed her teeth in answer and kept her eyes on the key in the door.

'Home?' He sounded surprised. How much had the *magi* told him?

'A friend's house.'

'Now?' he asked.

'What's it to you?'

He stood up slowly.

'You are fear of me?' he asked.

Beauty took another step towards the door and lifted her hand towards the key. There was a latch to turn, too. She'd need both hands. Darav edged sideways around the armchair towards the door.

'Stay away from me,' she warned him.

'Don't worry,' he said, and stopped. 'Hana say you need help . . . maybe some money . . . so I think . . .'

'You think what?'

'That, you know, maybe I give . . .' He waved vaguely with his hands; a gesture that took in the whole flat. 'And you . . .'

'Do you want to go back to your country?'

Beauty said it slowly and clearly so that he understood. It was a simple threat.

'OK, OK.' He raised his hands in surrender.

'Hana got it wrong. I don't need no one's help.'

Beauty glanced at the door, not wanting to take her eyes from him, and reached out for the locks. The key turned easily but the catch above it wouldn't budge. She brought her other hand up to help, and sensed his sudden movement towards her.

'Don't go like that. I . . .'

His hand reached out to the lock. She slapped his arm down and the catch clicked open. Beauty pulled at the door but his foot jammed it shut again. She turned to the Kurd and slapped his face as hard as she could with the ball of her open hand, like they did to her at home. It caught him on the cheek and his head banged against the door. He cried out in pain and stepped back. Beauty tore open the door, slammed it behind her and held on to the handle in case he tried to get out. She looked over her shoulder at the light above the lift. It was far below her on the ground floor. The neighbours? Who would open their door at this time in a place like this?

Beauty let go of the lock and ran to the staircase.

After six flights she stopped to rest her foot and listen for sounds from above.

Voices echoed up from the stairwell.

Doors slammed far beneath her.

But there was no noise of footsteps following her. Beauty looked around. This wasn't a good place. The walls were damp and the lights flickered.

On the twelfth floor she called the lift, pressing the button repeatedly as it climbed slowly. She squeezed past the opening doors, then stood unprotected, her eyes fixed on the exit to the staircase, until the doors slid shut.

When she reached the ground floor she burst through the lobby and into the car park. Through the bushes she could see the yellow light of the taxi. 'Wait!' she shouted.

The brake lights went off and the car pulled away.

'Please wait!'

She took out the phone and pressed redial.

'*You have insufficient credit for this call. Please arrange a . . .*'

The battery died.

Al-lāh!

Think!

Nicola had told her she lived near the centre. She'd walk towards the town, find a phone box and call another cab.

Beauty checked that there were no signs of her brothers. It wouldn't be far to walk past the lit-up row of shops until the darkness swallowed her.

Across the street a black guy in a long padded coat, tall hat and ear flaps watched her approach.

'Wa gwan?' he said, and loped a few steps towards her.

'Yeah right,' she muttered.

'A-where ya go?'

'That's my business,' she said, not looking at him.

He bounced along beside her.

'Rest yerself me girl. Me na trouble ya.'

'I aynt your girl.'

She risked a quick look at him in the light of the kebab shop. His beard was greying and matted in small clumps, and the whites of his eyes were beige. He shook the nearly empty can in his hand.

'I've got to go,' Beauty told him.

'Whe'?'

'Er . . . All Saints?' she said. Why had she told him?

'On foot?'

'In a taxi.'

'Na taxi na pick ya up.'

'I'll walk then.'

'Ya na wanna go down there,' he warned. 'Too much bullet. Ya'll get dead, ya so.'

He walked the length of the closed shops with her and stopped, peering at her closely through a haze of Special Brew and marijuana.

'Hey, ya dat pretty coolie-girl look up from da window dere?' He gestured over her shoulder. 'Whe' ya run go?' he asked, nodding at her bag.

She didn't reply.

'OK sista. Watch wa ya do. Man trouble ya, ya tell 'em ya a friend of me. Derrek. Everyone know me 'bout yah.'

He watched the small figure walk away, drained the can of beer and threw it in the bin outside the kebab shop. His woman was waiting for him.

Beauty settled the bag on her shoulders more comfortably and headed towards the town centre. The man had scared her with his warnings about All Saints. Cars passed, and some taxis, but they didn't stop when she waved. Squinting into the darkness, she prayed for a phone box.

Was that one ahead?

Please, let it be one!

It was! She struggled in. The door was stiff and trapped her bag as it closed on her. She pulled some coins from her jacket pocket and switched on her mobile. The screen lit up, the battery icon flashed and the phone went dark again. She picked up the handset of the public phone. It felt light and there was no noise when she held it to her ear. Frayed wires poked out of the side of the box, unconnected to the receiver in her hand. Who could she call anyway? She didn't know a taxi number, and what was Nicola's address? It sounded like Baby Street, but how could it be that? And where was the piece of paper with Nicola's number?

Al-lāh!

Was this punishment already?

I aynt going home.

She pushed open the heavy door and struggled out into the street. She'd have to try and find the train station. At least there would be lights and people.

I'll go there. I can sit in the waiting room until morning.

What kind of people you gonna find there?

Allah'll help me.

Will He?

Toba, toba astaghfirullah. He got me this far.

The black road glistened damp under the street lamps. Beauty shrugged the bag onto her shoulders, checked that no one was following, and peered into the gloom ahead. There was nobody coming. If anyone did, she'd cross the road. Once she got to town it would be safer. There would be people around, and police, too.

But someone *was* walking towards her. Two men. She turned left at the traffic lights on Sun Street and hurried past the Royal Mail sorting office. The sprawling depot was lit up and quiet. She reached a bend in the road and looked back at the junction. The men rounded the corner and came up the slope towards her.

She turned and hurried on. The road dipped and the street lamps ended. She stopped in the darkness under the arches of the silent railway bridge. They were still coming. She tried to walk faster but the cobbles were slippery underfoot.

She felt safer when she reached the glow of the Bilston Road Junction, but was dismayed by the intersection of ring roads, tramlines and subways.

Which way was the station?

Left.

She passed a signpost and tried to make out the letters. 'A-B-C-D.'

Was that a word?

Cars slipped along the bright street as she headed into 'All Saints and Blakenhall Community Development' and away from the train station, towards Willenhall. It frightened her that her brothers might be peering from every car. At least there were no people walking here. Apart from the lady up ahead. Perhaps she was waiting for someone, or a taxi. Another woman out alone at night was good. Maybe she didn't need to be so scared. God would look after her, as long as she didn't doubt it.

16

After a car stopped to pick the woman up, Beauty was alone in the street again. Maybe the lady had just got off a train round the corner. There was no one following her now, but the fear of the cars remained. It seemed like they slowed down as they passed her.

That one definitely did.

When she reached the place where the woman had been standing, there was nothing apart from the rusting gates of a closed factory. What had that lady been doing?

She sat down on a wall to rest. So what if people stared? As long as it wasn't her brothers.

Al-lāh, please don't let them be looking for me.

But the prayer felt empty. Beauty closed her eyes and tried again, searching in her heart for the fullness that came with words sent up to God.

'Yo, sister!'

The voice jolted her awake. A silver BMW had stopped. Two Asian faces were at the open windows, their hair sculpted with gel.

'How much do you want?' the boy in the front seat called out.

She heard laughter over the Bhangra music. What did he mean? A pair of miniature orange boxing gloves and a Sikh *khanda* swung from the rearview mirror.

Beauty stood up and walked back towards the town

centre, ignoring the car. She felt it crawling behind her but didn't turn round.

They're just kids messin' about. Keep your eyes down. They'll go away.

The car drew level.

'Come on, how much do you want? There's four of us in here. We ain't never tasted no *pudi* from Pakistan before.'

Now she understood.

'Fuck you, asshole!'

The car was a few metres ahead. She could smell their perfumes from the open windows.

'And I aynt your sister, egghead!'

The face at the window turned to say something to the driver. The brake lights went on and the car stopped.

'You Paki bitch, come here!'

Beauty ran.

The car caught up with her, the boys shouting from the windows. The wall to her left ended, became a grass bank and a side street. It was blocked off to cars. They couldn't follow her.

She ran past houses and front gardens, parked cars and open gates. She kept running and tried to listen for steps behind her, but didn't dare look back.

When the pain in her foot forced her to slow down Beauty looked over her shoulder and stopped. There was no one behind her. She leaned against a wall, hands on her knees, panting. Were they still searching for her?

Al-lāh, please!

She straightened up and peered over the wall at a dark and silent house. Should she hide in the front garden? A caravan on bricks filled most of it, and a narrow path led to the door of the house through broken washing machines, gas cylinders, cookers, piles of paving slabs and car tyres. A noise from inside the caravan startled her.

There's someone in that thing.

Al-lāh please, where am I?

Ward Street, the empty factories and foundries of All Saints and Blakenhall, and the All Saints Working Men's Club. As she neared the junction, the lights of a car swung into the street, flashing as they rose and fell over the speed hump. She dropped down alongside a parked car, held her breath and waited. The gravel dug into her knees as she watched the light sweeping up the pavement towards her. The car slowed down and stopped. She could hear tabla drums through the open windows.

'I'm telling you she ain't here bro.'

There was a pause.

'I ain't getting out of the car to look. You go, blood.'

A door clicked open. Beauty stood up, saw the driver climbing out of the car, and ran. She reached the end of the road as the car reversed, its body-kit scraping over the speed humps. She saw headlights as it accelerated and caught up with her as she turned the corner and –

'FOOKIN' 'ELL!'

Mark Aston rubbed his chest where the girl had hit him, and clocked the motor that had pulled up on the other side of the street.

'Here, y'm that Pak . . . that bird off the course,' he said.

Beauty recovered from the blow and recognized him – the racist bloke with the cap.

'Who's that lot?' Mark asked her, nodding to the car. Asians. Mostly they were pussies, but he'd seen a few in jails in Leeds and Manchester who knew how to look after themselves.

'I dunno,' Beauty said. 'They were following me.'

Is he gonna leave me here?

Mark took a few steps towards the face in the passenger seat window.

'You gorra fookin' problem, rag'ead?' he called out, opening his arms in invitation. The electric windows slid up and the car pulled away slowly.

'Knob'eads,' he said. He wouldn't have minded if they'd got out of the car; it might have been a laugh.

He turned back to the Paki bird. She looked scared.

'You OK?'

Beauty nodded. 'I was looking for a friend's house.'

'Wha', round 'ere? Where is it?'

What's the name of the street?

'It's in . . .'

Please, what's it called?

'I can't remember it,' she said.

'You sure y'm all right?' Mark asked. 'You look like shit.'

Beauty took a ball of tissue paper from her pocket and pressed it against her nose.

Mark fastened his jacket and was about to move on.

'Tay a good idea walkin' round here on yer own, like. You gonna be all right geddin' 'ome?'

Beauty didn't want to be alone in the street again.

'I can't go back home. I left,' she said. Would he care?

Mark noticed the small rucksack on her back. 'What you gonna do then?'

'I dunno. I'll go to the train station.'

'They kick you out when it shuts.'

Mark could see she wouldn't last the night, not in her state. But did he want a Paki in the house? The dogs wouldn't like it.

'You can crash on my sofa tonight, if you like. There ay no one else there. Jooss me dogs, but they dey coom in the house, jooss Honey, cuz she's expecting puppies.'

Beauty looked at the white man standing in front of her in the light of the street lamp, his thin pale face and the cap tipped to the back of his head.

'I ay a nutter,' Mark said, seeing the fear in her eyes. 'You can have a cup of coffee, a chat if you want, and go to sleep. I ay gonna bother you. Anyway, 'sup to you.'

The streets around her were dark and quiet, the empty factory buildings haunted at this time of night.

'You sure thass OK? I aynt gonna get in your way?'

'Nah, y'm all right. We'll have to walk though, unless you've got a few quid for a taxi.'

The driver was a Sikh in a turban and long grey beard. No one spoke, and it was only a short journey to Prole Street. Beauty passed the coins to the old man through the glass partition when they arrived.

'*Dunnia kya horee hé?*' he muttered, loud enough for her to hear.

What's the world coming to? I'm running away, thass what.

She got out of the taxi and slammed the door.

Something in the street smelled bad. It was coming from the dark passageway running down the side of Mark's house. Beauty peered through the iron gate and heard the snuffling of animals.

Kutayn! She'd forgotten.

'Coom in, y'm letting the heat out.'

Beauty stepped into the suffocating air of dogs, and a smell of acrid, stale piss filled her mouth and nose. She gagged at the stench and covered her mouth. The white bloke's back was turned and he didn't see.

Al-lāh, how can I stay here?

'It's a bit untidy,' Mark said, turning the cushions of the sofa over to hide the stains of the night before.

'Sit down, I'll mek us a coffee.' He went through to the kitchen, and the fetid air came in sharp and damp as the door closed behind him.

Beauty looked at the sofa and sat down, her bag on her knees. The carpet was brown with stains, and thick with dog hair. Empty beer cans were everywhere. Dirty shoes and clothes lay on the floor next to plates of unfinished, *haram* food. She put her hand in front of her mouth, but nothing could keep out the smell.

Al-lāh, why have You sent me here?

17

The rucksack jumped again on Beauty's back as she struggled to run in her sandals. A toothless woman burst out of a caravan and tried to grab her arm as she passed. She broke free, tripped, and felt the gravel digging into her knees and stinging her hands. She struggled to her feet and ran. A car appeared beside her, the face of her older brother shouting through the window, as she rounded the corner into the mullah's brother's fat belly. She was eight years old again, sitting on his knee. He held her small face in a sweaty hand and crushed his bearded wet lips to hers . . .

Beauty's head jerked up from the arm of the sofa; a dog leapt back and sat thumping its tail in greeting.

She wiped her mouth in disgust. The thing had licked her.

How long had she been asleep?

Beauty looked around the room in the grey light coming through the torn curtains. It was her first white person's house. Did they all live this way? Everybody said they were dirty, but they couldn't all be like this, could they?

Cold air and the smell of piss came from the kitchen. How could an animal have opened the door? She pressed back against the sofa as the dog inched closer and rested its head on her lap.

'Please, get off me, I'm begging you!' she said. Did it want her to touch it, like white people did?

She patted the dog's head with her left hand, the one that she wouldn't use to eat with.

Honey banged her tail against the sofa and looked up at her.

'Can't you talk?' Beauty asked, as the creature pressed closer against her. '*Feshab, kuta*. You'll have to let me stand up.' How could a dog have a name?

Beauty got up, stretched, and went to the kitchen doorway. She could taste the smell.

'*Al-lāh!* Is this a kitchen?'

The sink was under a smeared and splattered window. Cupboard doors hung open, a cooker and fridge sat where they had been dumped on their arrival, and a washing machine, the clothes half pulled out, had flooded the floor around rolls of carpet and bundles of the local newspaper. Through the muddied glass of the back door she saw the form of a dog rear up and rest its paws on the window.

Beauty picked her way around the bin bags of clothes and pools of water and climbed the steep, airless stairway. The door to the bathroom stood open and she stared inside in horror. The worst hole-in-the-floor in Bangladesh was cleaner than this!

She wiped the seat with wet toilet paper and looked away to avoid seeing the colour of the damp wads she dropped into the water. The door wouldn't shut properly so she sat with one leg stretched out to block it in case the white guy came in. She'd have to wash later, some-where else. She let the first squeeze from the toothpaste tube slide down the plug hole and brushed her teeth with her finger, rinsing her mouth with her right hand. That much was safe. If you weren't able to wash properly, it wasn't *haram*.

How long can I live like this?

*

Back in the sitting room she cleaned her face with a moisturising wipe and put on some make-up in a hand mirror. The bags under her eyes made her look like a *ganjuri*.

Where'm I gonna sleep tonight?

What about your mum? Did Ama sleep last night?

Beauty put away her makeup, pushed her hand down to the bottom of her rucksack and felt for the sock with her jewellery inside. The white guy had told her where she could sell it. She'd struggled to answer his questions about herself, and before long he'd left her alone in the glow of the heater. She could leave it on all night, he'd told her. Them things didn't cost much to run, and the meter was wired anyway.

The sock felt lighter. Beauty shook the *chouri* onto her lap. Where was the *tickli*? That *halla naguni* must have stolen it. The Somali bitch.

She clenched her fists until her nails dug into the palms of her hands. Cursing people was wrong, and at least she still had the bangles. They weighed three *tulla* and had cost thirty thousand *taka*.

Is that gonna be enough to stay out?

She put on a pair of jeans and a clean kameez. The dog watched her.

'You OK?' Beauty asked.

It sneezed.

'Yarumk'Al-lāh!'

You gone crazy? Talking to a dog?

Why not? It's one of God's creatures, aynit?

'Can't you say one word?' she asked the animal. She noticed the bitch's swollen teats. 'Are you the pregnant one?' The dog cocked its head at her. 'You are, aynit? Lucky you.'

Am I gonna see that day?

The old man and Dulal had told her many times that

she would die when she was twenty-five, that she'd get ill in her stomach and die. Hadn't the mullah's family paid *ulta-imams* a fortune to curse her?

Twenty-four or twenty-five, he'd said.

Would it be long enough to feel the joy of holding her own baby? And who would the father be?

Peter Hemmings finished shaving and tried to smooth out the frown lines on his forehead with moisturising cream.

He looked into his pale and joyless eyes. The honeymoon period of his freedom from Kate was definitely over, and with it he'd found only emptiness. There had come no new lease of life yet.

He went back to the bedroom and picked out the clothes that would at least make him feel handsome for the day – straight beige cords, dark brown suede loafers and a white herringbone shirt.

It occurred to him that he might be in need of stimulating company. The fierce debates he used to have with his own friends had always made him feel alive. He had even liked arguing with Kate's friends. Their clichéd arguments were easy to take apart, but they'd soon started avoiding him at social gatherings. He was too serious for them, and he didn't take cocaine.

Peter threw back the curtains to let in some light and check himself in the wardrobe mirror. But the grey dawn made little difference to the gloom inside. God, what a dump! Was this where he'd end his days, slumming it with the proles? When he'd first seen Wolverhampton town centre it had made him want to leave the country. Cheap chain stores, bakeries and pound shops – Pound-Saver, PoundStretcher, PoundHound. The dreariness and obese lumpen families were overwhelming.

He tried to drum up some satisfaction that Kate wasn't there to ask him who he thought he was dressing up for, as she sipped the nettle tea that he brought her every morning, in the bed she never left until midday. She'd surely got the hint now; she'd even hung up on him the last time they had spoken.

After coffee and a cigarette, Peter smoothed down his shirt front, pulling out the right amount of slack to cover his growing paunch, before making sure he had everything he needed for work and stepping out of the house. Drizzle fell on the scattered remains of a kebab on the pavement. As he turned to lock the door a movement in black caught his eye. A headscarfed Asian girl was coming out of the house two doors away: Mark's house. As she walked past him, her face partly covered by a hand pulling at her scarf, he caught a glimpse of dark eyeliner, the outline of her cheek, her slender red-jewelled nose and delicate mouth. Peter stared after the girl as she hurried to the end of the street, turned the corner and vanished.

He must have made a mistake. How could such a vision have appeared from a hell-hole like that? From Mark's house? That thug? Did Asian girls do that kind of thing? Muslim girls? Weren't they out-of-reach, mysterious beauties, untouchable and unreal? Perhaps she'd come from the black family's house next door to Mark.

By the time he reached Bushbury, Peter had had enough of the self-important opining of the Radio 4 presenters and switched them off. Silence was better than the *Today* programme. He watched the first children making their way to school. It was too early for the young white mothers in red England shirts pushing prams.

At the roundabout for the M54 his thoughts returned to the Muslim girl coming out of Mark's house. He was sure it was his house. Peter didn't know the bloke that well. Maybe he had all sorts of friends. Not that he'd noticed any mixed couples in Wolverhampton before. In

London he had, but they were anglicised middle-class Hindus, he presumed, and they had the air of people who had met on campuses and married soon after graduation.

His thoughts wandered at the traffic lights in Bloxwich as he pictured the headscarfed girl passing him in the street, and the fine profile of her face.

The van driver behind him sounded his horn.

18

Beauty Begum found an empty café and asked the large woman in a pink apron behind the counter for a pot of tea and a piece of flapjack. The smell of frying *haram* food didn't bother her. Let other people eat what they wanted.

It's a free world, aynit?

The woman called her 'dook', and said she'd bring it over.

'We ay busy at the minute,' she said, and winked at the pretty Indian girl.

Beauty chose a seat with her back to the wall, away from the windows. She had an hour to wait until the Jobcentre opened. She reached across to the next table and picked up a newspaper. It would pass the time and give her an excuse to drink the tea slowly.

She hurried past the topless white girl on the inside page, and tried to work out the stories from their photos: an open-mouthed bearded man, fist outstretched, shouting about something – Pakistani probably; that Prince boxer next to a picture of a smashed car; the beaten-up face of a man lying in a hospital bed next to a smaller photo of a group of hooded white boys; a row of girls with oiled bodies and bikinis; girls in white underwear lying on a bed touching each others' thighs, with speech bubbles coming from their mouths.

She looked up as a small Indian man slipped into the seat at the table next to hers.

'Oright?'

Beauty kissed her teeth and studied a picture of a Sikh with a large nose throwing a cricket ball.

'You go to that RiteSkills course too?' he insisted, spreading his toast.

'So?'

She knew his type. London was full of Asian perverts like him, trying to pick up young girls in the street. Unless you were wearing a niqab. And sometimes even then.

'It's a bit early, innit?' he said, looking at his heavy gold watch.

'I've got to go to the Jobcentre.'

Beauty watched him suck margarine from his hairy, gold-ringed little finger. He was short, his high heels barely reaching the floor. His curly, blow-dried hair was dyed black. Yellow margarine clung to the hairs of his dyed moustache.

'It do' open till nine o'clock, y'know,' he said.

'I know that.' Beauty covered her face with her hand and turned the pages of the newspaper again, staring unseeing at the row of near-naked bodies.

'Nice girls in there?' he asked.

She shut the paper.

No Asian bloke's gonna say anything rude to me again!

'What you doing out so early?' she asked him. 'Perving at young girls in cafés? What does your wife say about that?'

The little man tried to laugh it off, but Beauty had gone before he could answer.

Mark Aston went downstairs in his shorts to make some coffee. He'd heard the Paki bird – sorry, Bengali – leave the house earlier. He sat down on the sofa, scratched and looked at the small rucksack by the front door. He'd told her she could leave it while she sorted her shit out up town. He'd be at home later on. Where else would he be? Bob hadn't rung him with any work for today, and he couldn't be arsed going to that course.

Waste a fookin' time – better off giwin round the garages and looking for a proper fookin' job.

He rolled a cigarette. At least he had enough 'bacca left for the day, but that was all, apart from the sixteen pence on top of the television. The only other thing he could think of was to get a ten of weed on credit, and sell half of it to Pete. Then he'd have something to smoke and a fiver to get a few cans.

Beauty hurried down Darlington Street towards the Crown House Jobcentre, keeping close to the shop windows. Her brothers wouldn't do anything to her in front of other people, but she didn't want to see them anyway. Perhaps they wouldn't think to look for her there. Dulal would probably send the little one to watch the RiteSkills place.

A group of silent people waited outside the closed doors of Crown House. Beauty tried not to look at anyone. She thought about what to say to Jackie, her adviser, but was drawn to the worried expressions of the others' faces. A black guy paced about muttering. An old lady in a violet mac smiled at Beauty when their eyes met. A white boy leaned against the wall in a black tracksuit and white Nike plastic cap, one foot raised under him.

They got problems, too?

The doors opened at nine o'clock and the black guy rushed inside. The white boy let Beauty pass before peeling himself off the wall and following her into the building.

A uniformed black security guard took up position next

to the glass doors and metal detector, and gave each person a quick glance.

Beauty waited in line. She gave her surname and National Insurance number to the receptionist at the Client Enquiries desk, and explained that she needed to see her adviser urgently. She took her ticket and sat down away from other people, but as the queue lengthened the seats began to fill up near her.

Don't let anyone sit here.

A thin, pale-faced Asian woman in jeans and an army jacket, with bulging eyes and unkempt hair, came towards the empty seat next to Beauty, dragging a large-eyed five-year-old boy in an anorak. Beauty smiled at the boy hiding at his mother's side, and leaned forward to poke her tongue out at him. The child squirmed out of view behind his mother.

The woman dragged the boy out to stand in front of her.

'Sorry,' she said. 'He's really naughty.'

'Are you naughty?' Beauty asked him. 'He's beautiful,' she said to the mother.

'Apni?' she asked Beauty. Are you one of us? *'Kya toom Pakistani ho?'*

'No, I'm Bengali,' said Beauty. 'Are you from this place?' she added, to avoid answering more questions.

The woman was happy to talk about herself as they waited. She'd left Manchester with her Hindu boyfriend five years ago to have their baby. Her family didn't want to know her or the kid and she hadn't seen them since.

Five years without seeing her Ama! For a Hindu bloke!

Beauty prompted her, and listened to the flow of words as she stared into the boy's large eyes. At least this lady had a child to look after.

She doesn't have to worry about herself.

When her number was called Beauty was relieved to get away from the woman and her story. She made her way past the other advisers' desks and the backs of their 'clients' to the far end of the room.

A plump, middle-aged woman in a blue skirt and jacket stood up and smiled.

'It's Beauty, isn't it? How are you? Take a seat.'

Jackie remembered her well. The girl had sworn at her when she gave her the application form for the Basic Skills course.

Beauty sat down on the blue office chair and said nothing.

'How can I help? How's the course going?'

'I had to leave home.'

Beauty bit her lip and looked at her hands on her lap.

Jackie understood. She'd had diversity awareness training in Walsall. 'Are you OK?'

'Yeah, I'm fine,' Beauty said.

'Have you got somewhere to stay?'

She thought of Mark's bathroom. 'No.'

'Have you got any money?'

The question hurt, but there was no one near enough to hear. 'I can get some – maybe a hundred pounds.'

'Have you got any friends you could stay with?'

Beauty shook her head. Jackie felt she was asking the wrong questions. Weren't there often mental health issues surrounding cases like these?

'And you can't go back?' she asked. The girl shook her head again without looking up.

'Are you pregnant?'

'No!' Beauty said.

Was she? After a night at the white bloke's house? Isn't that what her mum had said? No. That Somali witch had laughed at her. You had to lie down with no clothes on like she had seen Hana doing. She shook the image out of her head.

'Have you suffered at home from violence or abuse?'

'No! They aynt like that!'

'I'm sorry, I have to ask.' There would be more money and resources available for her if she'd suffered domestic violence. Or if she was pregnant.

'It's family stuff,' Beauty said. 'They want me to get married.'

Jackie nodded. 'Are you in any physical danger?'

'No!'

Am I?

Jackie had seen the stories in the newspapers of women found buried in suitcases with their throats cut. There was no point in asking the girl much else. She tried to imagine what the girl might have been through. You could never tell with Asians. This one seemed different, more alert than most of the dead-eyed zombies she usually saw, prodded along by their brothers or fathers, or by mothers who spoke no English. Jackie was fed up with it. Now that 'mandatory referral for training' had started, she saw the thunderous-looking Indian women, on her walk to work in the mornings, hobbling and waddling across town to the various private training providers – another pointless exercise, from what she had heard so far – which had sprung up everywhere. At least her caseload had shrunk, though; she'd lost nearly half her clients. Some had found jobs to avoid being sent on the lengthy courses; others had simply signed off. Most, however, had tried to switch over to Incapacity Benefit. But the word from the DWP was that IB claimants were next on the hit list. They had six months at most until she'd have to start weeding out the serial malingerers among them.

She gave Beauty the list of refuges, telling her to come back at two o'clock when they could go through the domestic crisis forms together. The girl deserved more help than most of the troubled white kids she had to deal with. Like the one coming towards her in the black tracksuit and white cap. Jackie sighed.

'Hello, Chris.'

'Yeah right,' the boy said, sitting down and resting his elbows on her desk. 'I still ay bin fookin' paid. What you diwin' about that?'

19

Beauty knew the lady had felt sorry for her and wanted to help, but it was shameful answering her questions. At least she hadn't had to talk badly about her family, and she might get enough money – five hundred pounds the lady had said – from the Crisis Fund to get a room to rent. Maybe she could find an old white landlady, with a cat, and she could look after them both.

Who's gonna take a Paki girl in?

She walked back up Darlington Street, searching the faces ahead for her brothers. The pawnshop Mark had told her about was opposite the other Jobcentre, near the bus station. Cash Generators, he'd said it was called. They bought everything.

She found it easily. The windows were full of televisions and stereo equipment, computers, cameras and Play-Stations. A small display area was reserved for jewellery. Beauty looked at the rows of sovereign rings, bracelets and necklaces. Cheap, white people's stuff. Not like the proper Asian gold in her pocket.

People came and went as if it were a normal shop. Maybe it wouldn't be so embarrassing after all.

A young man with spots and a crest of dyed blond hair directed her down some steps to the buying counter, where a small queue of people waited. Some clutched plastic bags or stood with boxes of household appliances between their legs. A man emptied a rucksack of DVDs onto the counter, and a tall shop assistant checked each case for the disc.

'We can give you a pound a film,' he said.

Beauty could only see the man's wide frame and shapeless washed-out clothes, but she heard the anguish in his voice.

'You gimme two quid each for the other lot!'

'These aren't major titles. Do you want to sell them?'

'I'll have to, wo' I?'

The assistant made a pile of the DVDs and carried them to a partition at the end of the counter. The goods were checked again, the man signed a form, received the money and left, shaking his head.

Beauty looked away.

This is shameness.

Another assistant, a fat man with a badly tucked-in, beige nylon shirt, appeared from a side door. The queue shuffled forward. Two Indians took mobile phones from a supermarket carrier bag and put them on the counter. The fat man whistled.

'These 'm ancient!' he said, unpacking them. 'I can't give you more than . . .'

The men waited.

'. . . four pound fifty.'

'Each?' one of the men asked.

'For the pair. These things belong in a museum.'

The two Indians looked at each other.

'Kya pessa lélu?'

'Ha, lé lé.'

'We'll take it.'

Beauty looked away again as they came out from behind the partition.

*

When her turn came she took the gold bangles from her pocket and put them on the counter, proud of their rich colour.

'Do you want to sell or pledge?' the fat man asked her. She'd get more if she sold them, he explained, rather than borrowing against them. The price would depend on their weight. He gathered up her bangles and went to the side room to weigh them.

Beauty stood at the counter and waited. At least she'd have the money for a B&B for a few days. She could have a bath, and sleep.

The man returned.

'I can give you forty-five pounds for them.'

Forty-five pounds? They were worth three times as much. She felt sick and her face burned. She looked up to protest, but stopped. Forty-five pounds for five years of misery. She wanted to snatch them out of the fat man's hand, but knew she couldn't.

She went to the cubicle to sign the form and poked the thin roll of bank notes into the pocket of her jeans under her kameez.

Faisal Rahman watched his older sister hurry away from the shop and back towards the town centre. *Bhai-sahb* had let him bunk off school to come and look for her, but it had been his idea to hang around outside the Jobcentres.

20

Beauty headed back towards Dunstall Park. She'd know tomorrow whether she would get a crisis loan from the social fund, and how much it would be. Her adviser had told her that based on her age, number of weeks signing on and her ability to repay fortnightly, she might get three hundred and twenty pounds. Jackie had read the questions aloud and filled in the forms.

As for the RiteSkills course, she would have to stay on it.

Her brothers would find her there, Beauty said.

Unless she moved away from the area, Jackie told her, she'd have to carry on attending. If she wanted a placement in a care home for the elderly, it would keep her off the course and out of the way of her family. Jackie could arrange it for her straight away. She could start on Monday.

Old people who have no children to look after them.

Beauty agreed to try.

In the meantime Jackie recommended going onto Incapacity Benefit in case the placement didn't become a permanent job. She'd need a sick note from the doctor, though.

Beauty told her she wasn't ill.

Stress from family matters, Jackie said, and that she'd had to leave home. That's all she would have to tell the doctor and he'd understand. Lots of sick notes crossed her desk each week, she assured her.

On Newhampton Road Beauty ignored the admiring glances of men, her eyes fixed on the pavement, and stopped at a phone box to call the B&Bs from the list Jackie had given her. The cheapest was twenty-five pounds. She had enough for one night. She'd get her bag from the white bloke's house, thank him and go.

What about tomorrow?

Mark Aston was hungry and hadn't moved for an hour. When he heard the faint tap at the door he got up from the armchair and looked through the grey net curtain.

Beauty came in and sat down on the sofa where she had slept the night before. There was less rubbish on the floor, the beer cans and plates of food had gone, and the air was not as bad. Had he sprayed something?

'How d'you get on? What d'yer adviser say?' he asked her.

'She told me to go on the sick. Incapacity Benefit.'

'What with?'

Beauty scratched her forehead to cover her eyes.

'Stress,' she said.

What is that?

Mark nodded. 'Good idea. Fookin' 'ell, yer adviser mooss like you. That'll be an extra tenner a week. Did you apply for the crisis loan?'

She had.

'You might get three hundred quid. Depends how old y'm am. You caar use it for rent you know?'

'I know. The lady done the form for me.'

Mark raised his eyebrows. Pakis got special treatment at the Jobcentre. Everyone knew it.

'I just came to get my bag and say thanks for last night.'

'It weren't nothing,' he said. 'Jooss a few . . . Asians . . . in a car.' It was a shame they hadn't got out. Then she'd have seen something. He'd have battered the lot of them, with or without Bob. And put a few dents in the door panels on that fake M3. Maybe even kicked in a back-light unit.

'D'you fancy a brew?'

'No, I should get out of your way.'

'Have a cup a tea,' he insisted. 'You got somewhere to stay then?'

'I'm going to a B&B.'

'Black two sugars waar it?' Mark said, returning from the kitchen with two mugs.

Beauty took the cup and wiped the rim with her sleeve. *Bismillah hir Rahmaanir Raheem.*

Mark rolled a cigarette and watched the Asian bird on his sofa. 'Fit' wasn't the right word for her. Pretty. He couldn't make out what her body was like. Paki clothes didn't show much.

'Anyway,' he continued. 'I were jooss cleaning up. The place ay usually like this. I had to let the dogs in cuz of the bad weather.'

Beauty nodded and looked at her tea.

'So what you gonna do then?' he asked.

'Stay in the B&B until that moncy comes, and look for somewhere to live.'

'I've bin looking for a lodger to rent me spare room. You could rent it for a few days even,' he suggested. 'A fiver a night?' She'd been here one night already.

'I can't stay here!' she said. 'I mean . . . you done enough.'

'You wo' bc in me way. Anyway, I like Indian food.'

'Thanks, I'll bc finc.'

'Is it cuzza me dogs? They wo' come in now it ay raining. And the room's clean.'

The spare room was above the kitchen and looked out over the backyard. He was right, it was clean. The purple pile carpet had kept its colour and the walls were white. The room even smelled faintly of paint. A large double bed with an orange velvet headboard and a new-looking mattress stood along the far wall.

Beauty went to the window and looked down at the dog in his backyard, at the colourless, damp concrete of the surrounding houses, and the trees that hid some of them from view. There was no road and no one to look at her. It was tucked away, sheltered from everything.

Can I stay here? With a white bloke?

They went downstairs. Mark wanted to know. He needed the money.

'Think about it,' he said to Beauty. 'How much is a B&B? You could spend that on a set a sheets an' a duvet cover; towels – yer gonna need . . .'

There was a knock at the door. The dogs barked in the yard. Mark got up from the armchair to see who it was through the ripped curtain.

'It's two Asian lads.'

'Is it them? Is it my brothers?'

'How the fook do I know? Wodder they look like?' He peered again at Faisal Rahman and Dulal Miah. 'One's 'bout fifteen, in tracky bottoms,' Mark said. 'The other one's older.'

Al-lāh! How did they find me?

'Please, don't answer the door. Don't let them in, I'm begging you.'

'Do' worry, I ay gonna.'

A fist pounded on the door. Beauty ran through the kitchen and out into the yard. The dogs barked louder around her, and clawed at the doors inside their kennels.

Mark followed her outside.

'If they do' give up I'm giwin' out there. They wo' come here again.' He looked around for a useful weapon. The shovel.

A clean-shirted arm appeared above the fence two doors down and pegged a pair of pants to a washing line.

'Oright, mate!' Mark called out.

Peter could just make out Mark's head over the fences. His dogs had been howling for some time. He raised a hand in greeting.

'Here, listen,' he heard Mark call out. 'I could really use a favour.'

His head disappeared from view.

Peter groaned. Christ, did he want to bring one of them round? Why did he have so many if he couldn't look after them?

'Come wi' me,' Mark said to Beauty. 'He's safe.'

He opened the back gate and she followed him along the narrow path which ran between the yards.

'Pete, can me mate jooss sit round yours for five? I got to sort something out. Wo' be a sec.'

Peter looked at the headscarfed beauty in front of him and felt his heart quicken and the blood rush to his cheeks. 'Hi . . . I'm Peter.'

The girl nodded, chewing her lip, and ignored his outstretched hand.

'Sorry, I didn't catch your name,' he said.

'Beauty.'

Peter moved around the kitchen thinking of something to say. That he'd seen her this morning leaving Mark's house?

'That's an unusual name. Is it . . . ?'

She avoided looking at him. 'It's Bangladeshi.'

He wanted to say 'it suits you', but the anxious look on her face told him it wasn't the right moment.

The sound of dogs barking and raised voices in the street came through the open front window. Peter went to look out.

'What's happening?' Beauty asked from the kitchen.

'Mark's waving a spade at two Indian chaps. They're going.'

He drew back from the window as the two passed. Had they seen the net curtain twitch? What was he getting involved in?

The girl had followed him into the front room. 'Have they gone?'

Peter saw the torment in her eyes. 'Who were they?' he asked.

'My brothers.'

'Are you OK? Come and sit down.'

Peter guided her to an armchair and went to the kitchen to fetch her a glass of water. Who was she? Why were her brothers looking for her? How could she be called Beauty?

Mark let himself into the kitchen.

'Oright?' he said to Peter at the sink. 'Nice one for that, cheers.' He spotted the cups. 'I'll have one if y'm making it. Two sugars.'

'Everything all right now?' Peter asked.

'Sorted,' Mark said, loud enough for Beauty to hear. 'They ay gonna come back here in a hurry.' He went into the sitting room and sat down on the sofa.

'What did you say to them?' asked Beauty.

'That there waar no Pakis here. And if they came back I'd knock 'em through the fookin' floor and set me dogs on 'em.' Mark saw her eyes widen. 'Fookin' 'ell, you should've heard Honey, man. Proper giwin' for it, she were. Yer brother shat hisself.'

Beauty winced.

Al-lāh!

'Here, they ay gonna set fire to me house, am they?'

Peter watched the frightened, pretty girl. He'd seen the stories on *Midlands Today*, involving Muslims mostly, burning each other's houses down and stabbing their daughters/sisters/wives/cousins to death over some primitive concept of 'honour'. Mark seemed to take it lightly, enjoy it even. What was going on? Were these two an item? How could that be?

'Am y' coomin up the towun tonight?' Mark asked him.

Peter didn't think so. He had to be up early.

'D'you fancy giwin' out?'

Beauty looked up. *Is he talking to me?*

'That aynt my thing,' she said.

Mark nodded. 'What d'you wanna do about the room?'

'I dunno,' she said. Would her brothers come back? Or would they get someone else to watch the house? And how could she stay here and bring trouble to these strangers?

Al-lāh, what do I do?

'Them pair ay gonna show up 'ere again. It's probably the safest place in Wolves.' Mark turned to Peter. 'I told her to stay 'ere, rent me spare room, the clean one, for a fiver a day or whatever, 'stead of staying in a B&B, and save her money till she's got enough for her own place. At least she'd be wi' friends.' He indicated himself and Peter.

'Why not?' Peter said. For that matter she could have his spare room. Free.

'What d'you reckon then?' Mark prompted.

'I suppose so, for a few days,' she said.

I can't go home ever. Not now.

'Right, nice one. We can giw up Asda and I'll show you them sheets. Finish yer tea, I'll jooss fetch the keys to the truck.'

Peter waited until he'd gone before speaking.

'Are you OK?'

Beauty nodded.

Does it matter any more if I talk to strangers? They think it's normal an' I aynt gonna say anything bad.

'Have you known Mark long?' the man asked her.

She kept her eyes on the coffee table. 'We met the other day, on a course.'

'So, those were your brothers?'

It was family stuff, she said.

21

The Ford Transit bumped and jolted over the speed humps on Graiseley Road. Beauty sat in the passenger seat holding on to the door handle, while oddly shaped metal bits jumped on the dashboard and on the floor around her feet.

Mark swung into the car park at Asda and pulled up across two spaces. He went round to wrench the door open for Beauty, and she hurried to keep up with him as they walked to the entrance.

Asian eyes followed them down the aisles towards the home furnishings department. Couples nudged each other. She shifted under their looks and the bright lights. Mark seemed happy to linger and find the bargains. Beauty went to look for bleach, sponges and rubber gloves.

'We need bog roll 'n' all,' he called out.

As they waited to pay at the checkout, Mark asked her if she was happy with the money they'd agreed on. She got the hint, pulled out the roll of notes from under her kameez and offered him twenty pounds.

'Is that all right?' she asked.

'Beauty!'

She looked up at him.

'I mean, like . . . nice one,' he added. He paid for his sausage roll and they left.

When they got back to his house she made her way through the obstacles, up the stairs and into the clean bedroom. She covered the bed with a mattress liner and the new lime green sheets, smoothed down the empty duvet cover and stuffed the pillows into new yellow cases. Mark knocked and came into the room, a can of beer in one hand and a portable television in the other.

'Thought you might want this. I'll fetch you a table and I should have a lamp 'n' all.'

He plugged the TV into the wall, yanked the aerial around until he was satisfied with the picture and ran through the channels.

'I fixed this misself,' he said.

'Really?'

'Really.'

He returned with an anglepoise lamp, a flat brown alarm clock radio, a ring-stained bedside table, a clothes rack and hangers, a full-length dusty mirror, and her rucksack, at which point she stopped him. She had everything she needed, she said. She arranged her belongings on the bedside table and decided to wait until he had gone out before she cleaned the bathroom.

Mark called up that there was a cup of tea for her and she went downstairs.

EastEnders was on. When two lesbians kissed noisily on screen Beauty looked at Mark as he ironed his clothes.

'You OK, then?' she asked him.

'Sowund. Wha' 'bout you?'

'I'm OK now. Thanks again for what you done.'

Mark sniffed at his shirt and threw it on the back of the armchair, satisfied. 'Thass all right, got misself a lodger, dey I? Even if it is only for a few days.'

The kissing on the television had stopped.

'What was that all about with yer brothers then?'

'Oh, you know. Asian stuff.'

'*Ami tamar marray sude*,' Mark said in Bengali.

Beauty stared at him in surprise, her ears and cheeks burning. She covered her mouth, but her laughter soon filled the room. 'Do you know what that means?' she asked, clutching her stomach and wiping her eyes.

'Yeah, course. I wanna fook your m –'

She heard his Bengali accent again and her laughter broke out. The scowl and frown left her face, and her white teeth flashed. Mark was pleased that he'd made her laugh. She was a damn pretty girl.

He'd heard it from two Asian lads he'd shared a cell with, he told her. It was a long time ago, though, he added hurriedly. They'd also told him how it was for sisters, in Asian families.

At eight o'clock he put on his jacket to go up town. There was a spare key if she needed to go out, and Honey was outside if Beauty wanted to let her in. She did. Mark opened the back door and the pregnant creature came to sit at Beauty's feet, nosing for her hand.

He watched his bitch.

'Y've got a friend for life there,' he said to Beauty. 'Probly sleep outside yer door. If you get scared, giw round to Pete's. He said 'e do' mind.'

Beauty locked the door behind him and went upstairs to the bedroom.

It would only be for a few days, until the money came.

She sat down on the bed, pressed her face against the window and looked out at the darkened yards and the lights of the houses through the trees.

What if Faisal saw Mark at the course? He'd know she was here. What if? What if? She was tired of her thoughts, and of feeling hunted.

When they gonna give up? If I had a boyfriend?

No. If you was pregnant they'd have to.

Or if I moved far away.

And what would she do if they stopped looking for her?

She pictured herself in a small flat, high up maybe, or on the ground floor with a small garden and high fences so no one could see in. She'd get a cat and play with it; she'd look after it, and they would hide together from everyone. Beyond that she couldn't imagine.

She lay back on the bed and closed her eyes. The blackness and sparks behind her lids were familiar. Images from the last days replaced each other in the darkness. She shuddered at her brothers outside in the street, and felt shame for the two Indians selling their mobile phones; she pulled faces at the Asian couples who stared at her in the supermarket, and told her little sister what white people's houses were like inside; and she was running in the dark street, her rucksack jumping on her back, turning the corner. No one was there to save her and the car pulled alongside, her brothers' faces staring at her in silence.

She started awake at the noise. Honey barked and scratched at the bedroom door. A thud came from the kitchen below and Beauty sat up, straining to hear.

The dogs outside were quiet; but she had to go down and check.

Honey followed her downstairs and through the darkened kitchen. When she stopped to peer into the sitting room the dog brushed past her, sniffed at the front door and growled.

Voices.

Beauty went out to the back yard, the dogs stirring in their kennels. The knock at the front door carried down the passageway and they started barking. She fumbled for the latch on the back gate and ran along the path to Peter's house, stumbling in the dark.

The light was on in his kitchen.

22

Peter lay on the sofa with his eyes shut, blowing smoke at the lampshade and brushing ash from his chest when it fell. He played out scenes of himself on a petal-strewn four-poster bed in a marble-columned palace amid the lakes and mountains of Rajasthan. A demure-but-eventually-yielding veiled Mogul Indian princess abandoned first her religion, and then herself, to him in the midnight moonlight.

He heard the sound of tapping from the kitchen. It was most likely to be Mark, but his heart beat faster at the thought that it might be her.

Peter opened the back door and Beauty appeared from the darkness. He stopped smiling when he saw her anxious expression. 'What's happened?' he asked.

'There was someone outside the house. Mark said you wouldn't mind if I came round.'

Peter closed the door and locked it. The figure of his dreams didn't have angry brothers.

'Are they still there?' he asked.

'I don't know. It might be a friend of Mark's.'

'I'll check.'

He took his keys and went to the front door. He'd get something from the car, see who it was, and come back.

He returned, locked the door and slid the bolts into place.

'There's no one there,' he said.

Beauty sat in the armchair while Peter made tea. He put the mug on the coffee table in front of her and sat in the chair opposite. Where had Mark gone? he asked her.

Where do white people go?

'To the pub?' she guessed.

The words were strange to her, but it sounded like a normal, white answer.

Peter watched his Indian princess, her hands in her lap. Demure.

'Do you think it was your brothers?'

'Maybe,' Beauty said. If not them, Dulal could have got someone else to come looking for her. No one she would recognize. The Pakistani boys at his work would do it. Pakis would do anything.

Peter scratched around for another opening. 'Families can be difficult sometimes.'

Beauty picked up the mug of tea. 'I left home, aynit,' she said, and hoped it would be enough to keep him from questioning her further.

Apart from the possibility of danger outside, Peter was enjoying himself. Her reluctance to talk was a challenge. Unyielding at first.

'Do you mind if I ask why?'

A flash of irritation crossed her face. 'They wanted me to get married.' She took a cigarette from the packet he offered her and lit it. What else was he going to ask?

Peter watched the smoke curl up around her.

'Was that . . . an arranged marriage?'

She nodded.

'And you didn't want to?'

Peter slid the ashtray across the coffee table to her.

Beauty flicked the tip of the cigarette and shook her head.

He had a right to know, didn't he? Wasn't he helping her too?

So what if I tell someone? Do I have to hide it inside of me always?

'They were gonna send me back home again.'

Peter was entranced, his eyes drawn to her headscarf, her sensuous mouth and slender neck, the slight swell of her chest, her long shirt and the outline of her thighs in the embroidered trousers. Her eyes avoided his but her discomfort at his gaze and the silence excited him.

'It's called a salwar-kameez,' Beauty said. She didn't feel threatened. The man lounged on the armchair, the top buttons of his shirt undone. This one fancied himself too much, but she felt he was a wimp, not a dangerous pervert. And she didn't want to go back to Mark's empty house.

Peter didn't mind letting her know he was giving her appreciative looks. As long as he was careful not to go too far. For the moment she was too scared to leave.

'What are you going to do now?' he asked, feeling that the silence was no longer to his advantage.

Beauty crushed out the cigarette. What could she do? Had she really thought about it?

'Find somewhere to live and sort my life out, I guess.' Wasn't that what normal people said?

Peter saw a chance. Of course she'd have to find somewhere else to live. You could smell Mark's house from halfway down the street. Should he offer her his spare room now?

'Is everything OK at Mark's?'

Beauty nodded.

'Isn't it a bit . . . ?'

'What?'

Peter wrinkled his nose.

'No,' Beauty said. Mark had saved her life that night. She wasn't going to cuss him to no stranger.

Silence fell in the room again. Peter watched her sip tea. Perhaps he should try and lift her spirits. She'd been in a dark hole of despair, a prison. She'd run away from a forced marriage and a life of slavery. Surely she would want to embrace all that life had to offer.

'At least you're free now.'

Beauty let herself look at him. He'd stopped perving.

'To do what?'

She thought of her mother. Ama would be shuffling around the flat, moaning and crying, unable to sleep.

'I don't know . . . meet whoever you want. Anything . . . everything,' Peter said.

But what was *he* doing? He could hardly recommend smoking drugs and masturbation as a useful way of spending one's life. That was just for the time being though; hadn't he been in a kind of prison too?

The house was quiet. Beauty glanced at the man opposite her. How old was he? Didn't he have any family?

'Haven't you got a wife?' she asked, and blushed. That wasn't a white question.

Peter thought of Kate. 'No.'

She looked around the room, at the books, the computer and television. Not married. If she lived on her own, nobody would be able to tell her what to do, what to cook and clean. She wouldn't have to spend her life with a man more than twice her age. Someone who pinched and prodded her when he wanted.

Peter's voice pulled her back. 'Do you think your family will stop looking for you?'

'*Insh'allah*,' she muttered to herself. Would they? One day?

Not unless I was married, or had a kid.

Peter caught the word and sat up. If God willed it? Predestination? Christ, did people really believe this stuff? Could he dissuade her of it as a first stage in seducing her? It might be an interesting intellectual exercise. And there was nothing else to do.

'So do you believe things are destined to happen?' he asked.

Beauty held his eye for a moment to see if he was mocking her. 'Whatever's wroten in your book, thass gonna happen.' She looked down again. 'Thass wroten in the Qur'an.'

What do I know? Let him explain it.

'What do you believe?' she asked.

Peter composed his answer before exhaling it, slowly.

'I believe,' he said, 'that as long as no one is stopping you, then you have the free will to make choices and decide your own future. If it's all been written down beforehand, then how can you be responsible for the decisions you make and for what you do?'

He watched her face for a reaction. Had he made it clear enough? Leaving aside his designs on her for a moment, would she understand the implications for herself, that she was in control of her destiny, that she could break free of the shackles of a religious mindset that would only enslave her to a paralysing fatalism?

Beauty listened. That word again. *Free*. Was she really *free*? She'd chosen to leave home, to say no to a marriage she didn't want; she could have said yes like so many girls did. Was that what he meant?

She watched the man gently rubbing the patch of chest hair at the top of his shirt with his fingertips. What was he smiling for?

*

Peter was enchanted by her discomfort, innocence and *naiveté*. He felt alive. This was for real, not like one of the fatuous conversations he'd endured at Kate's dinner parties, among the Italian designer kitchenware. A person's physical and spiritual survival might depend on what he said.

It crossed his mind that he wouldn't have been so concerned had she been overweight and unattractive.

'Look, I don't want to knock anyone's religion,' he said. 'Everyone's free to believe in whatever gods they want.'

Beauty flinched. There was only one God! *Al-lāh*. The One. What did this bloke believe in?

He can't be worser than a Hindu.

'What religion are you?' she asked him.

'None,' he said. 'There is no God.'

Beauty choked on the tea and put the mug down.

'You don't believe . . . ?' She couldn't say the last words. Their meaning was darkness. If there was no . . . *toba, toba . . .*

'I don't know anyone who does,' Peter added.

Beauty stared at him.

He doesn't believe in anything?

What madness is this?

Dulal used to call her a *fucking Christian* and *Ehudi*, but they'd never accused her of this.

'That doesn't make no sense.'

'Why not?' Peter asked. It made no less sense than the idea of a Divine Creator. He watched the thoughts passing across her brow. Surely she had thought about this before! What else had she never considered?

Beauty couldn't think. The questions swirled around her. 'Where did . . . how . . . ?'

'Did everything get here?' Peter offered.

She nodded.

'A massive explosion of gas . . . out of nothing.' There.

That should rock her foundations. And for the killer blow . . . 'How did people get here?' he asked. 'We evolved, descended, we grew . . . out of monkeys over millions of years.'

He sat back, satisfied with her open-mouthed reaction. She *was* hearing this for the first time!

Beauty looked at the man on the sofa. Was he taking the piss?

Fa ranná.

It wasn't good talking like this.

What if he's right?

What if there is no . . .

She stood up.

'I have to go,' she said.

It was too soon for Peter. He'd never known a conversation hold such promise.

He followed Beauty along the dark path until they stopped at Mark's gate.

'Come back any time you like,' Peter said. 'It was just getting interesting.'

The dogs growled at the sound of his voice.

Beauty couldn't see his face in the darkness. What was he . . . a man or a devil?

'Will you?' he urged.

'Yeah, maybe,' she said. 'And thanks for, you know, before.'

The gate clicked shut behind her.

The dogs barked and Peter hurried back along the path.

23

Mark sat in the passenger seat of Bob's Transit as it crept around the avenues and side streets of Bushbury, his eyes scanning the front gardens and passageways for the scrap that people left out to be taken away. First thing in the morning was the best time, before anyone else did the rounds. They'd already found two baths on Showell Road, and a couple of television sets. They were good for the copper in the back. You had to smash them open to get at it, but the yard paid top dollar for it. They should have a good day.

Mark needed it. Seventy quid would sort him out for a while. The house was due a damn good clean, now that someone else was there. The place was a fucking tip, he knew. He'd seen the horror on Beauty's face, and heard her retch when she came out of his spare room.

Anyway, who was she to complain? At least he had a roof over his head.

Still, the money would come in handy, if she stayed on for a few weeks. He could get some more breeze blocks from Bob to sort them kennels out. Clean the house out proper. And she'd be no bother as a lodger. She was all right, for a Paki.

She ay a Paki.

Asian, then.

Bengali.

'Keep yer fookin' eyes open, will y'? There's two radiators over there,' Bob said, stopping the van. 'Fooksake, where's yer fookin' head?'

'Sorry mate. Giss a hand then.'

'Caar you diw 'em on yer own?'

Mark tipped his cap to the back of his head, relit the roll-up and jogged up the drive of the house. He pulled both radiators to his chest, staggered to the van and pushed them on to the back.

'D'you 'ave to make so much fookin' noise?' Bob said, as Mark got into the cabin. 'There's people asleep.'

'They was fookin' heavy. Still, not bad so far, eh? D'you reckon we'll pull a hundred and fifty quid?'

'We might, if you keep yer eyes open. Heavy night was it? Who d'you end up with?'

'No one. I went to Flanagan's for one or two. I was home at twelve.'

'Had enough of that tart then?'

Mark thought of Kelly. He knew he shouldn't have gone to Flanagan's. She'd sidled up to him at the bar and rubbed her tits against his arm, and his cock with her hand. He'd pictured her arsehole, and told her to stop.

Didn't he want her to come back to his house later?

No. He had a mate staying.

That dey matter, Kelly said. If his mate were fit he could join in.

It was a bird.

'Am y' shaggin' her?' she asked.

The van bumped and clanged its way down Fourth Avenue, past pale yellow houses and arched cement porches. Mark stared out of the window. It wasn't so bad round here. At least there weren't any Kosovans.

He thought of the Asian bird in his spare room.

Shagging her? It didn't seem right. He couldn't picture her . . . bent over . . .

'What's the fookin' matter with you? Dey you see that cooker?'

Bob stopped the van, and together they lifted it on to the back.

'Come on then, spit it out,' Bob said. 'Y've bin quiet since we left.'

'Nothing. I'm sowund.'

'No you ay. Y'm sitting there jumping and twitching. And you look like a fookin' tramp.'

'We'm diwin' a tramp's job, Bob.'

'The money's all right, ay it?'

'Yeah, I know. But I do' wanna do this forever.'

'That's it? Listen, it's like I keep saying. You need a good woman. Look at me and Karen. She put me straight.'

Mark looked at the round-bellied, cheery-faced older man. It was true. She had sorted him out, smartened him up and got him working more.

'What about an Asian bird?' he asked.

'You wha'?'

'I got one staying in me spare room at the minute.'

Beauty woke to the noise of dogs barking and Mark shouting at them from the bathroom. She listened as he went downstairs and slammed the front door. Silence fell on the house again.

She'd lain awake when she got back from Peter's house the night before, struggling not to think about what he had told her. He was quite a nice bloke, softer than she expected a white person to be, but he'd said some terrible things.

There is no God . . .

No *tochdir*, no destiny, nothing wroten in her book?

Was he right?

Did Allah know that she would commit a *zinna* by disobeying her parents and living with a strange man? And if so, how could it be a sin if everything was already decided?

But Beauty knew Allah existed, so the white bloke must be wrong, mustn't he?

It didn't seem so bad thinking about these things in the daylight. She stared at the ceiling and tried to remember what else he had said.

'*We grew out of monkeys over millions of years.*'

Everyone knew that monkeys were men who didn't go to the Mox on Fridays. Or was that just a kids' story?

And what else did white people believe? If there was no God that meant there was no heaven or hell. No punishment, no *zinna*. So what happened after you died? Where did you go?

Beauty shuddered at the blackness that arose in answer. She threw back the covers and got out of bed, scratched her head and looked about her for a scarf.

Anyway, how could someone who didn't believe in anything be right? The Qur'an said that Allah made people, and that everything you did in your life was wroten down before.

How do you know? You can't read it.

After you die you go to heaven and hell.

How d'you know?

What did white people think?

'*There is no God!*'

What about Christians?

Was she stupid for not knowing these things, and how could she find out?

At the care home they might think she was thick if she gawped every time she heard something new.

They might not give her the job.

Beauty lifted the wicker blind to let in the sunlight, opened the window and listened to the birds singing. They were free, flying from tree to tree, looking after their babies and singing songs to themselves. They didn't have to worry about anything.

She jumped when the phone rang.

01902 421352

Call waiting.

Beauty pressed the green button and listened.

'Hello? Is that Beauty?'

A woman's voice.

'It's Jackie from the Jobcentre.'

She'd found a placement for her in a care home for the elderly. Did she want to go and see it and talk to the manager?

Today?

Yes. It was easy to find. She'd have to get the 72 bus to Rough Hills. The manager's name was Maria. Should Jackie phone and say Beauty was going?

Can I do it? What if they give me something to read?

Yes, she would go.

Why shouldn't I work? That's what normal people do, aynit?

White people.

No woman Beauty knew had ever worked.

And it would be a good thing looking after people who had never had children, or whose kids had died.

Toba, toba astaghfirullah.

24

The doors of the bus hissed open outside the Sunny-side Residential Care Home for the Elderly. Beauty walked up the driveway of the old house, rang the bell and waited. She caught her reflection in the glass of the porch. Would they want a Paki?

The door was opened by a plump young woman in blue trousers and a nurse's top.

'Y'm all right, loov?'

Beauty scrawled her name in the visitors' book and followed the girl along floral-carpeted corridors. The air smelled of stale food.

'If you'd just like to wait in here with the service users, I'll go and find Maria.'

Beauty wondered what 'service users' were, and followed her into a large reception room. She stopped in the doorway, open-mouthed. How many people there were!

Ehcter, deuter, tinter . . .

Twenty? More?

Elderly 'service users' sat in armchairs along the walls, one thin seat touching the next. Some dozed, their heads tilted forward or to one side, others stared ahead unseeing. A television in the corner of the room showed a daytime chat show.

There were no brown faces. Had they seen a Muslim

girl before? Working here? The women wore long skirts and cardigans; some of them had bandages under their rumpled tights. The few men looked smart in jackets and V-neck jumpers

'Hello, chick,' a voice said. 'You coom for the job, have y'?'

An old woman from the row of chairs beside her leaned forward. She had a large purple bruise on one cheek and her eye was red with blood. She motioned Beauty towards her.

'Coom and let me have a look at you, sweetheart. I do' see so well any more.'

Beauty stood in front of the lady and allowed herself to be inspected. A cloudy eye stared at her while Beauty noted the lady's neat blue skirt, white blouse and pearl necklace. The woman held out a trembling hand and Beauty took it. Was that right?

'I reckon you'll do very well 'ere,' the lady said, smiling.

Beauty smiled back.

Sweet buddhi.

'Don't mind me bruises. It 'appens, when y'm old,' the lady said.

She looked Beauty over again and winked.

'You'll get the job. They caar find anyone to look after us. Why do' you go and sit down, loov? That Maria will take forever. We'll talk again, eh chick?'

Beauty said that she would, and went to the table by the window. She felt awkward as she smiled at the faces that watched her, and avoided the eyes of those that didn't.

They never had children to look after them when they got old, so they come to these places, aynit.

That's good. Back home they'd die, if they was poor and had no one.

But it wasn't a very nice place and she felt sorry for the

old people. The smell was bad and the furniture tatty. Pictures on the walls of men on horses were faded and crooked; the Silver Jubilee teacups on the hooks of a narrow dresser were chipped.

Outside the window, cars flashed past on the busy road, the high-rise flats of Chapel Ash beyond. It was a clear day. Low hills were visible in the distance, beyond the city.

What's out there?

'Where are you from, dear?'

Beauty looked into the pale blue eyes of a woman sitting near the table.

'Er . . . London.'

A man's voice growled. 'She means where's your family from. India? Pakistan?'

The face of the man opposite was unsmiling, his hands resting on the top of a walking stick standing between his knees. He was smartly dressed, in polished brown shoes and a brown jacket. A shaving cut touched the collar of his white shirt.

'Bangladesh,' Beauty said.

The man grunted.

'Don't mind him, dear,' the lady said. 'He still wishes Enoch Powell was his MP.'

Beauty didn't know what she meant but nodded, and stole a quick glance at the man staring at her from under thick white eyebrows.

Could she do this? Dressing, bathing and helping at meal times, her adviser had said. Would she have to help this man in the bathroom?

The girl who had opened the front door reappeared and beckoned to her. Beauty was relieved to get away from the man's gaze. The lady with the bruise wished her good luck as she passed.

She was led along corridors to an office, and left alone. The small space was cluttered with a paper-strewn desk, a filing cabinet and a medicine chest on the wall. There were photos on a noticeboard of groups of bare-shouldered young white girls on a night out, their arms around each other, clutching glasses or bottles of beer.

Maria turned out to be not much older than Beauty, a pretty girl with long, dyed black hair and badly applied pale foundation covering her spots. She wore a tracksuit and short vest that showed a strip of blotchy pink belly and a pierced navel.

'Iss Beauty, ay it? That's a wicked nayum! Wish I had a nayum like that.'

Beauty relaxed a little. 'Manager' had sounded important. Maybe this wouldn't be so hard.

'I ay the manager . . . she's away. I'm a Key Worker. Got promoted last week, dey I. Jobcentre sent me here eighteen month ago. If you can handle a bit of poo and wee, you'll be fine. Fancy a cup of tea 'n' a fag?'

Beauty followed Maria past the open doors of small bedrooms and into a big kitchen with long metal surfaces and huge cookers. A large woman in a white apron and hat, with bloodshot cheeks and a red nose, was pulling trays from an oven.

'Ello loov!' she called over the noise she made.

Maria threw open the back door and Beauty stepped into bright sunlight and a garden surrounded by thick bushes and tall trees.

They sat on a wooden bench and Maria told her about the Home, the manager and some of the other girls who worked there. Most of them were sowund. She'd got her best mate Louise a job there, jooss. They were desperate for staff. If Beauty got on OK they'd probably start paying her in a couple of weeks.

Maria stubbed out her cigarette and went to make tea.

Beauty leaned back on the bench and squinted in the sunlight at the well-kept lawn and the flower-beds.

I can do this!

I'll get a job and somewhere to live.

Maria returned with a blond-haired girl in a grey tracksuit and white England shirt and introduced her as Louise, who also thought Beauty's name was wicked. The two girls smoked and laughed, and asked Beauty about herself.

Did she have a boyfriend?

'No,' Beauty said, and reddened.

Didn't all Asians have arranged marriages?

'Most of them.'

So a girl didn't know her husband before she got married?

God! That was really bad! Louise could never do that.

Neither could Maria. What happened if it turned out he had a tiny cock? Could you get divorced?

Beauty laughed with them. Even if it was rude she didn't feel they meant any harm.

Could a girl have a boyfriend before she got married? Louise asked her.

'No.'

So Beauty had never had one?

'No.'

Was she still a vir – ?

Hana's twisting naked legs and the Iraqi's –

'Yes.'

The girls were silent. Did they feel sorry for her? Did they think she was simple?

Maria's best mate from school had married an Asian bloke. He was really sweet and kind, took her everywhere, bought her lots of nice things. But Maria hadn't seen her since she'd got married last year.

'You can't go out with an Asian bloke,' Beauty said. 'They change after you get married.' *Apart from in films.*

Had Beauty's family found her a husband? Maria asked.

But she didn't want to answer. 'What about you two? Have you got boyfriends?' she asked.

Louise's divorce had just come through the other day. She'd gone out drinking to celebrate.

Maria's chap was a useless stoner who sat about playing computer games all day.

Neither of them had kids. Everyone else they knew did. Had had them ages ago. They'd both like a babby one day, but with the right bloke. One who'd stick around.

Maria wanted someone who had, you know, a bit of initiative.

Louise had met a nice bloke down Flanagan's the other night. He was quite a bit older than her, but he was good-looking and had a proper job. Beauty should go out with them one night. There weren't any Asians there though. What type of bloke was she looking for?

'I'm not,' Beauty said.

25

Going to the Parkfields Health Centre was risky, she knew, and Beauty walked into the surgery without looking at the block of flats where her family lived. Jackie had phoned her to remind her to go.

The waiting room was full of people from all over the world, and the receptionist told her to wait for a cancellation. She sat down between an old Sikh and a large, grimacing Somali woman, and watched the door. If her father walked in she would have nowhere to escape. But what could he do to her in here?

No one had phoned her since she'd stayed out that first night. That didn't mean they'd given up, and she had checked the cars in the street every time she left Mark's house. Would Dulal send someone to watch her? He probably thought a dumb bitch like her wouldn't last more than a few days. But if she could work and earn enough money to survive . . .

I aynt never going back.

'*You can meet whoever you want.*'

Was it the white girl who'd said it? She couldn't remember.

Forget that.

They hadn't seemed like slappers. Louise was divorced and lived with her mum, and Maria lived with her boyfriend. Were they doing anything wrong, and why shouldn't Beauty live like that?

You're Muslim.

Beauty looked at the pictures in the waiting room, at health warnings she didn't understand, drawings of dissected body-parts she didn't recognize. Was that an ear?

A queue had formed at the receptionist's window. A white mother let her child make too much noise before scolding him harshly.

My kids aynt gonna do that.

What kids?

An Iraqi-looking woman in a niqab sat down in the empty chair on the other side of the Somali lady. Beauty caught their whispered exchange.

'*Asalaam alaikum.*'

'*Alaikum salaam.*'

The Iraqi said she was from Libya.

Where was that?

Beauty stood up when her name was called and made her way past people's knees. So what if they looked to see who had such a name? Why should she be embarrassed by it? Hadn't those girls said it was *wicked*?

The door to room number three opened as she reached it, and she was glad to see the doctor was white. You couldn't trust Asian doctors. They gave you village advice and told your parents everything.

A clean-shaven man in his mid-fifties with side-parted, fair hair and a tweed jacket welcomed her and closed the door. Beauty sat on the chair beside his desk.

'What can I do for you?' he asked.

'The lady from the Jobcentre said I should come and see you,' Beauty said, not looking up.

'What about?'

Beauty studied her hands. This was embarrassing.

'Getting Incapacity Benefit.'

Doctor Russell put down his pen and turned to the Asian girl in front of him. She avoided his eye.

What was it this time? Since the Jobcentre had introduced these schemes the number of patients claiming an incapacitating ailment had doubled. Half the people outside his door were waiting to explain their new disabilities to him. What they didn't know was that a mental health nurse and a Department for Work and Pensions panel were waiting along the corridor to assess their availability for work. Patients didn't like it. They didn't have enough time to get their stories and symptoms straight. They balked at seeing a 'mental' health nurse. It was their own fault for pretending. Depression was what most of them said . . . or backache, which was just as hard to disprove.

What would this girl say? She might be a genuine case. He doubted her parents allowed her to work anyway. But Doctor Russell had given up on Asian females. If there was something genuinely wrong, and there often was, you met a wall of silence when you probed too deeply. And some of these village peasant parents couldn't grasp the concept of clinical depression.

At least this girl had been honest about her reason for coming. Most of the scroungers out there pretended they'd never heard of Incapacity Benefit. He enjoyed sending them shuffling along the corridor. But it was a waste of his precious time.

'What seems to be the problem?' he asked.

Beauty looked at a poster of the muscle system on the wall.

'My adviser said she thought I was . . . I had . . . stress.'

She didn't like to say the word, but knew she might have to say more. She'd planned how much.

The doctor watched the girl fumbling with her hands.

'Why did your adviser say that?'

'I had to leave home,' Beauty said, and glanced at the doctor. The doctor was looking at her but his eyes were kind, not scary.

Would he understand what that meant? Did it mean she couldn't work, or that she was ill?

Doctor Russell waited for more.

Seconds passed before the girl spoke.

'There was . . . things . . . going on at home,' she said. 'They wanted me to get married –'

He held up his hand to stop her and watched her twist her fingers in her lap. He could fill in the blanks: forced marriage, physical and psychological pressure, anxiety, guilt, depression, self-harm and attempted suicide. It was enough to fell an ox, never mind the nonsense his own daughter claimed to suffer from. This girl would need specialist support and counselling.

There was a newly-opened Asian women's group and mental health facility in Wolverhampton, he told her. The mental health nurse just along the corridor could refer her. In the meantime Amitriptyline would help stop her from worrying. He told her to read the instructions carefully. If she suffered from any of the symptoms described she should stop taking them immediately. She could collect the prescription on the way out.

There wasn't much else one could do for her or others like her, apart from deporting their close male relatives. And whither, if they were born here? Besides, it wasn't in his power.

Doctor Russell watched the Asian girl close the door, wrote up his notes and buzzed through to reception. They could send in his next appointment. Adrian Bennett. Fifty-five years old. Unemployed.

Backache or depression?

Beauty was glad she hadn't had to tell the man any more. What was coming next? More questions? And she didn't want to go to any Asian women's place either. If she was going to start work in a couple of weeks she wouldn't need Incapacity Benefit.

Telling strangers your family stuff for a few quid aynt good. Thass gotta be a zinna.

She didn't have to stay long with the mental health nurse. She mentioned her arranged marriage, that she had had to leave home, and answered 'no' to all the questions: she had no trouble sleeping or concentrating, no feelings of hopelessness, tiredness, of having let herself or her family down, no loss of appetite and no thoughts of self-harm. But the nurse looked at her as if she didn't believe it and offered to refer her to the Asian women's centre, if she wanted. They had a hostel too. And she needn't worry about the Jobcentre. She'd ask the doctor to give Beauty a three-month sick note.

Beauty took the piece of paper with the telephone number of the Shanti Asian Women's Service, thanked the woman and left.

She waited for her prescription and sick note at the receptionist's window, and hurried away without looking at the block of flats on the other side of the dual carriageway.

26

It was almost dark when she got off the bus in the town centre and headed towards Mark's house.

Was that home now?

She looked over her shoulder to check her little brother wasn't following, and felt safer when she reached the early evening movement at the park in Graiseley and the row of shops. People stood outside the chip shop and bookies, cars vibrated with the rumble of amplified bass speakers. Young white men, cans of beer in one hand, let themselves be pulled across the park by English bull terriers, Rhodesian Ridgebacks and Japanese Akitas. Perfumed Kurds with bulging groins and dark-stubbled faces stood outside their own barbers, comparing phones and cars; an Indian newsagent came out of his shop; white kids on bikes circled slowly. And no one seemed to take any notice of Beauty. The Iraqis didn't nudge each other as she passed.

It felt good walking through these people unnoticed. But who were they? How had they come here? What did they do? Did they have families?

Beauty turned into Prole Street and made towards the van outside Mark's house. The lights in the windows were on, the front door open. A short white man with a round belly came out, his thumbs hooked into the pockets of his dirty jeans. Gold flashed on his little fingers, wrists and neck. He smiled and nodded at Beauty when she stopped in front of him.

Mark appeared in the doorway behind him, staggering with the weight of a washing machine.

'Out the fookin' way Bob, I caar see fook all.'

Beauty watched Mark struggle out of the house, his fingertips straining to grip the machine to his bare chest. She saw his filthy hands and the taut muscles of his thin arms, the blue outline of home-made tattoos and the muscles and ribs of his back. His reddened face was pressed against the white metal, the sinews bulging in his neck as he passed her. He raised his eyebrows in greeting and smiled through the effort.

Mark tipped the washing machine onto the van, and pushed it in among the rest of the furniture from his sitting room. He faced Beauty, breathing heavily.

Bob rested an arm on the tailgate. 'This yer new lodger?'

'This is me mate, Bob,' Mark said to Beauty. 'Cheers for the help, Bob.'

'You managed it.' The man winked at Beauty. 'He's a strong lad.'

Beauty didn't mean to look at Mark again, at his tight white chest as it rose and fell from his exertion, at his flat white stomach and pelvic bones disappearing into low-hanging beltless jeans.

Mark saw her glance at him. Birds loved it . . . lean and mean – but she turned away, and it felt cold in the street.

'S freezin' out here,' he said. 'You coomin' in for a drink, Bob? You'll have one won't you, Beauty?'

If you put some clothes on.

The older man climbed into the cab of the van.

'I'll leave you two to it,' he said.

Beauty winced.

The engine rattled into life. 'I'll tek a look at that timing belt tomorrer,' Mark said above the noise. 'It's burning oil 'n' all.'

The van left them in the street. Beauty prepared herself for the bad air and followed the topless man into his house.

Mark pulled on a T-shirt and tried to hide his satisfaction with his new sitting room. By two o'clock he and Bob had collected nearly two tonne of scrap from round Wednesbury-way and he'd come away with sixty-five quid. Bob'd had a load of stuff he didn't need, including a sofa, and Mark had managed two runs to the tip to dump his old furniture by the time Beauty got back. He'd kept his computer chair, the dresser and the TV cabinet, but the rest had gone. Bob's old leather three-piece still looked mint, and he'd given Mark eight litres of emulsion as well. He still had to clean out the kitchen but at least the front room was looking good.

Beauty was surprised. And the white bloke was grinning, waiting for her to say something. She looked around the room and nodded her approval. Had he cleaned up for her?

'Just did a spot of clearing out,' he explained. 'Bob gimme some things he dey need. He ay got dogs, well not in the house anyway, so it's all . . . clean.'

Beauty nodded again.

'It looks nice.'

'Innit,' Mark agreed.

He told her to sit down and went to the kitchen to make tea. Beauty waited and looked around the room. The rotten carpet had gone and he'd washed the wooden floor beneath. The surfaces were clean and the rubbish thrown out.

'Do' worry about Bob, he dey mean nothing by it,'

Mark said, returning with two mugs. 'He's a good mate. More of an old man to me than me own.'

Beauty didn't ask him what he meant. How could a stranger be more than your own father?

Mark rolled a cigarette and asked her how she had got on. Beauty told him about the care home and the job that might come out of it, that the doctor had given her a sick note, and that the crisis loan had arrived in her bank.

Mark was impressed. And three or four weeks' rent money up front would be handy.

'Sorted,' he said. 'You can stay on here till yer first wage comes through, if you like. I'm gonna do the whole place up. Mek it nice like.'

He looked away when their eyes met. Beauty didn't know what to say. She needed to stay somewhere until she had more money, but how could she live with a man and dogs?

What about that Asian women's place?

The phone vibrated in her pocket. Beauty didn't recognize the number on the screen.

Mark waited for her to answer so he could tell her more about his plans. By the look on her face it might be her family. He hoped they wouldn't convince her to go home.

Beauty pressed 'OK' and held the phone to her ear.

'Bew-tee?' Her mother's voice was weak and scared. Beauty felt her eyes begin to sting. *Ama!*

Mark stood up and went to the kitchen. He'd still be able to hear from there.

'*Balla asson'ee? Sharifa keta horra? Baht hai lisson'ee. Bhai-sahb ye keta hoi la?*'

He listened anyway. He was surprised to hear the flood of Bengali. He'd never heard her talk so much. She didn't make it sound so bad. Not like the ignorant Pakis in the shops all gabbling away. *Gora* this, *gora* that. That's when you knew they were slagging off white people.

'*Ai tam nai. Ami kham erchta faissee gorro roybar zaga assé. Sinta horrio na. Sinta horrio na.* I love you.'

The line went dead. Beauty looked at the phone in her hand.

Mark heard her sniffing and went into the sitting room.

'You OK?' He offered her a roll of grey toilet paper.

Beauty thanked him.

Things were OK. They weren't looking for her, not yet anyway. Her mother had told her that Dulal was convinced she'd be back within a few days. Let her come home on her knees, begging for forgiveness, he'd said. And if she didn't, he'd bring her back.

But it was easier to deal with her brother's punches than her mother's pleas for Beauty to go home. And why had Ama hung up suddenly? Someone must have come into the room. The old man would scream if he found out she'd phoned.

Maybe they told Mum to ring, and make out she was suffering.

'Families, man,' Mark said.

Beauty smiled.

'Was that yer mum?'

She nodded.

'Was she telling you to go home?'

'Not really. I just miss her. Sorry.' Beauty pressed the tissue to her nose again.

'Do' mind me,' Mark said. 'Ay they gonna come looking?' He looked at the pretty Bengali girl on his new sofa and hoped not.

It was just about the rent money, right?

'They think I'll go back in a couple of days.'

Mark wanted to cheer her up. She looked miserable. He knew what it meant to be alone, trapped inside yourself, trapped in jail, trapped in a house where no one came to visit. You needed someone to talk to. Not about anything in particular. Just things.

He drew the curtains and switched on *Midlands Today*. The halogen heaters would make it cosy. She could watch TV while he fixed the computer.

'Y'm all right now though. Y've got a roof over yer head, if you want it, and a job lined up.'

Beauty looked at Mark as he sat hunched over the back of the computer fiddling with the wires, at his closely shaven dark hair and sideburns and the sharp line of his jaw and chin. He was right, wasn't he? Not long ago she'd been running through the streets, with nowhere to go and no money. Who was he? How come he was in the street just when she had needed someone? Maybe this was her *tochdir,* her *kishmut.* Fate, or whatever white people called it.

Maybe Al-lāh sent him.

To make me live with a strange man?

It aynt haram if you're in danger.

'Anyway, y'm better off on yer own in this life,' he said. 'Least, that's what I reckon.'

'Don't you get on with your family?' she asked. How could it be better with no mother or sister near you?

Let him talk.

'Put it this way . . . they dey get on wi' me.'

Mark closed one eye as smoke drifted into it.

'Give 'em too much grief as a kid,' he said.

Beauty thought of her older brother and the times she had cleaned up his puke when he'd come home drunk. And the smell of ganja coming from his room.

'All kids do wrong things. Thass normal,' she said, and looked at him to see what was in his eyes.

'Not like me,' he said, and was silent. She might be shocked by how much time he'd spent inside. But why was he bothered what she thought? 'Anyway, I caar blame 'em. I was bad.'

He looked at her to see the effect.

'I ay like that no more,' he added. He wanted her to know that he'd changed. And that life wasn't better on your own.

'What did you do?' Beauty asked. What if he'd killed or raped someone? He didn't seem that type. You could tell a pervert by his eyes. *The way they look at you.* The mullah, his brother, cousins, men in London, Iraqis . . .

Mark watched Beauty tapping ash into the saucer on the arm of the sofa. He wondered what her hair looked like under her scarf.

'I started pinching cars when I was eleven years old.'

'Why?' Beauty asked. *Stealing!*

'For a laff. Getting chased by the old bill.'

'Thass fun?'

Mark thought about it, the flashing lights in the rearview mirror, the understeer and handbrake turns, ditching the car and running.

'Ye'man!'

But the time inside hadn't been fun, and that period in his life was over. He decided not to tell her about the thefts of two hundred motor vehicles he'd had Taken into Consideration. Pinched to order, most of them. You got three hundred quid for a Cozzie back in them days. At fourteen he was making and spending a couple of grand a month.

'I ay diwin' that shit again. Put my family through hell, dey I? Thass why they ay bothered wi' me now, d'you know woddamean?' He shrugged. 'I ay bin in jail now for nearly two years, and I ay giwin' back. I wanna show me mam.'

'What about your dad?' Beauty asked.

'I ay sin 'im since I was six.'

He wrapped two wires with tape and cut it with his teeth. Why was he telling her all this? He'd never mentioned it to the counsellors in jail. Not even the ex-wife. It felt right telling Beauty. Like they were in it together.

'I ay blamin' 'em though. I were a pain in the arse, but I'm diwin' all right at the minute. Got me dogs, and the rent paid by the social.'

Beauty looked around the room and nodded.

Mark was pleased with her approval. 'And I could sort me business plan out if I dey have to go on that fookin' course. You won't have to if y'm on Incapacity. What did the doctor say?'

'I told him I had to leave home,' Beauty said. 'He gave me a sick note for three months and some pills.'

'You do' wanna be tekkin' pills. They gimme tons a that shit in jail. Proper messes wi' yer head, them things. Mek you feel ten times worse. What am they?'

Beauty took the slim box of tablets from her pocket.

'Wossit say about the side effects?' Mark asked. 'Thass what you godder watch out for.'

'I dunno,' she said, passing the packet to him.

Mark took it from her. 'Caar you read?' he asked. He didn't make it sound bad.

'I got a problem with it, aynit.'

He didn't laugh at her, and she didn't feel embarrassed in front of him. It felt right to tell him. 'I didn't go to school much,' she explained. But she didn't tell him that they'd tried many times to make her read. She'd sat at tables at home and stared at the letters on the page. She copied the words when the mullah's pervert brother shouted, but none of it made sense. And she'd believed them when they said there was something wrong with her. She was thick, she'd never be able to do it. Anyway, what did it matter? She was a girl. What her brothers did at school was more important.

Mark passed back the pills. 'I taught misself to read in jail. Went to a few lessons, like. It's a piece a piss.'

Beauty didn't want to shame herself in front of him. 'I tried loads of times. I'm a bit thick,' she said.

'Bollocks. Iss like riding a bike or driving a car – you godder practise. Tay hard. I'll teach you if y'm staying for a while.'

Beauty watched him as he turned back to the computer. Wouldn't it be good to tell Sharifa that she could read?

'I could have another go, I suppose.'

Mark took the screwdriver from his mouth. Did that mean she might stick around?

'Nice one,' he said, and grinned.

He'd clean out the kitchen the next day.

27

Peter looked at the light around the curtain of Mark's sitting-room window. Was Beauty there? Should he knock?

He went back inside and closed the front door. His house was silent, the television unplugged. Neither would do any more. He wanted her to come round, had felt in limbo since he'd last seen her. It bothered him that he hadn't been able to enthral her with the prospect of her freedom. Her mind was a blank canvas waiting to be filled. He knew that he'd once had the words to describe mankind's accomplishments and make a person's heart sing. But if he was no longer able to summon up his own sense of wonder, how could he inspire anyone else? And what did that say about the time he had spent shunning the madding crowd's ignoble strife and devoting himself to the pursuit of knowledge?

It was different when she was there. Her innocence and ignorance were an inspiration, as well as her exquisite looks. He'd felt alive in the thirty minutes of her visit, had lain awake for hours afterwards fantasizing about guiding her through all the pleasures of life which she'd been denied.

And peeling off her clothes, although he'd tried to keep this to a minimum.

He paced from the back door to the front and peered at

himself in the mirror at the bottom of the stairs. His eyes were glassy and red and he knew he'd smoked too much.

At least he still recognized his own image. Not like Baudelaire.

'*Today I felt the wing of madness brush my cheek.*' Or something like that.

If his thoughts could still turn to the poets maybe he could dredge up some *joie de vivre*. Maybe even a *raison d'être*.

But the Frenchman had died of syphilis in his early thirties. Beguiled and poisoned by a woman.

He returned to the kitchen and looked through the window into the darkened backyard, at the uneven outline of the slatted wooden fence and the roofs of the houses beyond. Once, he would have found some melancholy beauty in it. Or in the dreary faces of those he passed in the street. All that had gone.

What was the point of thinking about Baudelaire and the finer things in life unless *she* was there to share it? Beauty.

He sat down on the sagging sofa and shut his eyes. He wasn't thinking straight. She was just a charming distraction.

He'd go to Asda shortly. At least there would be housewives and forty-somethings to smile at over the fruit and vegetables. Or had that lost its allure too?

The minutes passed in silence. Would she come again? And did he really think he could have his way with her? Did he really want to? Surely his interest in her wasn't just sexually motivated. Had he really become that shallow, as well as dissolute?

No, he hadn't! She was good company, she was interested. Her eyes were keen and bright. It was proof that you could have a more stimulating conversation with a religious devotee than with a metropolitan phoney like Kate. She would have asked him what he was 'banging on about now'. Beauty had a nascent, timid intellectual curiosity. If he could overcome her irrational fears of transgressing the mores of her repressive belief system, he would be doing his bit for womankind. He could rediscover life's mysteries through her exploration of them. And he might yet intellectualize his lustful thoughts for her. Let undressing her become a metaphor for stripping away the blinkers of religious dogma, or *vice versa*.

And if not her, then someone like her. Unformed, enquiring and innocent. The girl he'd met in the pub when he went out with Mark, what was her name? Louise. Wouldn't she appreciate being lifted out of the darkness of satellite television and the hand-chapping grind of scullery work?

No. It had to be Beauty. The cultural gulf was a greater attraction. The promise of Eastern mystery. He tried to fight the thought that she was probably still a virgin . . . and of a wedding night on a flower-strewn bed in Rajasthan. Couldn't he have a quick peek online at some Indian porn? There must be some.

No! It was wrong. It debased his noble thoughts about her.

It was Kate's fault. She'd held him back for the last few years. Her endless talk of home improvements and 'clearing out the loft', the pseudo-intellectual conversations at dinner parties with her lowbrow media-generating and consuming friends (where everyone's opinions were of equal validity by simple virtue of being opinions) had almost left him without the will to live.

With the right woman he might have done more over the last five years. His thirties had passed him by. Kate hadn't understood his brilliant mind, he decided. Maybe that wasn't even necessary in a woman. Perhaps all you needed was someone quietly supportive, who understood that she didn't understand but who wanted to; a woman who hadn't imbibed an over-inflated sense of her centrality in the universe from the pages of glossy magazines. Did such women exist? Otherwise you were better off alone. At least you weren't pulled down from the stars – the rightful place for a thinking man like himself – by trips to Homebase every Sunday afternoon.

Kate. Her text message asking him whether he loved her had so far gone unanswered.

Of course I do. It had always been easier than telling her the truth.

Kate Morgan hung up. Peter wasn't answering. That was three missed calls. What was he doing? Why didn't he ring back? He knew she'd be anxious; that she needed to talk things through with him, to discuss their relationship and where it was headed. Wasn't she his partner? They were supposed to be in love, weren't they? Didn't that mean being together, doing things together, sharing?

'Bastard,' she said aloud.

She was *physically exhausted* and *mentally drained*, and couldn't afford to wait forever. Life was slipping by. She wanted to share it with someone who made her feel special, like a . . . woman, someone who loved her *for who she was*. Was that too much to ask? If Peter wasn't able to make that kind of commitment, then what was the point of being with him? She could get other men. She knew they looked at her in the street. Revolting van drivers still honked at her in summer.

But the thought of being alone until she found another man was frightening. At least Peter listened. Maybe he did still love her? She knew she was difficult to be with, high-maintenance, but that's what love was all about, wasn't it? Maybe he just felt challenged because he didn't have enough money to buy a house. The thought had crossed her mind before.

She needed to be positive.

Didn't she have a right to be happy, too?

She'd go and see him.

She'd need a repeat prescription of antidepressants before she went. Maybe some more Citalopram, or Lofepramine.

That would show him what he was doing to her.

Peter splashed some water on his face, checked himself in the mirror and left the house. He drove the short distance to Asda, safely past the chip shop and the murderous-looking gangsters, yobs and hags in Graiseley Park.

The bright lights of the superstore blinded him momentarily, and he wandered around, unable to decide what to eat. There was an entire aisle of sliced white bread. He looked into other people's trolleys for inspiration but everything was in boxes. A couple of women flicked their hair at him among the cheeses, but they reminded him of Kate. How soon before they started talking about house prices and saying things like 'I'm thinking of knocking that wall through into the lounge to make one big space'?

Peter knew he could never go back to that type of life. But what were the alternatives? Giving up altogether? Staying here and slumming it with the underclass in the freezer section? Why not? It couldn't be more worthless an existence than living in London, on the edges of what passed for society. Were the downtrodden welfare masses, filling their trolleys with oven-ready chips, less fitting company for him? He watched an impoverished, elderly man in a thin coat inspect a bag of chicken nuggets through pale, watery eyes, and place it carefully in the bottom of his basket, next to a bottle of tomato ketchup, with a liver-spotted hand.

Peter was no ragged-trousered philanthropist. There was nothing romantic to be found in Asda.

And there was nothing to eat either. He put the basket back and went to the car. What if Beauty came round while he was out?

It bothered him that he could find nothing with which to entertain himself, other than the thought of the Bangladeshi girl and her possible reappearance.

He was restless, that was all, and had latched on to the nearest thing to drag him out of his *ennui*.

But he feared spending the rest of his days in a bare sitting room on someone else's sofa. In Wolverhampton.

The West Mids.

Alone in front of the computer.

After Beauty had gone to bed, Mark sat at the computer and scrolled through the list of tunes he'd downloaded. He couldn't get into the chatrooms. But for the first time since the line had been cut, he didn't mind.

She was nice. And he liked talking to her. Beauty.

He'd told her about growing up in Burntwood, what it was like in jail, and how he was never going back. He'd asked her about her brothers and gripped the arms of the chair when he heard how often they used to beat her up. They needed a damn good kicking.

But she didn't tell him much, he knew. Something bad had happened to her. He recognized the dead-eyed look she had sometimes. He'd seen it in other boys in care, when they were talking of one thing and thinking about another.

Mark smoked and swung round slowly in the chair, thinking of ways he could help her. He fantasized about protecting her in the streets from her brothers, or from those Asian blokes in the car. He'd take a couple of blows, knock one out and headbutt the other on the bridge of his nose, then push her into a car that he'd have to hot-wire. Maybe get chased across Wolves and lose them with his superior driving skills.

And he liked the idea of teaching her to read.

Beauty lay on the bed and listened to the wind in the trees outside. The dogs barked when they heard Mark in the kitchen below. She liked the different threats he yelled at them through the open window.

He's all right.

She wondered again whether Allah had sent him, and tried to imagine what would have happened that night if he hadn't been there. She might be at home already, packing her bags for Bangladesh, or that other place.

As soon as she had enough money she'd find her own place to live. Even if God had sent him, she shouldn't live with him if there was somewhere else to go. That would be *haram*.

For now it was OK.

Aynit.

They weren't doing anything wrong, apart from sitting in a room together. Why should she feel guilty about that?

I don't.

He was a good man, you could tell. He looked like a typical scary white bloke, but she felt safe knowing he was there. He seemed to understand, and didn't ask too many questions. And he'd had a bad life. Did all white people do things like him? Did they all have families like that?

Beauty felt sorry for him. His father had left him when he was only six years old. How could a man abandon his child? And his stepdad drank alcohol and beat him, the first time when he was eight after the police brought him home. He'd climbed into a place for broken cars. By the time he was sixteen he'd stolen over a hundred.

She couldn't tell if he was proud or sorry. He looked embarrassed, but there was a cheeky smile on his face. Beauty didn't mind. Was it his fault? He'd had no father and his mother didn't care for him. Still, he should have known it was wrong when he got older.

He'd stopped now, he said.

She asked him about prison, too. He told her how he'd been in just about every jail north of Birmingham, constantly moved around, rarely able to settle for more than a few weeks at a time; how the main thing inside was to keep busy and work, do all the courses you could; and how he'd warned the guards not to put him in a cell with any queers. Anything but that. Often they put him in with Asians. That's how he'd learned how to say rude things in Bengali.

Ami tamar . . .

Beauty slipped the scarf from her head, closed her eyes and smiled at his accent and the thought that she had made a white friend, one like him . . .

. . . and saw his flat stomach, the bones disappearing into his jeans, the tightness of his muscles as he carried the washing machine . . .

Fa ranná. That is not good.

But was it really so bad to think about it?

Think about what?

'This is a fucking zinna!'

Who said that?

'You fucking slapper.'

There was milk on her brother's lip.

'How many you done today, bitch?'

A white man's eyes stared straight into her.

'There is no God.'

Toba, toba astaghfirullah.
What kind of a devil is he?
'You're free to choose.'
'Hello love, have you come for the job?'
The lady's hand was so light.
'You'll come back and talk to me, won't you, dear?'
'It's all wroten before.'
'Beauty!'
The girls smoke cigarettes, and laugh. They don't care.
'That is a wicked nayum.'
How free they must feel!
'Are you still a virgin?'

28

Beauty woke up and knew where she was for the first time since she'd left home. She washed as best she could and left the house to go to work. It was early, but she wanted to be there on time. She was pleased to be going to help the old people at the home. They had no children to do it. And it took her mind off her own thoughts.

At the park in Graiseley a few white people were already out with their dogs. She passed the green-domed mosque on the corner of Dunstall Road and Waterloo Road, and from the bus stop watched the Pakistani men walk in slowly through the gates.

I aynt never been in a Mox.

Neither had her mum.

It was early when she got to the care home. The manager, Janet, was a nice lady. Fattish, with a friendly round face. Beauty liked her. No one had given her a form to fill in, or asked her about her reading yet. She would tell the manager today about her problem, and that she was doing something about it. If the white bloke was able to help her.

Most of the armchairs in the main sitting room were empty, but the lady with the curly white hair, who had spoken kindly to her on the first day, beckoned her over to the corner where she was watching television.

'Hello again, dear. Have you come to look after us?'

Beauty went to sit by her until Maria came to tell her what to do. The lady turned back to the silver-haired man and overweight woman on the screen.

'. . . *your son, Chris, was put into care when he was nine years old. That's right, isn't it?*'

'*That's correct, Jeremy, yes. He threatened to burglarize me.*'

'*Chris is coming out of prison next week. He's hired private security guards to protect himself from you. Can you tell us a little bit about that?*'

The lady shook her head.

'Three children with different men, and she wasn't married to a single one of 'em,' she said, leaning towards Beauty. 'Things didn't use to be like that,' she sighed. 'We had sweethearts and they'd do the right thing. None of this living together. I bet you're not doing that, are you, dear?'

She patted Beauty's hand on the armrest between them.

Maria burst into the room, flushed and out of breath.

'Oright, Ethel?' she shouted. 'Beauty, am y' coomin' for a fag? Lemme giw for a pee first, I'm boostin'.'

Beauty waited for her to go before she answered Ethel.

'Asian girls don't do them stuff.'

You're living with a white bloke.

That was different though, wasn't it?

The tall old man with the stick appeared in the doorway and walked slowly to an armchair opposite Beauty and Ethel. He tugged at the knees of his trousers and sat down.

'Morning,' he said to both women and opened the newspaper.

Beauty tried to smile.

'I was just saying, Norris –' Ethel called across the room to him, '– young people nowadays? It's shocking how they live.'

The man looked up. 'Damn right,' he said, looking at Beauty. 'This country's gone to the dogs.'

Ethel whispered to her not to worry. Norris was a grumpy old so-and-so and a bit deaf. But he was right, she said, about most things, and he kept everyone informed about what was going on in the world.

But the things the staff got up to! Their language!

'They talk to each other in front of us like we're not there.' It was enough to make your ears curl with embarrassment, the things they said.

Beauty nodded. Things had changed, the lady said. They didn't used to do them things – having different mens 'n' that.

'But we don't like to complain, do we, Norris?'

Norris turned a page and looked up when he realized he'd been addressed. 'Eh?'

'I said we don't like to complain!'

'I bloody do!'

Ethel whispered to Beauty that he'd been a hero during the War.

What war?

He'd fought in Singapore, Burma, India, North Africa and Italy, killed a Japanese soldier with his bare hands and had a chestful of medals for bravery. Fifty-six years he'd been married, but had no children.

Beauty stole quick glances at him as he lowered the newspaper to turn the pages; at his short white hair, thick eyebrows and long nose. He had a kind face, she decided.

Norris Winterton caught her looking at him and winked.

He killed someone.

She was sure he'd had a good reason. And he was an old man, so respect to him.

*

Maria re-appeared, uniformed in a white tunic and blue trousers.

'Morning, Norris!' she shouted.

She nodded to Beauty. 'You coomin' then?'

Maria sat down next to her on the bench in the garden. Beauty liked the girl's cheerfulness, but she looked tired today.

'How's it giwin'?' Maria asked. And could she scrounge a cigarette?

Beauty offered her the packet. 'You OK?'

'No, I fookin' ay! I'm pissed off,' Maria said.

'How come?'

'Me boyfriend's a fookin' useless twat, that's why. He jooss sits rowund the howuss all day gerrin' fookin' stowund with 'is mates. The place is a fookin' tip when I gerr'ome from work. And another thing . . .' She lowered her voice. 'I was savin' up for a boob job, you know. To boost me self-esteem?' Maria looked down at her chest. 'I'll be tucking 'em into me trousers soowun,' she added. 'But he's only gone and spent the money on a fookin' noine bar a hash.'

She'd had enough of him, she said. Apart from not working and spending her money, he never wanted to do anything or go anywhere. He came to bed late every night, and when they did, you know, do it, it was over really quickly. 'D'you know woddamean?'

Beauty didn't, but nodded.

If her boyfriend didn't work why didn't she kick him out? Not that she should have been living with him.

Why not? And what are you doing?

'I would not put up with that,' she said. It was all she could think of to say.

The day passed quickly. Beauty followed Maria – 'shadowing', they called it – and liked the work. Some of the residents needed help with everything. Beauty had looked after her grandmother in Bangladesh when her mum went back to England so she knew what to do. They had special ways here to lift and turn people over in bed, and a big metal thing to lower them into the bath.

When the shift ended she sat next to Ethel and had a cup of tea while everybody watched *Midlands Today*. She didn't want to leave. It was comfortable in the sitting room, and it felt right being there to help these old people. Beauty had always expected to take care of a mother-in-law, but now that that dream had ended, looking after Ethel and the other ladies was a good thing to do. And she hadn't thought about herself all day.

The bus was warm and the windows steamed up. She looked at the older white people around her and wondered if they too had done things like Norris.

He killed a Japanese.

Is that like Chinese?

And how come old white people were so different from the young ones? Asians shook their heads, too, about how the world was changing. Nowadays no one knew if their kids were going to grow up gangsters. *Gunda, sharabi.* Drinking and taking drugs.

Or worse.

Tabligs.

Beauty got off the bus and walked through the town centre. The streets were full of people going home. Young men in suits, Asian boys with gelled hair and razor-thin lines of beard, and bored-looking white blokes came out of closing shops and banks. No one seemed to take any notice of her. Did she look like a normal person now? She was on her way home from work, like them.

Home?

She passed the long queues at the bus stops on Darlington Street and glanced at the Asian girls in long black trousers, Sikh mostly and some Hindus, judging by their jewellery, with tong-straightened hair and too much pale foundation.

Why do they paint themselves white?

They were having a normal life. Why shouldn't she?

I'm Muslim.

So what? I can't live?

And so what if she had problems at home? So did these girls. White people, too.

I aynt feeling sorry for myself.

'Yo!'

Beauty started and looked up at the black-clad figure of Delford Johnston. He had a scabby cut under one eye.

'*Asalaam alaikum,*' he said seriously.

The dangerous one.

She mumbled the return greeting and made to step round him.

'Don't go, my beauty! Come on, I'll let you buy me a drink.'

He needed the money for another pint. Until his missus arrived. He held open the door of the pub from which he had appeared.

It was dark in there and smelled of cigarette smoke and beer. Beauty looked at Delford's unfocused eyes.

He's drunk!

'I aynt your beauty. Thass my name. And a Muslim shouldn't drink.'

Delford brushed her words away with a gold-sovereigned hand. He knew how to handle her type. Fiery ones needed smothering and smiles.

'You can't live your whole life like that, you know. Come on, I'll look after you. You don't know who you're with.'

Two other tall black men touched fists with Delford on their way into the pub.

'Yo, Delford. Safe.'

'Respect.'

'Ya cool, dred?'

As the door closed he called to them in a heavy Jamaican accent: 'No boda gan yam all a dem food dere! Me gonna broke your backside pon da pou-ul table!'

Delford turned round, laughing heartily, but Beauty had gone. He looked over the tops of the passing heads, and kissed his teeth in disappointment.

What a little cracker she was!

Beauty hurried along the crowded pavement and turned left into Waterloo Road, glad to have got away.

Gunda, aynit. Drinking, too.

She wasn't frightened of him. He was too old-looking.

But what kind of a Muslim was he?

He aynt. He's a convert.

So was my mum's grandfather.

And the old man's great-grandfather.

They were Hindus once . . . toba, toba. Who am I to say the black guy aynt a Muslim? Am I?

It's in my blood.

But how could it be? What did that mean?

He aynt a good Muslim if he's drinking modh.

'You can't live your whole life like that.'

There were fewer people as she walked away from the town centre. A young woman in a jilbab was coming towards her. Was she going home from work too?

Probably married, aynit.

These days, some husbands liked their wives to work. Not all men were monsters.

Or did this girl have trouble at home too?

Bas! Everyone's got problems. You're nothing special.

Look at them old people in the home. They never had no children to look after them. Feel sorry for them.

Beauty passed the orange struts and stands of the football stadium and a bronze statue of a man in shorts kicking a football. As the two women passed one another, their eyes met briefly.

29

Peter spotted Beauty in Dunstall Road on his way home from work. He pulled into Prole Street, parked outside his house and waited for her. An idea had formed since he'd last seen her. Something that might help them both. If she agreed, it would keep him entertained for a good while and away from the internet, while the benefits for Beauty were obvious, weren't they? How would that primitive next door ever help her? How long could she live with the offensive smell which came from his house? And where would Beauty meet an interesting and good-looking chap like himself?

But he recalled the onan-athon of the previous evening with a twinge of shame at the potentially disturbing turn his online searches had taken: *Ass-filled-Arab-Chicks.com* – dead-eyed Moroccan women oblivious to their mock-tent surroundings and the prodding males; *Headscarf Hotties* fellating hirsute Middle Easterners; *Burka Babes*. Exciting while he lasted, the post-orgasm clean-up was depressing; the image of the bruised skin of Casablancan heroin addicts remained with him as he lay in bed exhausted. More alarming had been his unsuccessful attempt to find pictures of educated Iranian women doctors in degrading poses.

Peter checked his reflection in the rearview mirror, ruffled his hair and undid another button of his shirt.

Never again, he promised himself, and so far he had managed to avoid the psychological implications of his fantasies. He was embarking on a noble project. It was up to him to save Beauty, to drag her from the darkness of religious superstition. Only then would she be free.

Beauty walked quickly, her head down. As she approached the house a car door opened in front of her, blocking the pavement.

Peter James Hemmings put out a well-polished half-brogue and a beige moleskin-trousered leg.

Beauty didn't look up and moved round the obstacle.

'Hi!' Peter said, appraising the tight-fitting kameez under her jacket and the . . . headscarf. 'I didn't see you there. How are things?'

The leather soles of his shoes crunched grit on the pavement.

Beauty stopped. 'Yeah, I'm all right,' she said. Across the street she watched a car reverse into a space, the engine racing noisily. A Pakistani woman got out to lift her young daughter from the back seat and noticed her *talking to a white bloke*. The child stared at Beauty over her mother's shoulder. Beauty stared back, and thanked Allah they weren't nosy Bengalis.

Yes, she said, loud enough for the woman to hear, she would accept Peter's offer of a cup of tea. She poked her tongue out at the child.

Let the Paki neighbours think what they wanted. Were they so holy inside?

Peter went into the kitchen to make tea.

Beauty stood in his front room. Through the net curtains, she watched the Pakistani woman emptying shopping bags from her car and wished she hadn't come.

Asians seeing you go into two different white blokes' houses wasn't good.

Why? What are we doing? Just talking.

And she didn't mind that part. Weren't there things she wanted and needed to know about? Like what else white people thought if they didn't believe in God.

Toba, toba astaghfirullah.

Anyway, nothing this bloke could say would change her mind.

But if you sit in a man's house he's gonna get the wrong idea, aynit.

Peter poured the tea in silence and passed Beauty a side-plate across the table. He watched her chew a small piece of biscuit, her hand in front of her mouth, and wondered how to begin. He needed to enthral her with his interesting and handsomely earnest conversation, not scare her again with his godlessness. Her lack of exposure to the light of reason made her a delicate flower. Too much sun, and she might wither.

'How is everything?' he asked.

'OK, I guess.'

'The work placement?'

'Uh-huh.'

'How's Mark?'

How was she supposed to know?

'He's fine, I guess.'

'Your brothers?'

'I aynt seen them.'

'Well, that's good, isn't it?'

'Is it?'

The image of her two brothers faded, and Beauty looked at the white man in his smart clothes.

*

Peter searched for another opening. Wouldn't she want to explore life, study something, discover a talent she never knew she had, make friends and meet a nice man . . . like him? Perhaps it was time for Stage One of his plan.

'Well, I'm glad I bumped into you,' he said.

Beauty touched her scarf.

Why?

'If I bought the ingredients one day,' he continued, 'would you show me how to make a real Bangladeshi home-cooked dish and . . . have dinner with me?'

He avoided saying 'curry' in case it was a stereotype.

Beauty's stomach cramped with hunger. It was impossible to cook at Mark's. He'd cleaned up, but she didn't trust the pots. Chips, kebabs and packets of biscuits from the shop was all she had eaten since she'd left home. She wanted rice, and to suck the *bitorhadi* from inside the sheep bone. Or better still, *hutki sheera*! Stinkyfish!

She looked to see if he was making fun of her, but his face seemed honest. Would he like her curry? White people only ate Indian food from restaurants.

'You aynt gonna like it,' she said.

Peter was relieved to see her smile for the first time. The frown passed from her brow, and her lips parted to reveal perfect white teeth.

'Why not?' he asked.

'There's lots of chillies.'

'That's OK. I like hot food.'

Beauty covered her smile behind the teacup. Boy, would she show him! She'd make him a proper one, hot like the old man always wanted it. Just in case this good-looking bloke did get the wrong idea. But was it right to come here? What did 'have dinner with me' mean?

You can't cook for an unmarried man in his own house.

Why not? What was wrong with it? And hadn't she

come to find out things so as not to look dumb everywhere she went?

'Can I arx you something?' she said, surprised by her
boldness.

Peter poured more tea for them. 'Of course.' Stay as
long as you like, he wanted to say.

'What you said last night? If there's . . . no God?'

Toba, toba . . .

Peter noticed that she touched her cheeks with the tip
of a finger while pretending to wipe her lips. Was it some
medieval gesture to ward off the evil eye? Christ! This
was backward stuff.

'Uh-huh,' he encouraged.

'. . . then what do . . . white people think happens when
you die?'

She raised the cup to her mouth and avoided the man's
eye.

Peter marvelled at being party to someone's first atheist
conversation, although he was wary of scaring her off
again. Could she handle humour with her religion?

'Well, no one's ever come back to tell us what it's like,
so it must be good,' he said.

She didn't laugh.

'Look, I don't know what happens when you die,' he
added. 'Nothing, probably.'

The fine lines of her eyebrows arched in surprise. 'Is
that what people think?' Beauty asked.

There was more she wanted to know, like if there was
no God and no hell, how did bad people get punished?
But she knew her questions might sound simple, until
she'd had time to think about them.

She stood up and thanked him for the tea.

So, would she come to dinner, Peter asked her at the front
door. He'd cook if she showed him how.

Beauty looked into his eyes to see if there was some bad thought behind them. He fancied himself too much but he wasn't the dangerous type, she decided. Yes, she would, she said.

She stepped past him into the street and cast a quick glance at the parked cars to make sure they were empty.

Peter watched her go and closed the door, glad she hadn't fled this time.

Beauty felt his eyes on her as she walked the few steps to the other house. She was pleased with herself for having discovered something without looking stupid, and with the thought of having some proper food.

What's he gonna think if I eat with my fingers?

30

Beauty looked down from the bedroom window. The backyard was tidy and the dogs quiet. How long would she be here? A week? A month? Where would she be in a year from now? Since she'd left home she had only been able to think about the next day. Two at the most. With no *kishmut*, no destiny, nothing written before-hand, like the white bloke said, the future seemed even darker. Would she still be living in this town, near her family? Would she ever see them again?

Yes. I will. I will.

She'd make her own future. She'd work, and have enough money to rent a house. Sharifa would be able to bunk off school, and come and play with the cat. She'd cook her little sister's favourite food: *kurma* and *aloo*, *halazam*, *rasmallai*, *ladhu* and *zilafi* sweets, and plant onions and coriander in the small back garden which no one could look into. She'd go to work every day and look after the *buddhi* in the care home. Maybe, one day, her brothers would find out she wasn't doing anything bad.

They'll say you're going to pubs.

And taking drugs.

And sleeping with different men.

So what if they do? I won't see them.

I could go and see Ama on Fridays when the old man's

at the Masjid. Bhai-sahb sleeps and the kids'll be at school.

Dulal would know you was there. He'd wake up.

What if Mum doesn't want to see me?

The phone rang.

'Bew-tee?'

'Ama!'

'Bew-tee! *Ai yo!*'

'*Farr tam nai.*'

I can't go back.

'Bew-tee, *ami bé marr!*'

'Did you go to the Doctor?'

'*Na, na.* Bew-tee!'

'Ama!'

'*Torr abhai mair horra torr Bhaien tologhé!*'

The old man's fighting with the boys!

'Ama!'

'*Ami echhla!*'

There's nobody to help her.

'Ama!'

'BYAR MAHT AISSÉ – HOMLA FUAA.'

'*Hheé?* Ama! Ama?'

Her mother had put down the phone. Beauty sat on the bed.

Wedding talk.

'Who?'

Homla, her mum's cousin-sister's brother's wife, wanted to come and see her.

She wants me for her son.

Hadn't the old man told Homla she was married to the mullah? Or did everyone know she hadn't let him touch her? Maybe people thought she could get a divorce easily. *Talaq, talaq, talaq* over the phone.

Why don't they give up?

*Cuz they know I aynt married here. Just Muslim way.
And everyone knows we never . . .*

She lay down, closed her eyes and heard her mother's
voice and her choked sobs.

She's ill.

There's no one to cook.

*Bhai-sahb and the little one are fighting with the old
man.*

Wedding talk's come up!

Would the old man let it happen? Would he give up on
bringing mullah Choudhury here?

Maybe that's why they're fighting.

*Dulal doesn't care who it is. He wants me married so
he can start looking for a wife.*

Beauty stood up and went to the window. It was almost
dark. Lights had come on in the windows of the houses
beyond the trees.

*What they gonna say if Homla phones again? I'm
nearly twenty. The old man can't say no for ever.
Everyone knows I never married the mullah properly.*

Habib Choudhury had waited a long time to make their
Muslim wedding in Bangladesh right. She'd walked into
the room five years ago under her red wedding scarf and
sat down next to him. *Shorbot habani.* And held the cup
to his lips. Her cheek was swollen and her right eye
closed from the slaps of the night before.

I was fourteen.

She'd stared at each one of their faces in turn and
sworn never to forget what they'd done: the mullah, her
old man, the mullah's witch-mother. She'd cried when she
said *hobbul . . .* I do. Afterwards, she got beaten badly.

The mullah had brought her a few pieces of his
mother's jewellery. In the night, he'd tried to lie on top of
her but she'd screamed until he returned to his side of

the bed. People told him to give it time, and he went back to live with his mother without her. For one night, she had slept in the same bed as him.

Beauty sat back down on the bed and took her make-up bag from the bedside cabinet. She squeezed some moisturising cream on to a cotton pad and began wiping off her eyeliner.

Let them think of something to say to this new wanker. They can tell him I'm still mad.

People will find out you aynt at home.

So what?

Thass scandal. The big one will never get married.

Yes, he will.

Not in this country.

Let him go to Bangladesh and find a wife.

Al-lāh! Why now? Ama! She's suffering. This aynt her fault.

No one's gonna think bad of her.

They will. The old man will blame her. And the big one aynt gonna find a wife.

Beauty took the hand mirror from the pink bag and checked that the make-up had all gone. Her eyes looked tired.

Maybe it was all a trick. Beauty's mum's cousin-sister's brother and his wife would come from London. And the mullah's brother. That pervert. He'd want to stick his nose in. Then they'd tell her to go back to London with them. Just for a few days.

They know I aynt gonna fall for it again.

I can't go back. What if Homla's son is really there and he wants to marry me?

Is the old man gonna say yes?

That's why the big one's fighting, aynit? He wants me to get married.

What am I supposed to do?
If it's not him, it'll be someone else.
They aynt never gonna give up.
Unless I was . . .
You can't do that!

Al-lāh amarray shai jo horro!
Help me!

Mark ran up the stairs and knocked on the door.
'BEAUTY! YOU IN?'

31

Beauty sat up on the bed.
Al-lāh, this aynt good.

'D'you fancy giwin' out later? There's a do on at the club.'

'What club?'

'Where I bumped into you that night when them Asian lads was looking for you.'

Beauty stood up and straightened her headscarf.

I can't do that.

Mark scratched dried paint from his hands at the door. It might be hard to convince her, but he wanted her to come.

'Tay a nightclub. It's a family place, really. Bob's a member. One of his nephews got engaged, or had a kid, I caar remember which. There'll be food laid on, and a bit a music.'

Mark looked at Beauty. Would she come? He wanted to show her that he knew people. That he wasn't a no-mates loser.

'Giw on, it'll be a laff.'

Beauty tidied her few things on the bedside table.

He wants me to say yes.

I can't go. 'Look what the bitch is doing.' Thass what the big one's gonna say.

They think I'm doing those things anyway.

'Yeah, sure,' she said, and saw his face light up with surprise.

'Nice one!' Mark said. 'We can get a taxi back whenever you want. I'll put aside a fiver for it.'

He ran downstairs to feed the dogs and get ready.

'Going out?'
With a bloke?
Should she?
It aynt like that.
Aynit?

It wasn't a nightclub. He said it was a family place. She'd be safe with him and one day she could tell Sharifa that she'd been to a white party.

Could she really go?
Why not?

The taxi left them at the corner of the Willenhall Road. Mark felt good in his black jeans and polished shoes. He pointed out the spot where they'd run into each other, but Beauty didn't recognize it.

When was that?

They walked to the flat-roofed, red-brick Working Men's Leisure and Social Club. Beauty felt her bum was uncovered without a kameez hanging low behind her. She wore high boots with her jeans rolled up, a black printed T-shirt, her denim jacket and a black headscarf. Nothing Asian. Apart from the way she did her eyeliner and her headscarf.

The elderly man in a dark suit at the door nodded to Mark, and smiled kindly at Beauty. Mark signed in for both of them.

'I'll get this,' he said, and paid the forty pence entrance fee for non-members.

Beauty breathed deeply – *do they have Asians in here? Al-lāh!* – and followed Mark into a large, strip-lit lounge with lino floors and a pool table. Black padded benches ran around the outside of the room, separated by flashing fruit machines. White people sat at tables, young and old together. Children, too. Muffled music came from a room beyond.

Beauty flinched at the light and kept her eyes on Mark's back as he headed to the bar. She knew she was the only Asian there, and that eyes were on her.

What's he doing with a Paki?

Her headscarf felt tight and her scalp itched under it.

Mark nodded to the people he knew: Bob's sister and one of her neighbours. Beauty tried not to look at the faces around her, and stood next to him at the bar. A massive bloke, with thin dark hair swept over a balding head from ear to ear, came to serve them. She watched his belly tremble under the short-sleeved white shirt as he moved.

'Oright, Tone. Bob in yet?' Mark asked him.

'He's through there.'

The fat man nodded over his shoulder. The face of a pretty young girl appeared at the serving hatch behind him. She waved to Mark.

'That's Bob's niece, Hayley,' Mark explained to Beauty.

He ordered a pint of Carling. 'D'you wanna J2O?' he asked her.

'Has it got . . . ?'

'Do' worry, it's non-alcoholic.'

Beauty thanked him, and was glad he'd spoken quietly.

Mark stood in the doorway of the large function room, sipped his pint and looked around for Bob. He'd have pulled a few tables together for his family. Over there, near the bar. Away from the dance floor, for the time being.

Beauty carried her bottle of orange juice and felt awkward as he introduced her to 'Bob's Karen', and his niece Hayley, a girl of thirteen or fourteen chewing gum and looking about her to see if there were any nice boys there yet.

'Sit dowun, loov,' the woman said.

Beauty squeezed past the chairs to sit with her back to the wall next to the lady. Was that the older man's wife? She had short, spiky, dyed blond hair. Women's sovereign rings, bangles and men's chains and lucky charms covered her hands and wrists, and she had a tattoo on each forearm. Beauty couldn't make out the pictures and didn't want to stare.

Mark sat down next to her. Their legs were almost touching. 'Tay really started yet,' he explained. 'It'll get busy though, do' worry.'

Beauty didn't want it to get busy. What if he left her alone? What could she talk about with these people?

'There's food 'n' all down there. We can get some in a minute.' Mark would wait for the nod from Bob.

'Here, Kaz?' Mark leaned past Beauty and she saw into his ear. 'Is Steve-o doing the music?'

'Ar,' she said, and nodded to the door where a thin, pale boy was carrying a case of records to a low platform at the end of the hall.

'That's Steve,' Mark said to Beauty. 'One of Bob's nephews. Thass right, ay it, Kaz?'

'Ar.'

Bob came with drinks, and winked at Beauty. He was cleaner than when she'd last seen him. Beauty liked his cheerful face, tanned from working outside, his short grey hair and clean white teeth. His eyes smiled. He went away again, stopping to pat one man on the back and talk to another.

Mark pointed to other members of Bob's family as they came through the door. His sisters Elaine, Janet and

Wendy. And his brother John. Beauty nodded her interest. There were brothers and in-laws and neighbours. He told her who they were, and what work he'd done on their cars.

'Kaz's brother Alan gimme a loada work round December time. Said I did a damn good job 'n' all.'

Mark sat back and felt good. He was at home here. He knew everyone and everyone knew him. They liked him, respected him. He kept his word and knew how to graft hard. He could do just about any job they gave him. Apart from welding or panel-beating.

And they came to the table to greet him.

'This is me mate, Beauty,' Mark told them.

Beauty gave each one a quick glance and looked down again. It wasn't so bad after all. White people could be pretty friendly.

Mark and Karen talked about cars, vans, breeds of dogs and how much they cost. She was looking for a Dog de Bordoh. Or a Kayner Korser Italiano. About eight hundred quid, Mark reckoned.

He went to the bar for more drinks, happy to have the money to get some rounds in. He'd make sure Bob's missus was all right for drinks. And Beauty.

Hayley returned to the table with a can of Coke and a packet of crisps and sat next to her. Beauty noticed the young girl's denim miniskirt and blotchy pink thighs. Hayley opened the crisps and offered them to her.

'Am you Mark's new girlfriend?' she asked.

Beauty felt her face flush. 'No, no! I'm just staying at his house. We're . . . friends.'

Al-lāh!

The girl pulled crisps from the packet and put them into her red-lipsticked mouth. She had painted nails and two small gold coins on her fingers. Her arms were bare, and her young white chest was squeezed into a tight pink vest. She wore make-up on her pale face, and her highlighted hair was layered and straightened.

'He's buff though, ay 'e?' Hayley said.

Beauty coughed into her hand and touched her cheeks. 'Is he?' she said. 'I don't know about them things.'

'You wha'? Lookaddim!'

They both watched Mark returning to the table, a triangle of three pint glasses in his large hands.

Maybe he wasn't bad-looking.

This aynt good.

Mark sat opposite the two girls. 'Oright, Hayley, how's it giwin?'

The function room had filled with white people. Mark talked, while Hayley laughed and tried to flirt with him.

Beauty sat back and watched everything. Young girls in calf-length tracksuit bottoms, pink and white Reebok Classic trainers and pop socks weaved their way through the adults to the bar, and returned to their families at the tables with crisps and cans of Coke. Young mothers with ringed fingers, their hair pulled tightly back into ponytails, settled empty prams around the tables. Little boys tottered about in baby-sized Nike Air Max, short-sleeved checked shirts and gelled blond hair, clutching packets of crisps in tiny fists. They were dressed like their fathers, who stood at the bar talking and laughing, holding pints of lager and cigarettes in the fingers of one hand. The men made way for overweight middle-aged women, with large bare arms and short black dresses, carrying glasses of brandy. Gold flashed on fat fingers, chubby wrists and seasoned necks.

The noise grew. The tables filled with empty glasses, were cleared by the fat man, and filled again. Hayley went off to talk to boys. Mark chatted about his business plan and what he needed to get it going and how long it would take him to make the money. Beauty listened and was encouraging.

He aynt got no one. Al-lāh give him a good life.

'Go for it. Work hard and you'll get what you want,' she said.

Insh'allah.

Bob came back. They could eat.

Beauty told Mark she wasn't hungry, but he stood up and she had no choice. It would be rude. And she wanted to see what white people ate at a party. She'd tell Sharifa. One day.

Mark told her not to worry.

'S free.'

They made their way to the buffet tables and waited in the queue for a paper plate. There were metal trays of small sandwiches. Beauty took two with tuna and lay them flat on the plate to make it look full. The pink line between the pieces of bread on the next tray looked *haram*. She passed unheated, wrinkled grey chicken legs, sausage rolls, and a plate of orange balls. Would she sound thick if she asked what they were?

'Ay you sin a scotch egg before? Fookin' 'ell!'

Enda!

'Those are crisps,' he said, pointing to the various bowls. 'Ay you sin them before either?'

Beauty nudged him with her elbow.

Al-lāh, don't let me flirt!

She didn't mind him teasing her. He didn't do it like her brother would have done.

'*Dumb bitch!*' he would have said.

There were trays of southern-fried chicken and purple Chinese chicken wings, a bowl of chicken tikka masala, and white rice. Apart from the curry, the meat was cold and dry. She took a piece of the orange chicken and a spoonful of coleslaw. Mark took some of everything. She was disappointed by the food, and felt sad for the people carrying plates piled high back to their tables.

Is this all they eat?

She wished she could have made something for them.

There was no space for her plate among the glasses on the table, so she rested it on her lap. She pulled off the skin from the chicken leg, and the curled white sinew, which was *haram*. The meat was slimy and tasteless, but she ate the tuna sandwiches.

Beauty was happy looking at the people, and shocked by how much they drank.

Bob sat down next to her. He had a kind face, round-cheeked and friendly, and his eyes were shining.

'Y'm all right for a drink, am y'?'

He's drunk!

Mark talked to Karen's brother, Dave, about the off side bearings on his LDV, and noticed Bob sitting next to Beauty. He was glad the older man was making an effort with her. Bob knew he liked her. Why else would he have brought her to the club? Not that he'd said anything to Mark about it. That was a real mate.

And thank fuck no one had said 'Paki' near her.

'He's all right you know,' Bob told her.

She knew who he was talking about. Could Mark hear? He was busy explaining something with his fingers.

'He talks about you a lot.'

He likes me.

'He's 'ad a rough life, but he's got his head screwed on right.'

Bob drank a third of his pint and wiped his mouth.

'What 'e really needs is a good woman to sort 'im out. He's a sowund bloke,' he said. 'Loyal.'

'Uh-huh.' Beauty believed him.

'If he likes someone he'll do anything for 'em.'

Al-lāh! Does he mean me?

She looked up at the older man. His eyes were suddenly serious.

'Mark said you had some bother wi' yer brothers, or some Asian lads in a car.'

What had Mark told him?

'Listen.' He leaned towards her. She could smell beer on his breath. 'You get any grief off anyone in this towun, anyone, you come and tell me. They'll get . . . that.' He kissed his fist.

Beauty thanked him. There was something cold and threatening in his eyes now. She looked at the men standing at the bar, drinking and laughing with the *buddhis*. Bare forearms with faded tattoos under blond hairs; shaved and balding heads. Her brothers would die of fright in a room like this. It felt good to be safe in here.

'And see if you can talk some sense into that bloody niece of mine,' Bob said.

Small children stopped and stared at her. Beauty pulled faces and offered them crisps. People she didn't know came and said things she couldn't hear over the noise of voices and laughter and music. But their faces were friendly, and she smiled back. Bob came again to check she was 'all right for a drink'. Everywhere cheeks grew redder, eyes shone and she realized most people were drunk.

Why shouldn't they be?

Was it that bad?

If they didn't believe it was wrong.

Hayley came and went from the table.

'*Talk some sense into that niece of mine.*' *That's what the man said.*

Beauty watched the teenager struggle on her high heels towards the toilets. Her skirt was too short. But no man, brother, neighbour or friend of the family seemed to notice her *hombol* and *buni* sticking out. No one pointed at her, or pulled their grey beards and called her a whore, or tried to touch her.

Even so, some things you should only show a husband.

Bob made his way through the crowd, dancing the conga alone, saw his niece and slipped his arm through hers.

'Come on, you lot, what y'm all diwin' sitting dowun? We'm giwin' dansin'!'

Hayley pulled Beauty to her feet. She looked at Mark for help, but he was still talking to Karen's brother.

They were nearly at the dance floor. Bob was singing and holding the two girls tight. The noise grew as they neared the speakers and the dancing bodies.

Beauty looked over her shoulder for Mark.

Al-lāh! Amarray ita horrai yona! Don't make me do this!

There were tables at the edge of the dance floor. When Bob reached it and loosened his grip, she slipped into one of the chairs.

Bob looked round for Beauty, but Mark sat down next to her, and she was safe. Unless *he* asked her, too!

'Please, don't make me dance,' she said to Mark. She wanted to grab his hand. She'd touch his feet if she had to.

'Do' you lot dance then?'

'No.'

I don't.

The music made no sense to her. She watched Bob with his niece. They moved their bums and shuffled their feet. What kind of dancing was this?

You'll have to kill me before I do that.

Once she would have liked to learn Indian dancing, and dreamed of wearing nice saris like in the films. But the old man wouldn't let her watch them on television. They were half-naked *shaitani* shaking their bodies. But she knew he watched them.

The dance floor filled with people. Small children bounced up and down, the older ladies in black dresses kicked out their high-heeled feet. Bob danced with them, said things in their ears and they threw back their heads in laughter. Hayley did pop-star routines with a little girl in a tracksuit and vest.

It was nice to watch. They were good people. The dancing ladies were enjoying themselves. Mark pointed out people to her and they laughed together. Bob came and drank from his pint, his shirt buttons opening, and returned to twirl the shrieking women around.

How could any of this be bad? Beauty couldn't wait to tell Sharifa about it. The *buddhis* were her mother's age. But when had she ever seen her ama laugh like that? Would she ever see her mum's sad, sweet face as she danced the *damail* at her daughter's wedding with the other mothers?

Sharifa's wedding, maybe. I hope she sees that.

The whooping, bare-armed women spinning round in front of her turned her choked tears to laughter.

'Y'm all right?' Mark shouted above the music.

She was fine. It was just a bit smoky.

He went to the bar to get her another drink, and Hayley came and did a pop dance in front of her to a medley of sixties hits.

'Am you coomin'?'

'No, I can't. My leg hurts,' Beauty said.

Hayley sat next to her, panting. 'Do' you like this song?'

'I dunno, I never heard it.'

What is this rubbish?

'It's the Beatles!'

'I dunno what that is.'

'Ay you never heard of them? Fookin' 'ell!'

'I'm Asian. We don't do them things.'

I don't.

'Me mates do at school. They'm Asian.'

Hindu.

'It's easy. Come on, I'll show you,' Hayley said.

Beauty might have done, if she'd been alone with her sister. But not to this music. Not in front of men.

Mark came back, and Hayley went to writhe a few steps away from them. Bob danced over to his niece, his shirt completely open. Beauty saw the thick gold chain, his hairless flat chest and the tight, round belly below, before he disappeared again behind the laughing and cheering women. The smaller children were led away by their parents.

'He's well gone!' Mark said to her above the music.

The older man rubbed backs with one of the ladies in a short, strapless dress that showed her tanned, freckled shoulders. He turned to face her and jammed one leg between her thighs, and they pressed against each other, grinding to a Hispano-pop rhythm. Laughing faces surrounded them chanting, 'Off, off, off!' Bob had his back to Beauty and Mark by now, and she saw him fumbling with his buttons. Mark jogged her arm to keep looking, and Bob's trousers fell to the floor to a loud cheer from the ladies. Mark watched Beauty. Her eyes widened in disbelief, her white teeth showing in a frozen half-smile. Was Bob's pissing about too much for her?

With his back still to them, Bob clicked his fingers above his head and his shirt tail lifted. His small, white bum caught the disco lights and changed colours.

Beauty's mouth opened, and the ladies rocked back together, screaming. She turned to Mark.

'Y'Allah-goh!'

She covered her open mouth.

If the old man saw this!

'Let's hope he do' turn round!' Mark shouted above the howling and clapping and whistling.

Al-lāh! If her mum could see! She'd pee in her clothes!

A woman ran up and lowered her mobile phone in front of him. The camera flashed, the ladies crowded to see the photo and screeched with laughter.

Mark stared at Beauty. Her face, her eyes shone, and he knew he liked being with her. Loads.

They got into the taxi outside the club. As the car passed the places where she'd run and hidden *that night*, she shuddered for the girl that might still have been out there, hunted and tired, if it hadn't been for the white bloke next to her. Where was that Beauty now? Was she still wandering the streets with her bag?

Mark talked and laughed about the evening's events, and Bob's drunkenness. He'd had a good night. He'd shown Beauty that he wasn't alone, and that she didn't have to be either. He was happy that she'd enjoyed herself, had relaxed and laughed; and that Bob and Karen and everyone else had liked her. No one had asked him what he was doing with a Paki, or said anything about it. He'd have knocked them out if they had. Even Bob. Not that Bob would have said it. Wasn't he always telling Mark to find himself a decent woman? But Mark knew it might be hard for Beauty to accept a white bloke like himself as her own. Asians stuck together. He'd never heard of anyone going out with an Asian bird.

The taxi rattled over black cobbles under railway bridges, past dead, brown factories and into the light on the ring road. Beauty looked out of the window, through the drops of rain that spotted the glass. The car slipped past a figure on the other side of the road, dark-haired and limping, in a denim jacket and a rucksack. She twisted round to see who it was through the back window. But there was no one. Was she seeing ghosts? *Bhout?*

Beauty stayed downstairs with Mark until she finished her coffee. He talked about getting a proper job and finding a better place to live. He reckoned it would take him a couple of weeks to get the money.

She listened. He had a good brain, she told him, and it was always good to work towards something.

She put the cup on the new coffee table and said she had to be up early. Mark asked her if she'd had a good time. She had.

'Night, Beauty.'

Their eyes met for a second before she looked away. But for Mark it was enough. There was something there, some flash of understanding. The door closed behind her and he swivelled in his office chair.

Nice one.

32

Peter woke up late, stretched, and hawked to clear his throat.

Beauty was coming for dinner, or at least to show him how to cook. The gloom he had felt at her last visit had passed. The pity he had felt for her ignorance had given way once more to an exquisite thrill at it. It wasn't her fault she hadn't been to school. In fact, it was a miracle to come across someone who had had little or no stimulus, input or influence from human life.

He threw back the duvet and stood up. Forget that other stuff. He would be her spiritual and intellectual liberator, nothing more. And everything had to be right that evening. The poor girl's eyes had shone as she'd listed the ingredients he had to buy. Powders – red, yellow and grey – not to bother with the *gorom moshla*, which, it had taken him a moment to realize, was garam masala: that was for Pakistanis, apparently; onions, chillies (small, green and hard, she'd said), garlic, ginger, brown rice, fresh coriander leaves, and brown sticks – which might be bay and cinnamon; lamb shoulder, sheep or 'baby' chicken. A halal butcher would know what he meant. She told him how to have the mutton bone cut properly; the chicken skinned and in eight pieces.

He had a shower, shaved and put on a pair of straight, dark blue jeans and brown suede Oxfords, his white

Aquascutum shirt and a grey jacket. Outside in the weak sunshine everything seemed brighter, closer and more colourful than on a work day. He switched on the car radio in a buoyant, purposeful mood, and searched for something suitable. An echoing '*Midlands Underground 1-0-7, Midlands Underground 1-0-7*' and a black youth saluting his listeners:

'. . . *big shou' out to all my bredren. Big up all you sexy-body ladies. Hold tight all my Walsall soldiers. Hold tight my WV10 crew, all my B70 crew, the DY6 – keep it locked in, locked on. All my texters, all my signalists down in the block at HMP Featherstone – big yourselves up – trooss me this next choon is massive, y'get me?*

'*P-P-P-Pull it op selektah!*

'*Br-Br-Br . . .*'

A pump-action shotgun, loaded and fired twice, and a sultry New York black woman's voice:

'*Treat me good, treat me right*
Lick my body all through the night
Do it slow, do it fast
Suck my pussy and lick my ass . . . ass . . . ass . . .'

And a bass line that distorted the speakers of the stereo.

Peter stopped at the traffic lights on the ring road, opened the window and affected an air of urban boredom for the benefit of the woman in the next car. He was in high spirits, and the '4-4, Speed Garage, Bassline House and Bashment' on the radio made him feel like he belonged in the architecturally brutalized city.

The lights turned green and he pulled off as if in a hurry, which he wasn't, and considered having a sub-woofer and amplifier fitted to the car.

At the Bilston roundabout he turned the music down. He was nearly forty, for God's sake.

*

He headed towards Dudley and a small brick precinct with an Indian supermarket and greengrocer's. He parked outside the Apna Punjab pub and avoided looking at the five lolling Jamaicans drinking cans of beer, talking loudly in patois and laughing.

The small supermarket was busy, the aisles full. He could just make out the vegetables through the pastel and turquoise nylon-looking robes and scarves of overweight middle-aged Indian women, emptying crates of chillies into plastic bags. Peter waited, and tried to keep out of the way of turbanned men setting out more boxes of vegetables, and fathers with paunches and thick gold jewellery carrying sacks of flour and rice on their shoulders while calling their young children to follow them. Excusing himself frequently, he managed to nip in and out of the line to get what he needed. By the time he reached the tomatoes he'd had enough of the place, but he stifled the irritation he would usually have allowed himself to indulge in had he been at Sainsbury's, with Kate. It might look racist here.

Away from the vegetables, things were calmer. There was a butcher's at the far end of the supermarket, which doubled as a Western Union branch. Posters of smiling relatives in India advertised the service. A map of the Punjab hung on the wall, behind five white-aproned men chopping meat. It wasn't halal – he'd have to go elsewhere – but he lingered as he passed the attractive, slim young mothers in order to inhale their perfume, the shampoo of their layered and highlighted black hair and, he imagined, the washing powder of their freshly laundered blouses and tight jeans. What type of lingerie did Indian women wear?

The younger butchers nodded to the Bhangra rhythms coming from speakers hanging on the wall and a woman singer's sweet, high-pitched voice. Their shoulders twitched to the banging drums and the whistling that punctuated the chorus. It was happy music. The butchers smiled at the women as they passed large plastic bags of meat over the counter.

Peter went to the checkout at the front of the shop. The tall, fierce-bearded Sikh owner weighed and packed his vegetables in silence.

Outside, the Jamaicans had gone, and the Asian fathers and husbands were strapping their children into the back seats of silver or black BMWs and four-wheel drive Mercedes with chrome crash bars. Peter got into his car and watched the men. Pretty wives joined them. He looked at the single plastic bag on the passenger seat next to him, and back to the menfolk loading sacks of onions into the boots of their cars. Where did they get the money from? What jobs did they do? Were their marriages all arranged?

Peter drove out of the car park and headed back to Dunstall to look for a halal butcher. He turned on the radio to recapture his earlier mood, but the music had changed to the plaintive melody of a slow reggae tune.

'*How I envy you*
You got a woman home waiting for you
And a baby and boy running to you
I need to find a good lady like you got'

Was this what he was missing? Providing for and protecting a beautiful wife and children?

'*To have a family would be so sweet*
A joyful thing it would be
To have a woman and baby girl waiting for me
Would make me so happy-y-y-y'

Peter reached for the off switch.

*

Outside the halal butcher's there were crates of onions, ginger and garlic on the pavement. He made his way to the meat counter at the rear of the premises. Framed verses from the Qur'an in Arabic script and pictures of the Ka'aba in Mecca hung on the walls. The butchers sharpened their knives to the sound of religious Qawwali music coming from an old radio on the worktop, a man's voice yodelling in its range to the beat of a tabla drum.

The shop was dark, and there were few women. Men waited to be served. Peter presumed they were all Muslim and tried to guess their origins: Aryan Pakistani, high-cheekboned Somali, a wide-faced, dark-stubbled, south European/Slav/ex-Soviet Republic type, and a strawberry-bearded white convert in camouflage trousers. Peter felt uncomfortable in his Oxfords and jacket; and with his racial profiling of the customers. He studied the meat behind the glass.

The men in the queue in front of him chose carefully – shoulders of lamb, skinned 'baby' chickens, 'boiler' chickens, liver, gizzard, chicken 'niblets' and mutton chops.

'Yes, mate?'

Peter asked for a kilo of lamb shoulder, diced into small pieces. He watched as the butcher sliced away the fat and sinews and cut the bone on an electric saw.

33

Mark pulled out the soiled newspaper from Honey's kennel, threw in some bleach and hosed it out. He had to get them done before Bob picked him up. He didn't want to go away for two days, but he needed the money for a deposit on a new house. This place was all right for him, and for some of the rough slags he'd brought back here, but not for Beauty. He knew Asians were clean. The blokes in jail had been anyway. He'd said it in the pub once and had got some funny stares. So fucking what? It was true.

He'd cleaned the bathroom after she moved in, but he'd seen the bleaches and detergents she kept in her room, the rubber gloves and sponges. She didn't dare touch anything in the kitchen. It wasn't that she was stuck up. Just that she was more . . . ladylike than most of the birds he'd known.

He washed his hands in the sink and dried them on his trousers. The kitchen was better now that he'd thrown the carpet out and the dogs hadn't been in for days. She still hadn't cooked curry yet. Said she didn't know how, but he knew it was an excuse. He climbed the stairs, knocked on Beauty's door and went in when he heard her voice.

Beauty sat up, straightening her scarf. She didn't like to take it off until she went to bed at night, when she knew he wouldn't come.

'I'm off,' he said. 'Got a job on the motorway barriers with Bob.'

He'd be back the day after. Karen was coming to feed his dogs.

Was she gonna be all right?

Beauty didn't like the idea of being in the house on her own, but didn't want him to know. He had his own life to worry about.

She'd be fine, she said. She'd go to work and come home. Watch telly and stuff.

Was she sure? He could stay if she preferred.

She told him to go. He needed the money.

If she wanted company, he told her to fetch Honey. She'd take the face off anyone who tried to get into the house.

Honestly, she'd be fine, she told him.

Beauty watched Mark inspecting his blackened fingernails in the doorway. He was being sweet with her. She was sure that he liked her, but he wasn't pushy. He looked away when she caught his eye.

'When I get back we might have enough money for the deposit on a new house,' he said.

Mark didn't want to leave her. He knew she was pretending that it didn't bother her being in the house alone. He gave her his new mobile number and told her to call him if there was something wrong.

Or if she just wanted a chat.

He heard the Transit in the street outside, nodded to Beauty and left.

34

Peter kept himself occupied all afternoon and was relieved that his resolve not to switch on the computer had so far held. It was a good sign, a faltering step across the rope bridge between ape and true human being. Did that mean he had to give up his designs on *her*?

He had another shower instead, shaved, and tugged at the tusk-like nasal hairs that had appeared overnight. Eyedrops whitened the bloodshot of his eyes. He put on his loafers, rolled up his sleeves, and checked himself in the full-length mirror in the bedroom. Handsome.

Downstairs he laid out the vegetables in the kitchen and searched the radio for some Indian music. Or was that overdoing it? Probably. He found a 'community language' station, and turned it off until Beauty arrived.

She looked exquisite on his doorstep in a black salwar-kameez with embroidered trim and a dark brown headscarf. He stood aside to let her in, and ached at the sight of her slender neck.

Beauty followed him into the kitchen. She was looking forward to eating. And leaving, as soon as she could. The bloke looked at her too closely.

'What do I do first?' he asked.

Beauty put her cigarettes on the table.

'Chop the onions,' she said.

She watched him labouring over the onions and asked for another knife.

'Small pieces,' she said, and rolled up her sleeves.

Bismillah hir Rahmaanir Raheem.

Peter saw her lips mumbling something as she stripped the onions. Her gold earrings trembled as she moved. Some kind of blessing? *For what we are about to receive may the Lord . . .* Sort of.

'I found an Indian station by mistake earlier,' Peter said, switching on the radio.

Beauty listened to the sweet voice of Alisha Chinai: *Kajra re, kajra re mere kare kare naina.*

'It's from a film,' she said.

Peter had watched an Indian film the other night, he said. 'Did you like it?'

'Yes,' he lied. The songs were interminable, the film four hours long, but the women were magnificently beautiful. 'It was very . . . innocent,' he said.

'That's how they are,' Beauty said. So what if the actors didn't kiss, and Rani Mukherjee didn't take her clothes off?

Peter opened a bottle of red wine, and took some mineral water and a lemon from the fridge. 'Right, what's next?' he asked.

'Hot the oil. Fry the onions a bit, then put the garlic and ginger in after.'

She washed the meat at the sink, her lips moving as she did it.

'Can I ask what it is you're saying when you touch the food?' Peter asked.

Wasn't it a respectful question?

'*Bismillah hir Rahmaanir Raheem,*' Beauty said. 'It means . . . Allah the Mercy One . . . I dunno in English.'

Peter leaned against the sideboard and watched Beauty move about the kitchen. She washed the rice and put it in a large pan of cold water. He passed close by her and switched on the cooker. He was happy with her company. Lewd thoughts seemed out of place with the food, the music and the Arabic words.

Eat and go, Beauty told herself. If he tried anything, she'd give him two slaps. It was worth the risk for the food. She stirred the onions and enjoyed the stinging in her eyes, after so long. His house would smell, and his nice clothes.

He'd been almost the only white person in both shops that morning, Peter told her as she grated the ginger and garlic. In fact, generally people didn't seem to mix at all. You never saw mixed white and Asian couples. Why was that? Beauty scraped the meat from the chopping board into the pan, mixed it in with the melting onions and said she didn't know. Asian people liked to stick to their own kind.

Beauty covered the meat with water and sat down at the table. She lit a cigarette and watched Peter, his shirt buttons open, glass in one hand. He had a soft face and nice smile when he wasn't perving, which he wasn't anymore. He was lonely, it was obvious, and needed to talk. She didn't mind. Weren't there things she wanted to find out, that she needed to know? It was better to look stupid alone in front of him, one person; and he hadn't laughed at her the last time they'd talked.

She got up to stir the rice and sat down again. The meat would take some time to cook.

'Can I arx you something else about them other stuff?' she said.

Peter set out plates, knives and forks and sat down opposite her. 'Of course.'

He opened a drawer in the table, took out a small candle, lit it and placed it between them.

'You know . . . like . . . people who don't believe in God or heaven 'n' that?'

She stared into the flame.

Peter wondered where this notion had taken her. Did the prospect of worms scare her? Or that there was no soul? Had she realized that she wouldn't be punished for any 'sins' she might commit?

She looked up. 'How do they know what's right and wrong?' she asked, and looked away again, embarrassed.

Peter smiled. It was a good question. She'd obviously been giving this some thought.

Her face opposite him caught the glow of the flame as she waited for a reply. But how could he answer without conceding something to religion? That the principles of a liberal enlightenment, human rights and political correctness were derived from Judeo-Christian values? Tricky in one go. Perhaps some moral equivalence might serve his purposes better. If he were to stand a chance of turning his sensual and intellectual desires into reality, he'd need to be clever about it.

Beauty watched him rub his chin and wondered why he needed so long to answer.

'Well, I guess we all make our own choices,' he said. 'What's right for one person might not be for another.'

Beauty heard him, but had to repeat the words to herself in case she hadn't understood and said something dumb. Nothing he said made sense at first. How could everyone decide what was right or wrong?

Peter saw her eyes narrow as she considered his words. He had to open her up to other ideas, on sin, for example, without betraying the superiority of the belief system he wanted to make appealing. It might take more than an evening.

'Actually, it's more a "don't do to others what you wouldn't have them do to you" idea – a Judeo . . . a Jewish-Christian thing,' he said. It might be less alarming for her if he steeped it in something she could relate to. 'I suppose that's what most people believe.'

Beauty wondered what *Jewish* was. Christian she knew. *Issa* was a Muslim prophet. Her brother accused her of being a *fucking Christian* after he had found out she had let those two people with the magazines into the house. But what was the other one? What did they believe?

She went to stir her curry again. The rice was nearly done.

Peter poured himself another glass of wine while her back was turned.

'What's . . . *Jewish* . . . mean?' she said, returning.

Wine rolled over the edge of the glass as he put it back on the table. Surely to God she'd heard of Jews! Maybe she didn't know the word. Or was it true they were known as 'pigs and monkeys'? Isn't that what the Qur'an said? Or so he'd seen on a television programme once.

'You know, Moses, Abraham, Isaac, the Ten Commandments . . . Israel?' he prompted.

Beauty was embarrassed by the surprise in his voice. But the names reminded her of the sitting room in London, and the mullah's brother telling her stories of the times before Mohammed. Of Mussa and Ibrahim. And how the Ehudi would all go to hell.

'You mean *Ehudi*?' she asked.

Peter considered the etymology of the word. Ehudi. Yehudi? Menuhin? Ehud? Barak, Olmert?

'I think so,' he said.

She didn't know anything about them, except that the *Ehudi*'s prophets were Muslim prophets too. She remembered the strange men with long beards and sidelocks in black coats and hats she'd seen near Finsbury

Park years ago, and her cousin Marouf shouting at them from the car window. *Fucking Ehudi!*

She'd never known why he had sworn at them. They were old men.

'They're God's people, aynit,' she said to Peter. '*Allah-manush*. They believe, too.' The mullah's brother had told her that as well. He'd scolded her when she'd asked him how they could be God's people and go to hell just for being *Ehudi*, but she hadn't understood his answer. Now this bloke was saying that people who didn't believe in God had the same ideas as the *Ehudi* and Christians? So why did they eat and drink *haram* stuff, why did they have lots of boyfriends and children with different men?

And hadn't her brother always said that Muslims weren't like that; screamed it at her?

'If white people got them Jewish and Christian ideas you said, how come they do what they want?'

Peter looked at her across the table with curiosity. By 'white people' did she mean atheists? Non-Muslims? And is that what Muslims or Indians thought of white Brits?

'You can't do whatever you like. There's the law,' he said. 'Anyway, do religious people never do anything wrong?'

Beauty picked at the dried wax which had dripped from the candle. The mullah and that other pervert. Touching her. And the beatings. You couldn't blame God for that.

'They know it's wrong,' she said.

Peter watched her face lost in thought. What had she suffered? Guilt pricked him for the thoughts he'd found so hard to overcome. This was a wounded bird, not an object of lust.

Her curry was perfect and hot, and Peter hadn't seemed to mind her eating with her hand; the rice had scalded her fingers nicely and she had left her plate empty except for the stalks of a dozen fresh chillies.

Beauty passed her hand in front of her face and thanked Allah for the food.

Shobor shukor al-hamdu lillah Allah – tumar dana ha-ba lai siro din ola habai tai.

Peter sniffed and sweated on the other side of the table. She told him to drink milk if the curry was too hot. He finished eating and filled his mouth from a carton in the fridge. It worked.

Beauty lit a cigarette and blew out smoke with relief at having eaten so well for the first time since leaving home.

'Have you got any brothers and sisters?' she asked him.

Peter wrestled with the espresso maker at the sink. He was happy to give up on religion and philosophy for the moment.

He had an older brother, he said; didn't see him very often. They didn't get on.

'Has he got a wife and kids?' she asked.

He hadn't.

What about your parents? Don't they have a right to see their grandchildren?

But she didn't ask him.

'I suppose neither of us has found the right person yet,' Peter said, hoping it would open a more promising avenue.

Beauty flicked cigarette ash onto her plate. White people all wanted 'love' marriages.

Don't you?

'What's a right person?' she asked.

'I have no idea,' Peter said. Attractive and not over-weight (admit it), sexually curious but inexperienced, non-nagging. 'You tell me.'

He poured himself coffee, preparing to fit her description.

'If someone respects their parents, looks after them; if he works hard and takes care of his wife and children – thass perfect,' Beauty said.

Peter was disappointed by the assured answer. Was that it? What about intelligent, good-looking, witty?

'And the perfect woman?'

'Someone who looks after her in-laws and children, who makes her husband strong and keeps him in line,' she answered. 'Then you can love that person,' she added, and reddened. Why had she used that word in front of him?

Peter sensed her embarrassment. He stirred sugar into the small coffee cup and saw the Asian men at the supermarket, the providers and protectors, loading their cars with children and onions. Was that why their chests swelled, and they bristled with masculinity? Could he do that? Was there fulfilment to be had from playing the dutiful husband and father? Was that 'love'? Was that the appeal of an arranged marriage – in fulfilling your duties and enjoying your wife's fulfilment of hers? And what about his own parents? They were 'getting on', weren't they? Was he looking after them? Peter had always had a childhood belief in his parents' longevity, had always expected to go before them. Or was this just a selfish refusal to face up to his obligations as a dutiful son?

Beauty looked at the white man lost in thought. She'd shut him up finally. Maybe she wasn't so stupid after all.

Peter raised his head and considered the young woman across the table, the empty plates between them, his full belly. It felt right.

'I wanted to ask you something, too,' he said.

Beauty poked the wax from the candle into the flame. It was nice talking to him, and she felt comfortable in his house. He was different from other white people she had met; he didn't think bad of her Asian stuff; he wasn't rough. His house was clean and warm and you could eat properly.

'I know this might sound crazy,' he began.

Beauty sat up, alert. His voice had gone strange. She shouldn't have relaxed. Was he going to say something embarrassing?

'And I don't know what situation you're in or what your plans are, but . . .'

Beauty measured the distance to the back door. She could be there in a few steps. All this talk of love and the perfect man – had she been flirting with him? A little? The old man was right – she did bring trouble on herself.

'. . . I was thinking of moving house – somewhere near or far . . . it doesn't matter with my job,' Peter went on, 'and was wondering if you wanted to . . . share it with me, you know, as housemates?'

He looked at Beauty for a reaction.

The knock at the front door startled him. Who the hell could that be? Peter went to answer it. Probably that bloody yob come to get in the way. Wasn't he supposed to be away working somewhere?

Peter looked through the spyhole in the front door.

35

Kate Morgan stood on the doorstep, holding her coat against the *bitter* cold. It was a foul place, and had taken her hours to find.

His car was there and the lights were on in the house. Why didn't he open the bloody door?

She knocked again.

Peter froze. This couldn't be happening! He looked through the hole again. She was still there. He'd have to open the door.

'Hi! Why didn't you ring?' he said, stepping out of the house to kiss her on both cheeks.

'I thought I'd surprise you.'

Peter heard bitterness in her voice.

'Can I come in?' she said.

He stood sideways to let her pass, large in a waist-length, fake fur coat. 'Have you had your hair done?' he asked.

She ignored his question. 'What's that smell?'

'I've just had a cooking lesson from a neighbour. You must be hungry – let me get you something to eat.'

Kate headed for the kitchen. When did he ever cook? She took in the pretty Indian girl in a headscarf and black eyeliner, the candle and empty plates.

Beauty started.

'This is all very cosy,' the woman said. She ran her

fingers through her hair, and smoothed out her travel-creased clothes.

'Hi, I'm Kate. I'm Peter's *girlfriend*.'

Peter looked from one woman to the other. 'This is Beauty,' he croaked.

'Beauty? What a lovely name,' Kate said. She took off her coat and handed it to Peter. 'Could you get my bag from the car, please? I'd like to have a word with – Beauty, is it? – alone.'

Peter didn't want to leave them in the room together but he recognized the strident tone in her voice and went to get her bags.

Beauty stood up. She shouldn't have come. What trouble had she caused in a stranger's house?

'I have to go,' she said, and made to move round the woman.

'Please, I need to know. Is there something going on between you and him?'

Beauty flushed at the accusation. 'No!'

I don't do them things. I'm Muslim.

But Beauty couldn't blame the woman. She shouldn't have been in a strange man's house. 'He asked me to show him how to cook.'

The woman's angry eyes looked at her from head to toe. 'Come off it, I wasn't born yesterday!'

Beauty didn't know what the woman meant. 'I don't care when you was born!' she said, and took a step towards the back door.

Kate moved to block her path. 'Didn't he tell you that he had a partner?' Kate heard her voice tremble.

Beauty felt sorry for the man's pretty girlfriend with the pale skin and dark hair. 'He said he didn't have a wife.'

Kate felt the energy drain from her. That was just like him to think he was being clever, playing with words. Kate wanted to believe her. The girl's voice was at once angry and apologetic, her eyes sympathetic. But surely this 'Beauty' knew Peter was drooling over her? He was just the type to want some young, submissive Asian type.

The lady looked like she was about to cry.

'I shouldn't have come,' Beauty said. Had she encouraged him? Hadn't she seen how the bloke had perved at her?

'It's not your fault,' said Kate.

But Beauty knew that it was.

Kate clutched the back of the chair to steady herself. The exhaustion and hunger from the journey were making her dizzy.

'I'm sorry. I just get so emotionally spun out sometimes.'

She took Beauty's hand and squeezed it.

Leaning against his car, Peter smoked a cigarette, Kate's heavy weekend bag at his feet. (How many bloody clothes had she brought with her?) Before going back inside he'd let her find out there was nothing going on. The whole thing was a disaster. He'd blown it with Beauty, and Kate would put him through hours of anguished relationship analysis. This time he'd tell her it was over. Definitely. As soon as she started shouting.

The front door opened and he took a step towards Beauty. 'Thanks for coming,' he said, attempting a casual air. 'Sorry about the, er . . . interruption.' It sounded feeble.

Beauty glanced at him. It wasn't his fault. He was a man.

'Go and look after your girlfriend,' she said and turned away.

Peter watched the door to Mark's house close behind her. He picked up the bag and went to face Kate's ire.

The conversation went much as all the others had before it, except that when Kate got to the 'do-you-still-love-me?' part, he told her he 'didn't know any more'. After a moment to absorb the news, she burst into tears.

Peter was horrified to find himself becoming aroused.

Afterwards, her head on his chest, post-coital regret hit him hard. She'd moaned in his ear that she loved him, and he'd mumbled something barely audible in return.

Peter groaned in the dark. Why had he done it? Would she see it as a last act of affection between them as their 'relationship' came to an end, or as a sign that they could 'work things out'? Would they have to go through another round of bitter recriminations over the 'emotional investment' and the time she'd wasted on him? The best years of her life? It made her feel so 'worthless and unattractive', she'd sobbed. She'd always known he wanted a slave type, that he couldn't handle an 'empowered and independent' woman like herself, and here he was preying on a virginal Asian girl half his age. He'd told her it wasn't so, that he just wanted to learn how to cook a decent curry.

Peter looked at the slanting patches of street light on the ceiling. Why had her tears excited him? Was a woman's vulnerability sexually stimulating? Was he moved by Kate's pain, or had he done what he could to stop the nerve-shredding, guilt-inducing sound of her crying? He'd put his arm round her when she'd told him his coldness towards her was like a slap in the face. His hand had brushed against her breast, and for some reason he could not explain to himself, he'd been overcome with lust. For the first time in the history of their sexual relationship he was rough with her. And the anger he felt seemed to leave her satisfied.

Apart from regretting what he had just done, Peter worried that he was indeed chasing virginal innocents. Was it really the result of his own inadequacies and a deep-rooted antipathy to women? Hadn't he been on the verge of coming to a newer understanding of his purpose in life, and how to achieve fulfilment? Surely there was no place for such sexual neuroses. These were Western hang-ups.

Peter shifted under Kate's weight and tried to extricate his arm. Hair went up his nose and he brushed it away in irritation. His 'girlfriend' nestled closer against him.

Cars passed occasionally in the street outside.

He thought again of the Asian men in the supermarket. The husbands and fathers, with their wives and children, loaders of onions, shepherds of broods, passers-on of genes. It was a simple existence. And what of *her*? The future wife and mother? Devoted? Caring? Supportive, understanding, soothing, bright, sweet, slim, pretty, shy yet adventurous? Feminine!

There, he'd said it!

He imagined tossing the word like a hand grenade into the middle of one of Kate's dinner parties. There'd be baying howls of derision from her friends. 'Feminine?' they would shriek. What kind of a Neanderthal was she going out with? A repressed public schoolboy, Kate would say. Before it blew them all to pieces.

Peter smiled in the dark.

Where to find a woman like that? He'd buggered it up with Beauty, that much was certain. But was it only a person of religion who could be all those things? There was no God! Organic life was an accident, procreation its sole aim; human consciousness was a freak of nature to be used to ensure our survival, and religion merely a guideline to keep the family together as the basic unit of society. Different animals did it different ways. Meerkats stood on their hind legs to keep a look out for predators.

Peter yawned. What rubbish he was thinking! It was Kate's proximity, he decided, that reduced his mental capacities.

It was over between them. What they'd done tonight on the sofa changed nothing.

He wanted his own Beauty.

36

Beauty Begum climbed the stairs in the quiet house. Mark wouldn't be back until the morning, he'd said. She opened the door to her bedroom, switched on the naked light bulb and looked at the bare walls, the purple carpet, the orange headboard of the double bed in the corner against the far wall, and the lilac duvet cover. Her salwars hung on the clothes rack which Mark had given her, and her few items of make-up were arranged on the brown and white bedside table. She took off her jacket and sat down on the bed with her phone in her hand. Would her mum ring again tonight, late, after the old man had gone to bed?

She slipped off her sandals. It was still early and she knew she wouldn't be able to sleep yet. She stuffed the pillows into the corner, sat with her knees clasped to her chest, and pulled the duvet to her chin. She could still taste the marrow from the smooth pieces of leg bone, and the freshness of the hard, green chillies. She'd need to find somewhere to live with a proper kitchen. Soon. But she was grateful in the meantime, and thanked Allah again for what she had eaten.

Would she ever have her own kitchen? With her own children to cook for? Or a husband? She'd always been able to imagine the Bengali in-laws she would take care of. In her dreams they used to look a bit like her own mother and the old man. But kinder. The picture was fading now. There was still no face of a husband.

What Bengali would touch a *bugri*-runaway? Even if she met one herself, they'd never have a wedding with both families doing things properly. A simple, holy one with dates and water. Any Bengali bloke would throw it in her face as soon as they had a fight.

You were a fucking bugri when I met you!

Or Indian, Sikh or Paki. They'd throw everything in her face. 'You're this, you're that'; 'You're a Muslim'; 'You're a runaway'; 'You didn't have no family'.

Were white people like that? Everybody said they had lots of girlfriends before they got married and that they didn't take anything seriously. And white women had children with different men. You could tell from their TV programmes. White people's 'love' was like in the films. Every girl wanted that. Dreamed of it. The man was handsome and strong. You were shy when you saw him, your stomach turned over and your heart beat faster.

Asian way was more than that. He was a stranger at first but a girl would love him because he was her husband, and he would love her because she was his wife. And if she became the *koutti* and was strong enough to control her husband and make him big, if she became the pillar of the house and took care of his parents, then his love for her would grow. That was her job. He had to look after his family, work hard, and be generous to her brothers and sisters. That was a man's job.

Beauty looked at the bare walls from the corner of the room.

That was all gone. A kid's dream. Those men didn't exist. Not for her. It was better to be alone than to risk marrying a monster.

If only she had a child to look after! Just her and a baby. No man, no one to bully her, or throw mean things in her face every time he got angry. No one who threatened to divorce her if she wanted to visit her mum. She knew what Bengali men could be like. Cousin Sweetie's husband divorced her because she went back to Bangladesh for her brother's wedding.

Talaq, talaq, talaq, when she got back.

No. It was better to be alone. Like the white girls pushing prams she saw from the windows of the bus.

But how would she ever have kids?

The phone rang. Her legs were stiff as she crawled across the bed.

Mark sat against the wheel arch in the back of the Escort van, his knees pressed to his chest, and looked at his phone in the passing orange motorway lights. The metal ridges on the floor dug into him painfully as they bumped over potholes in the road.

Where the fuck were they?

Junction 25.

Twelve more till the Stafford exit. Half an hour along the A449 to Wolverhampton. They'd be back by six o'clock.

It had been knackering work shifting concrete central reservations on the M62 all night, but at least he'd earned some decent money. Two hundred quid for eighteen hours' graft. It was enough for his share of a deposit on a new house. If Beauty wanted. She'd get to know him better, see that he was a good bloke, that his heart was in the right place. She might get to like him. She did already, a bit. He'd re-home a couple of the dogs if he had to . . . Satan definitely.

He shifted his weight on the floor. It was too *basstud* cold to take off his jacket to use as a cushion.

The motorway lights flashed in the back of the van and lit up the bags of tools around him. Another junction.

It must've been pretty tough for Beauty getting used to how white people lived. He wanted to show her he was reliable and that he could take care of her. He'd told her about his plans to move, find work and get the mobile mechanic business up and running. She'd encouraged him. Apart from Bob, no one had ever done that before. Maybe his foster parents had tried, but by then he'd been too far down the road of car crime.

Mark strained to see the signs through the wire mesh and the front window.

Junction 23.

He'd give up the eight cans he drank every night, and all. He'd done it before. He'd save some money, and it would be a good gesture to Beauty. Show her he wasn't a pisshead. Anyway, he could get by on a couple of spliffs of an evening.

And if she didn't like him *that* way, then they could be mates. A mate was always good to have. They were friends already, weren't they?

If she stayed.

Beauty lay curled up on the bed. She shut her eyes and covered her ears with her hands, humming to drown her mother's voice. Words no daughter should hear. But the curses from the phone call grew louder.

Zibon ne tui tor horuta soke derchten nai! You'll never see your children's eyes!

She held her silent baby in her arms, its eyes closed, its chest still, and a doctor took it from her. Was it a boy or a girl?

And it was the night of *Shabe-Baraat*. She repeated the prayers of repentance. The *filista* should have taken her Book to God, for Him to tear out the pages of the good and bad things she had done that year. But the angels stayed on each shoulder, the Book still open, ready to carry on recording. Where was her forgiveness for the past year? Was He not listening?

And then she found a prescription for her mother's medicine in her hand and she couldn't read it. Mark wasn't there, and if she made a mistake her ama would die.

They wouldn't let her see her mother's body laid out in its white *haffon*. She pushed past them and grabbed her ama's feet, but they hit her arms and she had to let go. And her dead mother's voice spoke:

If I die I hope they don't show you my face . . .

Mark closed the door behind him and locked it. Beauty's jacket was on the sofa. He picked it up and hung it on a clothes hook on the back of the kitchen door.

He climbed the stairs quietly and threw himself on his bed. It was good to come back to a house with her in it.

Beauty opened her eyes to the grey light of dawn. Her head felt thick and her eyes stung.

She listened to the creaking stairs, glad that Mark was back, relieved not to be alone in the house.

Her skin looked yellow in the bathroom mirror, her eyes sunken and dark. She performed her ablutions properly for the first time since she'd left home, and felt better.

Ash-hadu alla ilaha illallahu wa-ash-hadu ann-na Muhammaden 'abduhu-wa-rasuluh.

37

The mental health nurse phoned later the same morning. Beauty could go along to the Asian Women's Centre any time today. They were expecting her.

The three-storey building stood back from the road, protected by high railings. The gate buzzed open for her when she rang the bell.

Beauty looked around the hall. Posters of mentally healthy Asian women hung on the walls, and leaflets were spread out on a low table written in several languages. She recognized the Bengali script.

What was she doing here?

She heard running footsteps above and the animal-like howl of a woman in pain. A door opened and a tall Indian woman came towards her, smiling and smoothing down her kameez. She had long, layered hair, and no make-up or jewellery. Her name was Puja.

Beauty followed her down a long corridor to an office. Had Beauty found them easily? Had she had far to come? How long had she lived in Wolverhampton?

Puja Patel offered Beauty a seat and had a closer look at the Bangladeshi girl. She seemed tired and harassed, but was looking after herself, which was a good sign. She asked why the doctor had sent her.

Beauty said she'd left home to avoid getting married.

The Jobcentre had told her to go to the doctor in case she wasn't able to work. Puja nodded. 'Are you working?' she asked.

'I'm working voluntary at the moment.'

The symptoms of mental health issues were often subtle. Many South Asian women were in denial about the suffering they had experienced. Every woman had a different tale to tell. Bangladeshi Muslim girls were often the worst affected by traditional family pressures and abuse.

This girl had found work and somewhere to stay. She was keeping it together. Still, she'd been referred. Puja would need to probe further, to satisfy herself that Beauty was not at risk. The Bangladeshi girl's reluctance to talk might be a front to avoid dealing with difficult issues. A natural defence mechanism. It could take weeks for a patient to open up. Sometimes they never did.

Beauty didn't need any help, and she didn't like the questions about her family life. Not from a nosy Asian. What did she understand anyway? She'd not suffered anything, you could tell from her eyes. Beauty was the one who should be working here. 'Listen, I went through a lot,' she said. 'But I aynt mental.'

Puja smiled at her use of the word, but she would reserve judgement. She knew what 'a lot' could mean. The ones who didn't go under often turned out tough. Which one was this girl? She'd invite her back to talk again, just for a chat, to see how she was getting on.

Beauty didn't want to come for a chat. The idea of working here had taken root. She knew what girls went through. She could help them. Her own kind. Wasn't she going through the same stuff?

'I don't need help,' she said, and asked what she had to do to get a job at the women's centre, like she was doing at the care home. 'Phone them. They'll tell you I aynt mental.'

Puja recognized the aggressive-defensive tone in the girl's voice. She wasn't out of the woods yet. But Beauty seemed to have a strength most of the women upstairs needed, and Puja was always short of volunteers, especially at night. Maybe she could help and comfort some of them. It might also be a way of getting her back to the centre, where Puja could keep an eye on her.

But it was tough work, physically. Would she be able to handle it? The women they helped were there for a variety of reasons. Domestic violence and abuse, self-harm and attempted suicide, eating disorders, depression and nervous breakdowns. Some had severe learning difficulties. They had a small team of counsellors and volunteers who tried as best they could to provide some comfort. They helped with accessing benefits, housing and jobs too. But funding was always a problem.

Beauty didn't understand everything. She knew what suicide was, but what was a nervous breakdown? What kind of abuse was the woman talking about? And didn't Beauty have learning difficulties?

Puja keyed in the security code for the heavy door at the top of the stairs and held it open for Beauty. She pointed out some of the residents' rooms and mini-apartments. 'We try to encourage independent living,' she said.

They stopped at the communal dining room, and Beauty looked through the glass panes in the door.

A dozen Asian women, Pakistani and Sikh, and several girls the same age as Beauty sat around a long table. Large Jamaican women in plastic aprons brought bowls of rice and curry, and plates of chapattis from a serving hatch. One Sikh lady had a black eye and a plaster over the bridge of her nose. A long-haired Pakistani girl had razor stripes on her forearms and bandages around her wrists. The women didn't eat much. The eyes around the table were dead. The lips of the older women mumbled continuously, but not to each other. An emaciated Indian girl in jeans and a fleece swept her plate of chicken and rice to the floor. The woman with the broken nose leaned towards her and patted her hand, while one of the Jamaican women came to clean up.

And on the floor in the corner was a girl in a black salwar with embroidered trim and a brown headscarf. Her knees were clasped to her chest, her face pressed between them. There was an untouched plate of rice by her side, and a small rucksack. She looked up and stared at the door, searching it, until her eyes met Beauty's through the glass.

Beauty stared back at herself, and her legs trembled.

'Are you OK?'

She started at Puja's voice, and looked back into the dining room, but there was no girl on the floor, no plate of rice or rucksack.

'I thought I saw . . . a friend,' Beauty said.

Puja took her to see other communal areas, a kitchen, the television room, a library with internet access. Beauty tried to concentrate. She felt sick and dizzy, and wanted to sit down. Was she going mad?

They reached a staff bedroom on the top floor. It was bright and clean. She looked out onto the main road and a primary school playground. Children in black trousers and blue sweatshirts chased each other, the noise of their excited cries reaching her over the traffic.

An eight-year-old girl with a long black plait, like Beauty's used to be, stood in the playground alone.

'What we really need is weekend staff,' Puja said.

Beauty came away from the window. 'How do you help them women get better?' she asked.

Puja explained that some were on courses of medication, counselling and therapy; others had learning difficulties and would return to their families. The victims of abuse and domestic violence were often the hardest to help.

She accompanied Beauty to the top of the stairs. 'Grab our literature on the way out. It will give you an idea.'

Puja couldn't force her to talk, but the girl agreed to come back.

Beauty had no idea what 'literature' was, but picked up the leaflets by the door.

Outside, the children's shouts sounded louder. She stood on the doorstep and searched the playground but couldn't find the girl with the long plait.

Dust blew into her eyes and the hissing brakes of a bus hurt her ears as she crossed the road. Were the drivers of the cars looking at her? She tugged at her headscarf and kept her eyes on the pavement.

I aynt mad. I aynt like them women in that place. People helping them to eat. I aynt like that. They must have went mental from the pressure. They couldn't take it no more.

She knew what they'd been through. How many of them had been touched by men, raped, beaten, forced to marry, forced to go back home, forced to have abortions, forced to give up their love-babies?

Corner-girls.

Evans Street was quieter, sheltered from the wind.

I aynt mental.

I seen a ghost, thass all.

They were the spirits of grown-up dead babies. She'd never seen one before, but she knew they existed. Her brother had seen one back home. Usually they lived in tamarind or mango trees. But in this country they stayed in parks.

Beauty quickened her pace past brown tower blocks, their windows occasionally boarded up, blackened by the smoke from fires. She knew what she had to do.

The house was quiet. Mark stopped typing his CV and swivelled in the chair. He'd slept well and had a good bath. He had two hundred quid in his back pocket, and was wondering how to spend some of it. On her. They could go somewhere for their tea, maybe. He looked up when the door opened from the street. She looked pale and beautiful, and stared at him as she caught her breath.

'Can you teach me to read?'

38

Beauty changed into a pair of jeans. She didn't like the idea of having 'learning difficulties'. And she didn't want that Indian lady to think she was thick either. She wanted to help those other women. She'd prove she wasn't loony, that she didn't have 'learning difficulties', by learning to read.

And if she had seen ghosts, that just proved people were right about them. It wasn't anything to worry about. Back home an old lady *bhout* had got inside her mum once when she was a little girl. She'd trodden on a shadow and the ghost came out of the tree. The old man had walked in ghost wind and got his neck twisted for two days.

But how can you see a ghost of yourself?

Mark waited for her and remembered the few English lessons he'd had in jail; how he'd struggled with some fucked-up spelling rules and spent hours on his bed after lock-in getting his head round it; and how he'd taught that lad he'd shared a cell with. If Beauty knew the alphabet it would be a start. She'd need to know the sounds each letter made, alone and together. He felt confident he could do it, and he was happy to help her. It would give him an excuse to be with her. Sit near her. It didn't go any further than that.

He couldn't, didn't, imagine sex with her. It wasn't right. The word was even embarrassing. She was probably still a virgin. That was a big deal.

Spending some time with her would be a good thing. She'd get to know him more and see that he was a good bloke.

Beauty came in and sat on the sofa. 'Promise you aynt gonna laugh?' she asked.

Mark saw the begging look in her eye. 'Do' worry. I dey learn till I were sixteen misself.'

He took some paper from the printer and searched for a pen on the computer desk. 'D'you know the alphabet?' he asked.

'A-B-C stuff?'

Beauty knew she would sound thick at first. There was nothing she could do about it. But she did know the alphabet.

'Giw on then,' he said.

'What?'

'Say it.'

'Loud?'

'Uh-huh.'

She recited it steadily to the end.

'Thass all right,' Mark said. 'Can you write it?'

She could, but not very well.

'Both ways?' he asked.

What did that mean? Big and small?

She could do that as well. She told him what the problem was. She knew the letters, but when they were put together it didn't make no sense. Even her own name. How could bee, ee, ay, you, tee, why make 'Beauty'?

Mark listened. It was like diagnosing engine problems. He searched for a simple explanation. Each letter made a different sound, he told her. Sometimes more than one. When you knew what they were, you could start putting the letters together. The letter 'A' could be 'ay' as in 'I *dey* do something', or like in 'at'; you didn't say 'bee', it was 'buh' like in 'buh-nana'.

He checked she knew what sounds each of the letters made.

Beauty asked him how she was supposed to know which way to say some of the letters, like 'c' and 'g'. He told her she'd get used to it. He'd keep it simple to start with, he promised, and wrote three-letter words on a piece of paper. They sounded them out slowly together.

She saw how to do it. You didn't always say it the A-B-C-D way. It was the first bit of each letter, 'd' not 'dee', 'o' not 'oh', 'e' not 'ee'. P-e-n. Pen. B-e-d. Bed. It was slow.

Mark sat next to her, helping, but not telling her the answer. He pulled the coffee table closer and wrote all the three-letter words he could think of. Beauty sounded out each one, letter by letter, over and again until the words took shape before her. M-a-n. Man. D-o-g. Dog.

She sat cross-legged on the parquet floor and read the words to him, surprised and delighted each time the snaking letters revealed their meaning. The tiredness from her sleepless night vanished. She felt awake, the room seemed brighter, everything was clearer, not just the words on the piece of paper.

I aynt mental.

I aynt got 'learning difficulties'.

I aynt dumb.

She could read. Not well, but she could do it. Mark was patient. He went over the letters with her until she got it right and didn't need his help.

*

Hours passed. He made tea and rolled cigarettes. She took one to please him. It tasted horrible at first and made her head spin.

Then he called out words from the list and she tried to write them down, repeating each word over and trying to work out the letters. It was harder than reading but when she got it right it felt good. 'I' and 'E' were difficult.

Mark watched her fingers grip the pen as she wrote. He willed her on and planned what to introduce next. He was pleased with her progress and his skills as a teacher. When he was satisfied she'd got the hang of it he introduced some harder stuff. Two letters together, like 'st' and 'th'.

Beauty's finger hurt from pressing the pen. She stretched and leaned back, brushing against his leg.

She was happy. She wanted to tell her little sis that she could read, and her mum.

No one had explained it to her like Mark had. Maybe she hadn't wanted to listen. Her family told her she was dumb, so she had been dumb for them. It helped block them out, their noise and shouts. Then the old man said she was mad, so she was mad for them.

No one had been patient with her or encouraged her like Mark did. No one had ever asked her how she got on at school. They didn't ask Sharifa either.

Mark was different. How was it that a stranger had done more for her than her own family? She knew he liked her, but he looked at her from far away. The white *gunda* was shy. He was a tough guy but he couldn't hold her eye for long. It was sweet, and she knew she'd be safe with him if they got a house together. He was kind, too. And lonely. He wanted people to like him. He was *arwa*, innocent, even though he was a scary racist type, with a cap tipped to the back of his head, the England shirt and dogs.

But he had done something for her they never had.

Al-lāh give him long life. Keep him shanti; give him money, good health, and kids that respect him.

From now on she'd pray for him every day.

Mark told her she'd need to spend a lot more time on her reading. They could do a bit every day. She could practise down here, or in her room. He talked about moving house, showed her the lists he'd picked up that morning from the estate agents and housing associations in Chapel Ash, and told her to circle the ones that said DSS/PETS OK.

Mark switched on the heater and they watched *EastEnders* and *Coronation Street* together, and his favourite programme – police camera recordings on *Car Crime Street Wars UK*.

39

The two women walked up Darlington Street towards the town centre. Beauty wondered how long this would take. She hadn't wanted to go with Kate. She only had her pink salwar to wear, the old-fashioned one her mum had given her, and had wanted to go to the launderette before it closed. The lady had pulled up in her car as Beauty was returning home from her morning shift. She'd begged Beauty to let her take her out for tea, to apologize for how she'd behaved. Peter had explained everything to her, she said. Beauty winced at the thought of these strangers talking about her and told the woman there was no need to say sorry. But Kate had insisted and it had been easier to go.

Kate Morgan strode ahead and looked at the shabbily dressed people, the women in cheap high street clothes from many seasons ago. It was another world. Kate was glad she hadn't worn anything too ostentatious. Her D&G overcoat and scarf, Diesel jeans and trainers were enough. Lots of designers made urban-chic clothes these days.

The Indian girl next to her – Bangladeshi, Peter had corrected her irritatingly – was a funny one. That thing she was wearing really was peculiar. Kate would have felt sorry for her, but *actually* it was quite embarrassing. She looked like an old woman with all the excess material bunched between her legs. Maybe she was religious. Or straight out of a village. Other Asians in the town didn't dress like that.

Beauty.

Her name was a bit cringeworthy too.

Beauty struggled to keep up. The lady didn't want to go into any of the cafés. They looked dirty, she said, so Beauty took her to the Wulfrun Centre instead.

The coffee bar was in a roped-off section in one of the plazas. As they slid into seats opposite each other, Kate apologized again for the night before. Her nerves had been on edge, she said. Her relationship with Peter had hit a rocky patch recently, and she hadn't known where she stood with him.

Beauty eyed the passing shoppers for her brothers' faces. Would they dare do anything if she was with a white woman in a public place?

'Everything's OK now,' Kate said.

She watched the pretty girl break off a small piece of cake and put it in her mouth . . . ever so daintily. Was she sweet and naïve, or was it just an act? And did it matter, now that Peter had shown Kate how he really felt? She'd let this one know about it, just in case. You could never really trust another woman.

She beckoned the Bangladeshi girl to come closer.

Beauty leaned forward. She was glad the lady was smiling and happy today. But why did she want to tell a stranger her private stuff?

'We had wonderful sex last night!' the woman said.

Beauty didn't move.

'He *literally* tore my clothes off.'

She tried not to hear her words. Her cheeks stung.

'Grabbing me . . . touching me everywhere. And he was so hard!' She'd never had such intense orgasms with him. 'You know that feeling when you *literally* melt?'

Beauty didn't want to listen, didn't know what the woman's words meant.

Yes, you do.

Kate sat back in her chair.

'It was such a relief,' she said. 'I'd been suffering these terrible anxiety attacks that he didn't love me any more. You can imagine what I thought when I saw you there! That's why I just had to say sorry for being such a cow. I'm usually a very chilled-out person.'

Beauty let out her breath. 'Does that mean you'll get married now?' she asked, and reddened in case it was another of her *arwa* questions.

Kate smiled at the girl's innocence. There was nothing to fear. She was a complete child; likeable, too. And she was a good listener, just what Kate needed.

'I don't know,' she said. 'I've felt so low about it over the last couple of years, I don't think I've got the strength left in me to keep on struggling. I was on the floor the day before I came up here.'

Beauty wondered what the woman had been doing on the floor. She watched the passing shoppers – white, Asian, black, Chinese, Iraqi faces – and hoped the lady would finish talking soon.

Kate scraped the cream from the plate with the side of her fork. 'Here I am, banging on about myself! What about you? Are you going out with anyone at the moment?' she asked.

Beauty wanted to tell her that Muslim girls didn't have boyfriends. Or if they did, they didn't talk about it.

'I'm waiting for the right bloke,' she said. Did that sound white? The woman nodded, so it must have done.

'That's what bothers me about Peter,' Kate said. 'Sometimes I think, "Is he the right person for me?" You know, a man's got to be supportive, sensitive and caring? As well as good-looking, interesting and all the rest of it. He has to make you feel like a woman?'

Beauty waited. Was there more?

'Then there's his bloody family!' Kate felt the familiar stabbing pain in the pit of her stomach at the thought of Peter's mother. She'd never been good enough for *Mummy*'s precious little boy. 'His mum's an absolute cow.'

Beauty winced. How could anyone say that? And how much longer would she have to listen to this? Was she supposed to say something? 'What about your parents?' she asked. 'Do they get on with him?'

'Well, that's another thing that's ruined my relationship with Peter . . . and all my other boyfriends actually,' Kate said. 'Nothing's ever been good enough for my *mother*. She's so overbearing and critical, you know, about everything I've ever done. It's really screwed my self-confidence and self-esteem with men.'

Kate ripped at the corner of a serviette. They'd never been there to support her when she'd been at her lowest points, she said. She'd done everything for them. Who was it who'd been there when her mum was weeping down the phone about how badly Kate's father treated her? And what about that time her mum had been *physically* sick in Kate's toilet, when Kate had told her that Dad had been out to dinner with another woman?

Beauty watched the growing pile of torn paper. What was the woman talking about?

And what was 'self-esteem'?

Kate looked up and saw the blank expression on the face of the girl opposite her. What could she understand? Unless you'd lived through these things yourself, you couldn't possibly know about the awful chains of guilt which Kate's parents had made her drag around.

'My mum's never done anything for me,' she said.

Beauty choked and coughed to hide it. Had she heard right?

She gave birth to you!

'She's an utter bitch,' Kate said.

Beauty felt the tears fill her eyes. Her heart beat in her ears. What kind of *shaitan* could say that about her own mother?

Al-lāh, if my daughter said that about me, I would stab her.

Kate noticed the girl's eyes shining strangely. Had she put her foot in it? Peter had mentioned something about her having only recently left home. Well, it wasn't Kate's fault, was it?

'Don't you get on with your parents either?'

Beauty's chest hurt.

'Peter said you'd left home?'

She couldn't breathe.

Don't tell her anything.

'I can't blame them,' she said.

You aynt never told no one.

This one needed to hear it though.

Beauty stared at the empty coffee cup on the table. 'He started touching me when I was ten years old . . .'

Kate closed her mouth.

'. . . and tried to rape me when I was twelve.'

She shut her eyes, and listened.

'My old man pretended he didn't know what was going on, cuz of the shame; then he blamed me for being a slapper; I started cooking and cleaning for the whole family when I was nine; they forced me to marry an old man when I was fourteen. And I never went to school.'

Beauty couldn't look up, didn't care what the woman

thought, didn't want to see her face, and felt no shame. Not any more.

And a man's voice beside her said: 'Causing trouble, sis?'

40

Dulal Miah stood on the other side of the rope and motioned away with his shaven head. 'Let's go.'

Beauty glanced at the white woman . . .

Help me!

. . . and back to her brother.

His jaws were clenched in the smile she recognized, which had always come before she got a beating. 'Nah, man. I'm staying here,' she said.

Man? No Bhai-sahb?

She saw his eyes narrow, nostrils widen, his fists grip the rope. *He's gonna lose it.*

'*Tarra amarray marri lar.*'

'So?'

'You gotta do what's right.'

'I aynt marrying no one.'

The white woman still had her eyes closed.

'Think about Sharifa and Faisal. How they gonna get married?'

'They'll find someone.'

'*Tui amarray arr derchtay nai.*'

Kate Morgan opened her eyes, saw Beauty's look of fear and an Asian man leaning over the rope, his hand on the girl's shoulder.

'Take your fucking hands off her!' Kate shouted.

Dulal looked at the faces turned towards him. White

faces. Fathers with blond-haired five-year-old children in short-sleeved shirts.

Kate felt the rage in the man's eyes turn on her, something deranged and uncontrolled.

'Who's the white bitch?' Dulal said to his sister, without taking his eyes from the white woman.

Kate felt as if she'd been slapped. 'I beg your fucking pardon!'

The chair tipped over as she leapt to her feet. Beauty felt more eyes turn to them as the lady screamed.

'WHO THE FUCK DO YOU THINK YOU ARE?'

Kate had *never* been spoken to like that in her life! She wasn't going to let this *ape* get away with it. Or come near Beauty, for that matter. Not after what she had just heard from the girl.

Beauty watched a white bloke in a red football shirt and heavy gold jewellery making his way through the tables towards them.

'*Bhai-sahb*, please, just go. I aynt coming,' Beauty said. Now there'd be more trouble.

The man appeared at Kate's side. 'Y'm all right loov?'

He nodded at *the Paki hassling two birds in the middle of the Wulfrun Centre, for fook's sake.* 'Is this bloke bothering you?'

He stepped over the fallen chair towards Dulal Miah.

'*Tar gor zolai limu,*' Dulal said to Beauty, and was gone.

Kate searched the crowd until she was sure he'd disappeared. The man in the football shirt picked up her chair.

'Thanks for the help,' she said, sitting down. 'We're fine now.'

'Am you shooer?' he asked.

Kate nodded.

The man shrugged and made his way back to his table.

The two women looked at each other in silence. Kate saw the anguish in Beauty's face, the horror of her words and experiences.

Touching me when I was ten years old . . . tried to rape me . . . beat me until I married a forty-five-year-old . . .

This was no TV news story to be dismissed, undeserving of consideration because it came from a backward and savage culture. It was something real, tangible, in front of her. And more serious than her own.

Beauty took a tissue from the sleeve of her jacket, uncomfortable under the woman's gaze. She didn't need pity. Not from someone who called her own mother a . . . *that word.* But she was grateful to her for making Dulal go away.

'Was that your brother?' the woman asked her.

Beauty nodded.

'Peter never said anything,' Kate said.

Beauty pushed the tissue back up her sleeve. 'I don't talk about it. I only told you, cuz . . .'

Kate averted her eyes.

The two women were silent again.

'My God, I'm shaking,' Kate said.

She held out her hand to show Beauty.

'What did your brother say?' she asked.

'That I'm killing them back home.'

'Did he threaten you?'

'No. What can he do?'

Tar gor zolai limu. I'll burn his fucking house down.

'You should not have to put up with this,' Kate said. 'You're a person, too. You're entitled to a life. I think you need to talk to someone.'

'Who?'

'A professional. And you need a refuge, somewhere away from all this.'

'There's one here for mental Asian women,' said Beauty.

Kate felt an overwhelming sadness for the young woman chewing her lip in front of her, the weight of long suffering across her features. Helping her would go some way to . . . 'Come on, girl, let's get you back to Peter's. You need a hot bath and a back rub, and we'll look for something on the internet – a quiet and safe place in the country where you can get some peace. I know where to look, believe me. You can't live like this any more.'

Peter wouldn't be back from work yet, and he would have left his laptop at home.

It was almost dark when Kate pulled up outside the house. She went upstairs to prepare a bath for Beauty. She'd brought her aromatherapy bath set with her as well as a new towel and dressing gown. OK, so the essential healing oils wouldn't solve anything, but they couldn't hurt. And it felt right to look after her. Considering . . . everything.

While Beauty was in the bath Kate went through Peter's cupboards until she found a comforting hot drink to make for them both. She switched on the heating and the lamp in the sitting room, drew the curtains, and pulled the coffee table up to the sofa so that they could both see the laptop.

The boiler fired up in the kitchen. Kate decided to get started on the internet. It would occupy her thoughts. She typed in 'Asian women refuge' and opened the links. She'd expected more. Most were havens from domestic violence offering community language speakers, counselling, therapy and help in accessing training, education and benefits. Few gave addresses. One, in Derbyshire, had photos of the premises: a converted manor house in large, well-kept grounds, with a river, chickens, sheep and vegetable gardens. To Kate it looked ideal. She returned to the search engine and tapped in 'Asian women's mental health', opened the first page, and scanned the links.

. . . *suicide and self-harm among young women twice the national average; psychosocial, spiritual and physical health problems; relationship difficulties within the family; izzat and family honour; the pressures from the family to behave 'well'; hard-to-achieve cultural expectations of women as daughters, daughters-in-law, sisters, wives and mothers; abuse and isolation; fear of speaking out . . .*

Kate stared at the screen. She could imagine the horrific effects that might have on a person's mental state.

Couldn't she?

When Beauty came down the stairs wrapped in the bathrobe, a towel twisted around her head, Kate didn't turn round. She looked pale.

Kate patted the sofa for Beauty to sit beside her.

'I found a few things,' she said. 'There's one not too far from here. It's a lovely place.'

Beauty felt clean and warm after the hot bath. The lady was trying to be kind, and hadn't said a word about herself since Beauty had told what she had been through; had avoided looking her in the eye, too.

Kate hit the 'back page' key, but she'd visited so many sites that the path didn't return her to the original results. She clicked 'History', tapped in 'Asian women' and scanned the list.

www.AsianWomenBound-And-Gagged.com

www.AsianWomenFuckedHard.com

www.AsianWomenUp . . .

Kate's throat hurt and she struggled to breathe as she scrolled down the list, but she managed to find the site she had been looking for. She opened the photos of the manor house. There was no need to see any of the websites Peter had visited. Nor to tell Beauty about it. She didn't need such degradation on top of everything she had suffered. Let the girl at least be spared whatever squalor lay behind the pages and pages of links.

'You see, it looks wonderful.'

While she rubbed her hair dry, Beauty looked at the photos of the old house, the green lawns and countryside around it. It was nice. Quiet. And the chickens running around reminded her of Bangladesh – the *good way*. But she noticed the woman's hand shake as she moved the mouse and a drop falling on the keyboard.

'You OK?' Beauty asked.

Kate took the scrunched-up tissue paper offered her and wiped her nose. 'It's nothing. It doesn't matter,' she said.

It didn't. Compared with what Beauty had been through none of her own crap mattered.

This new low of Peter's was just more of the same thing.

Peter Hemmings switched off PM News on Radio 4. It ended at six o'clock and there were only the listeners' banal emails on the day's world events to read out: one-line solutions to Middle East conflicts and global warming.

He was looking forward to getting home, and had been all day. In fact, he was surprised by how much he had thought of Kate while driving around. And not sexually, although there had been that, too; he'd even found himself becoming aroused, in Walsall, at the thought of what she could expect when he got home. Did that mean he actually wanted her to stay? Christ! Surely he couldn't have changed in such a short space of time?

How long would it be before her ways began to grate on his nerves again? Three days? Two? It would depend on the amount of analysis she made him suffer. It was his fault, he realized at the roundabout on Stafford Road, for failing to pull her out of the psychotherapy crap. He had no influence over her, nor could he have expected to: he'd failed to fulfil his duties towards her as a male. How long could a woman wait for a man to get through his extended youth and do the right thing? How long could she deny her reproductive needs? Wasn't that what he wanted, too? What else was there in life apart from fulfilling one's biological role? Yes, to intellectual striving and achievement, but maybe spiritual and philosophical contentment only came to those who provided for a wife and child. The creation of a new life would take him to a place of selflessness and cut the chains of his all-too-human weakness and vanity. Or was he losing it?

Peter parked in the street outside his house, relieved to see that Kate's car was still there and that there were lights around the curtain in the sitting-room window.

How long before his eye roved to the flesh with which the world was so abundant? If he had to satisfy his urges, would his conscience allow himself the occasional, carefully controlled fling?

It would, he decided.

It was part of the male condition. A genetic defect.

Peter walked to the front door and slid the key into the lock. He stepped into the sitting room as Beauty slipped past him and out of the house.

41

The bus stopped again. Beauty didn't mind the traffic. She was early for the shift at the care home. She'd washed, dressed and left the house as soon as it was light, glad to get out of her bedroom and be among other people. The white woman in a fast-food restaurant uniform sitting next to her leaned into the aisle to see why they weren't moving.

Beauty rested her head against the window and the voices returned from the night before.

'Tui amarray arr derchtay nai.' You'll never see Mum again.

Her brother's hand on her shoulder.

'Take your fucking hands off her.'

Where had the lady learned to speak like that?

She's white. They can say what they like.

Thass good, aynit?

'You do not have to put up with this.'

The woman was right.

Good she said it.

Beauty shuddered at the rage in her brother's face and lifted her head from the vibrations of the window. What did the white lady really know anyway? Beauty didn't understand what Kate's mother had done that was so terrible, but maybe they had problems too. *White stuff.* She looked at the white faces on the bus around her, women in their fifties on their way to supermarket jobs, and rested her head against the window again.

'*Homla's coming! You got to be there . . . or you'll never see Mum again.*'

Her brother's words were less scary with other people around. She'd turned over in bed a thousand times that night, sat up, smoked, and lain down again. Her head spun at what she had to do; the future; the choices she had to make. The white bloke was right. She was free to make choices and control her future. But what if he was right about the other stuff he had said?

There is no God.

And she had jerked up and smoked another cigarette in the light of the city sky falling on her bed.

From the window, Beauty stared at the reflection of the bus in a car showroom. Her eyes pricked with tiredness. She'd managed to sleep the night before but it hadn't seemed any different from being awake. Her head had felt heavy, something pressing inside, the same faces and questions swirling around her.

Who would make sure that Sharifa did well at school, that no one forced her to marry a freshie or an old man?

'*Get your fucking hands off her!*'

When would she be with her mother again?

'*You'll never see us again.*'

And she'd arrived at the place the white woman had shown her on the computer, with the green grass and the chickens and the stream. And for a few moments in the darkness of a stranger's house she'd managed to stroke the sheep and shoo away the cockerels scratching at the flower-beds, a dog at her side wherever she went.

Dogs is haram.

So what?

They were almost people, too. If only they could talk.

And she'd shaken her head and whispered aloud in the dark: *I am going loony*. And the ducks on the river at the bottom of the garden faded.

Anyway, could she live in a place like that and not think about . . . *stuff*?

Could she start a new life alone in a different city?

Why not? Lots of people did.

White people, though. Not Asians.

You'll never see us again.

She closed her eyes.

If only I could stay like this forever, in the dark behind my eyes.

And as she'd turned in the night, the sheet had wrapped itself around her like a shroud.

It felt cool and clean, and the spinning in her head stopped.

The bus lurched to a halt and she opened her eyes.

'For fook's sake,' a man said behind her.

Beauty pushed the tea trolley back into the empty kitchen and loaded the dirty cups and saucers into the dishwasher, relieved to have something to keep her from thinking. She enjoyed serving tea in the morning. The old people woke to the noise of rattling plates and teaspoons as she bumped into the sitting room.

Later she made a round upstairs with Maria to change the bed linen. The rooms were small, some of the sheets soiled from the night before.

Maria punched a pillow into a clean pillowcase.

'I kicked 'im out like you told me,' she said.

Beauty was smoothing down the blanket. Kicked who out?

Her boyfriend! I didn't tell her to kick him out.

'The basstud took all my stuff to Cash Converters – me jewellery, stereo, me fookin' MP3 player – the fookin' lot.'

Beauty stopped at the door clutching the dirty sheets. What trouble had she caused now?

'You gonna get it all back?' she asked. Maria joined her in the corridor.

'My brother's gonna sort 'im out,' she said.

Beauty took the clean linen from the trolley and followed Maria into the next room in silence. People she didn't even know would get hurt and Maria had lost all her belongings.

Cuz of me, aynit.

After lunch she went into the dining room to clean tables. There was only one resident there, talking to a social worker, or someone like that, so she thought it would be OK to carry on if she was quiet. Beauty moved around the tables squirting cleaning liquid, rubbing and wiping as she went. She liked the jobs she could do without worrying whether she was getting them right. Like making the tea, and helping the *buddhi* get dressed.

But Maria's story continued to bother her, and the part she had played in it.

She smiled at the old lady as she passed, the one who watched for the postman from the sitting-room window every morning. The health visitor, or whatever she was, a large woman bulging out of a blue trouser suit, sat opposite her.

'. . . he couldn't come,' Beauty heard the woman say. She spoke as if the old lady was deaf.

'So how have you been since I was last here?'

'Oh, quite well, thank you, dear.'

'And the staff are looking after you?'

'Oh, yes.'

'Have they been keeping you busy?'

'Yes, yes – we had a nice sing-song the other day.'

Beauty carried on wiping. The large woman sounded bored. If she didn't like old people why was she doing this job?

'They cut your hair as well?'

She talked to the *buddhi* like she was an idiot.

'And are they giving you enough to drink? Water's very good for you – it was on the *Today* programme this morning.'

Beauty saw the woman turn, and noticed the irritation on her face.

'Could you please bring my mother a glass of water?'

Beauty didn't understand. Where was her mother? There was only the old lady she was talking to, who lived in the home. The people here didn't have children. How could the fat woman be her daughter?

'What's wrong with you?' the woman asked her. 'What are you gawping at?'

Beauty stood open-mouthed. 'That's your . . .' She pointed, the cloth still in her hand.

'She's my mother, yes. I'm hardly going to visit someone else's, am I? Can't you see she wants a drink of water? Don't you people do your jobs properly?' She turned back to the old lady opposite her. 'Mum, what's this one like? Do I need to have a word with the manager about her?'

The woman's mouth moved, but Beauty couldn't hear anything.

That's her daughter!

Blood pounded in her ears and her chest felt painful.

They got kids!

She couldn't breathe; sparks drifted before her eyes.

What about the others?

What about Ethel?

*

Ethel was sitting on the edge of her bed, a framed photo in her hands. They dropped to her lap as Beauty appeared in the doorway.

'What's happened, dear?'

Ethel followed her gaze to the picture and turned it so that Beauty could see the faded image of a young woman with curly, shoulder-length hair lying in a field beside a baby girl in white knickers and a cotton hat. A young, dark-haired man in a suit stood behind them.

'He was a handsome chap, my Arthur. A good man. Twenty-five years ago, he passed away.'

Beauty was sorry for her husband, but had to know about the baby.

'Was that your daughter?'

'Yes, dear. That's Margaret – she was such a sweet child.'

'How did she die?'

'Heavens! She's not dead, dear. Whatever made you think that? She lives in Leicester. She's married to an engineer. I see her every month or so.'

Beauty searched the old lady's face for an answer. 'Why are you living here?'

'She couldn't look after me,' Ethel said. 'I'm a bit of a handful, I'm afraid. She takes me out to tea once a month and I go to hers for Christmas and New Year.' She winked. 'Between you and me, I prefer to stay here.'

Beauty closed her mouth and tried to swallow. 'Have them other people got kids too?'

'Yes, most of them. Why?'

Beauty felt her legs tremble and the room begin to swirl around her.

Al-lāh, help me!

A hand touched her shoulder and she heard a man's voice. *'What's the matter with her?'* A sharp smell made her open her eyes.

She was sitting in the armchair. Norris Winterton knelt beside her and passed a small brown bottle under her nose again.

'I think I've upset her,' Ethel said.

Norris got to his feet slowly. He poured a glass of water at the sink and handed it to Beauty.

'What's she been telling you?' he asked her, sitting on the edge of the bed next to Ethel.

Beauty took the glass and looked into his kind grey eyes.

That most people here got kids.

'I was just showing her a picture of Arthur and my Margaret, that's all,' Ethel said. 'She thought Margaret was dead, bless her!'

'She may as well be, for all you see her,' Norris said. 'Shocked, were you?' he asked Beauty. 'These old fools think their children give a damn about them!'

Beauty saw the anger in his eyes.

'Left to rot in this bloody place. You know the smell in the sitting room? Half of them piss where they sit. Not enough staff. They've only got four of those bloody tarts for thirty of us. Is that enough?' His voice rose, his face growing redder.

'Norris, stop it! You're scaring her,' Ethel said.

'Where are your children and grandchildren?' he shouted.

He stood up and headed for the door, turned to say something else and grabbed for the doorframe to keep himself upright, reaching to open his shirt with a shaking hand. Beauty jumped up, her head clear, and guided the old man to the armchair. He sat down heavily, struggling for breath.

'Run and fetch Maria, dear,' Ethel said to Beauty, reaching for the alarm beside her bed. 'Tell her Norris is having one of his turns.'

Maria rushed past her on the stairs.

'Find Louise! Tell her to bring his medicine from the office and phone an ambulance – quick!'

Beauty waited outside Norris's room for the paramedics to finish. They'd been with him for half an hour. Maria had told her not to worry. It happened two or three times a month, she said. He was always getting himself in a bother about something or other. But Beauty knew that it was her fault for upsetting him.

What if the man died?

Please, God, don't let him die. Allah, amar zan néughia. Take my heart instead.

A man in a yellow and green uniform came out of the room.

Please, God. Please, God.

With rest and quiet he'd be OK, the man said. They'd stabilized his breathing for now, but they shouldn't let him get excited. It was bad for his heart.

42

Beauty stared at the shoulders of the man in the seat in front of her. She'd stayed outside Norris's small bedroom until he awoke to make sure that he was all right.

It was my fault.

She hadn't wanted to leave Ethel alone either, ever again, but Maria had told her to go home.

Ethel said she would see her the next day, and not to worry about the silly old folk in the home: they did get visits from their children, but no one liked to talk about it. It wasn't fair on those who never saw theirs. Beauty felt dizzy again as she listened to the elderly lady.

Never saw their children!

What was the point of having them?

The bus jerked forward in the traffic and the radiator blew hot air from under her seat. Beauty felt sick. She pressed the stop button and got up when the bus slowed.

It was a long way to the town centre but she didn't mind. She wanted to walk and walk, and not think about what she had to do.

The wind rushed through the branches of the trees overhead.

Most of them got kids.

She glanced up . . .

'She may as well be dead, for all you see her.'

. . . and walked faster . . .

'If you die I hope they don't show me your face.'

. . . beyond the bus and the cars that had stopped at the traffic lights, until the trees and their ghosts ended.

An old man passed her with a walking stick, a small dog by his side which looked at her; and a white-haired lady in a faded pink raincoat and loose tights.

'I'm a bit of a handful, I'm afraid.'

It was getting dark. The pain in her foot slowed her down. Cars crawled past with the faces of children staring from windows. Beauty tried not to look at them.

White way, your kids put you in a house full of strangers and leave you there to die? She'd never heard of that before. Until the end, you stayed with your parents; you cared for them, dressed them and cleaned them; they needed help, like children, so you helped them, like they had done for you.

God said that's your job to look after your parents. That's what we're here for.

But what did she know, a dumb girl who believed in God? That white guy, Peter, had looked at her like he felt sorry for her. If white people's laws were based on *Ehudi* and Christian stuff, like he said, why did they throw their parents away when they got old?

Didn't they have laws for looking after their mum and dad?

Is that what people meant by being free?

Your kids gonna look after you one day?

In the town centre she walked close to the shop fronts and looked ahead for her brothers. She didn't need to hear Dulal's threats again; she knew them by heart. There was only one way out now, only one thing to do to stop her family hassling her. And knowing made her feel lighter, like she had felt in her dream, when all the pain had stopped.

At the orange football stadium she turned right into Linton Road and stopped in front of the Asian Women's Centre. She looked up at the windows of the three-storey building. Was the runaway with the rucksack still sitting in the corner? The playground of the primary school opposite was empty. Where was the little girl with the plait?

From Craddock Street she made her way to Mark's house through the side streets and narrow passageways of Graiseley, avoiding the eyes of passers-by.

Peter stood outside his house, lit a cigarette and leaned back against the wall. Kate said the smoke was giving her a headache while she packed her clothes. She was leaving him. *For good.* Peter couldn't decide whether he was happy or not. The realization of his long-hoped-for split-up had caught him by surprise. His 'wanting-her-to-stay' and 'looking-forward-to-seeing-her-after-work' had been short-lived. Not even a day. Confronted with his internet searches, including some of the pictures, he had at first tried to lie his way out before realizing it was useless and that it was better to let her rage run its course. Besides, 'it was a junk mail link I followed' seemed a feeble excuse when faced with the mass of pages she had found. Nor was moral outrage at the invasion of his privacy an option, judging by the *anger and hurt* she said she was feeling.

What kind of sicko had she been going out with? she'd demanded to know. Was that what he got up to as soon as her back was turned? It had been *so* humiliating to find out that her boyfriend would rather look at *that*, pointing to the screen, than have sex with her.

What could he say? That he'd been bored one night and decided to look at the worst of human sexual depravity? He'd kept to it as a line of defence. Did she really think he fantasized about midgets sticking their feet up his arse, or having clothes pegs attached to his scrotum?

What about all the Asian women he'd been looking at? It made her feel so *worthless and unwanted*, she'd sobbed.

Peter had tried to comfort her, but she'd screamed at him to get his filthy hands off her. Instead he said things like 'I can't handle this any more' and 'I don't know what I'm doing with my life', had even clutched his head for dramatic effect. And then he made the mistake of asking her if anyone else had seen it, which provoked another outburst of tears and recriminations. Peter had felt himself becoming aroused again at her misery, but it hadn't seemed opportune to make this fact known to her. Kate was alternately furious, hurt, dismissive and confident, depending on the nature of the 'home truths' she thought he needed to know. Peter had tried to appear suitably chastened. Indeed, it hadn't been one of his most splendid moments.

He'd slept on the sofa that night and never did find out if Beauty had been there when Kate had made her discoveries. Had the two women looked at the fruits of his internet searches together? What if Beauty told Mark that he was some kind of sexual deviant? What if Mark got together an angry mob of torch-bearing local residents to hammer on his door in the middle of the night? Should he move? Peter thanked God that he hadn't allowed himself to indulge in any online schoolgirl uniforms, and then felt embarrassed to have invoked Him in such a sordid affair.

He flicked the butt of the cigarette into the road. Jesus! Was he becoming religio-superstitious himself?

Peter looked up the street and saw Beauty rounding the corner. Even if she hadn't seen the porn, was there still a chance that she might take up his invitation to find somewhere to live together?

Beauty didn't notice the white guy until he stepped in front of her. She'd had enough of this *shaitan* and his devil words.

Ethel.

That's where his ideas ended up.

Peter could see Kate in the sitting room through the net curtains.

'Did you manage to think about what I said?' he asked Beauty, as she moved round him.

Beauty turned to face him and looked into his pale face and bloodshot eyes. She remembered everything he'd said.

'Yeah. I just seen your *free*.'

Peter watched her disappear into Mark's house. What the hell was she talking about? His treatment of Kate? The porn? Or had she been referring to something else?

It could have been anything, he realized.

A light rain began to fall. A siren flashed past at the end of the street.

Peter waited for Kate to emerge from the house. Was that it between them now?

When the front door opened he moved to take the bag she was holding.

'I don't need your help, thank-you-very-much.'

He followed her to her car, unsure whether he felt the usual guilt at hurting her, shame at the porn, or neediness after the withering look from Beauty. Did it matter? He wanted Kate to stay. There was something different about her, as if she'd woken up after years.

'Is that *it*?' he said, as she lowered the bag into the boot. 'Why don't you stay? Can't we talk about this?'

Kate slammed the lid shut. 'What's there to talk about, Peter? You tell me you love me – and I catch you drooling over a . . . a vulnerable young girl . . . and all that filth . . . You know, I feel really sorry for you.' Her anger was restrained.

She took an envelope from her coat pocket and headed towards Mark's house.

Peter looked about him at the houses in Prole Street, up through the drizzle to the grey sky, sighed, and went indoors.

43

Mark Aston sat in the armchair by the window of his sitting room and watched the street through the torn, grey net curtain. Peter was talking to a woman as she put a suitcase into the boot of her car. It must have been his missus, the one he said he wanted to dump. He was pointing to Mark's house.

Mark flicked the ash from his roll-up into an empty beer can and watched the woman walk past his window. She looked expensive, tall and fit with a good figure. He opened another can from the box at his feet and went to the door.

Kate was waiting with the envelope in her hand. She'd told Peter to go inside. It was none of his business why she wanted to see Beauty.

'Hiya!' she said as the door opened.

A rough-looking type stood in front of her with shaven dark hair and sideburns, fading home-made tattoos on his wiry forearms, and a beer can held between two fingers and thumb of a large, dirty hand.

'Oright?'

'Hi, is Beauty here?'

'Ar,' he said. 'Her's asleep. D'you wanna coom in?'

Mark took a swig of beer from the can. She seemed like a nice enough bird. Not his type, mind.

Kate felt eaten up by his eyes. She could tell this brute had never met a woman like her before, and flicked her hair. She was still desirable.

'No, it's OK. Could you give her this, please?' She handed Mark the envelope. 'Tell her I'm sorry I couldn't wait. I've got to drive all the way back to London tonight,' she said.

'K. Sowund.'

Mark slid the envelope into his back pocket and watched her hips sway as she walked to her car. He ignored the two *Pakistannies* in the Vauxhall Astra on the other side of the street. No point letting them know he'd clocked them. He switched off the sitting-room light and returned to the chair near the window to see what they did. These two looked different, but the car was the same as on the first day.

Mark knew he could handle them on his own and it would be a damn shame not to give them a proper beating. But this was Asian shit and there was no telling what he'd start. These fuckers were crazy when it came to their sisters. The Bengali lad he'd padded up with in Liverpool had got seven years for knifing his sister's boyfriend. Mark had listened to the stories because there was nothing else to do for twenty-three hours a day. *Proud of hisself, the fookin' prick.* Someone else would have battered him sooner than Mark had done.

He could talk to Bob about it but didn't want to involve him. He'd deal with it himself. But he'd have to move house quickly in case things turned nasty. And Beauty. And where would he get the money from? A landlord would want two months' rent upfront. If Beauty chipped in a couple of hundred they might manage with what was left of the money he'd made on the barriers, but he'd rather have done it on his own . . . to show her that he could take care of them both.

His eyes strayed from the Pakistanis to the other cars in the street and stopped at Pete's Fiat Punto under the street lamp. Four hundred quid he'd get in a chop shop for that. Tonight, if he wanted it. Maybe more for a two-year-old car. He'd have enough cash for them to move straightaway. Beauty wouldn't even know he'd gone.

Not while those two were still out there, though.

Mark watched the two men get out of their car. As they began to cross the street and come towards the house, he ran through to the kitchen and into the yard. The dogs clawed at the insides of their kennels, but he went to the last one. Satan had been used for fighting, and although Bob swore blind it was a Staffy, Mark knew different. The dog was leaner and had the flatter head and squarer jaw of a pit bull. Mark didn't trust the animal, and never took it anywhere without a muzzle. This time he wouldn't need a muzzle.

Beauty had stopped in the kitchen to fill a pint glass with water before going up to her bedroom. She was glad Mark hadn't been there when she got home. He would have noticed something wrong. She just wanted to sleep forever, to go away and never come back. She was scared, too, of what she was about to do.

She sat on the bed and looked around the room at her belongings, her two salwars hanging on the clothes rail, a pair of sandals, her few pieces of make-up on the bedside table and the packet of antidepressants next to her toilet bag. Not even a photo of her mum or sister.

You come into this world with nothing . . .

Afterwards she lay back on the bed and closed her eyes. She was sorry for the trouble she'd caused people: the white guy, Mark, and his neighbour, his girlfriend, the girl and the old man at the care home. Her mum and brothers. It wasn't their fault either. They were just doing what they were supposed to. They didn't invent the rules.

Life aynt fair.

Beauty kept her eyes shut and rubbed her stomach, full from water.

Toba, toba astaghfirullah.

Mark held Satan by the collar with one hand, the other gripping the dog's powerful jaws. He struggled with it along the dark passageway. The beast could feel his excitement. He edged forward to the corner of the house until he was close enough to hear whispered voices at his front door. A low wall extended from the end of the passageway to the pavement. If he could make the few steps without Satan going for him, the two Pakistanis would be pinned against the front door. If they tried to jump over the wall to get away from the dog they'd have to get through him, or go up the passageway.

No one would see.

He stepped out of the darkness.

Beauty felt the blackness grow around her. Her head felt light and the pain left her as she floated down through the bed.

Was this dying?

It felt nice. Quiet and cool, but not scary any more.

She opened her eyes as she slipped down.

How strange it was . . . so light . . . and free.

Shapes moved in the swirling darkness, figures emerged and disappeared into the shadows. A cloudy hand took form and a voice came to her from far away.

'You'll come back and talk to me, won't you, dear?'

Beauty tried to reach out as she passed but her fingers slipped through the old lady's hand.

A grey face billowed out of the darkness, black holes where its eyes should have been.

'My mum's an utter bitch.'

Beauty shrank back as the mouth spewed out the milk that the woman had drunk from her mother's breast. It would fill the lady's grave and drown her when she died. Beauty wanted to save her but knew she couldn't. That's what happened when you cursed the mother who had carried you for nine months inside her. You could never pay her back, not for one kick you had given her. If you carried her on your back for a hundred years it still wouldn't be enough!

What did she do for her mum?

Strange naked creatures writhed in the shadows around her, their legs entwined; beasts with two backs, moaning and grunting. She tried to close her eyes, but she had no body any more, just a sense of being.

Her mum sat in an armchair alone, her face lined and aged.

'Where are my grandchildren?'

Beauty cried out but no sound came and her mother vanished.

She slipped past a young girl in a red wedding sari. The girl's eyes begged her to stay. Sharifa! She was getting married! Where was her husband? Beauty reached out but her sister turned away, her image fading.

Her brother's face appeared close to hers, wet with tears. Why was he crying?

'You didn't do nothing wrong. It wasn't your fault,' she tried to say. Her brother heard her, and smiled.

She stopped floating, as if she had reached the bottom of something. There was only darkness around her.

But when she felt the baby inside her, the faces of her family surrounded her again, warm and smiling.

'Why didn't you tell us?'
'A new life is more important than anything.'
'Leave her alone now.'
'She's going to be a mother.'

A dog appeared next to her and nosed at her hand.
'Where am I?' Beauty asked.
'Y'm free,' said the dog.

44

Mark washed the blood from his hands in the kitchen sink and flattened the piece of skin on his knuckle gouged up by the Pakistani's teeth. His heartbeat returned to normal.

The two had been slow to react. They'd stared at the snarling pit bull and pressed back against the door.

Where was she? They just wanted to talk to her.

But one of the cunts had a bottle of accelerant in his hand. So Mark didn't have a fucking clue what they were on about. Mate.

Satan sprang, open-jawed, at the nearest man's thigh. The other bloke scrambled over the low wall as Mark's fist smashed into his nose and teeth. Mark would have set about him on the floor but his mate had managed to kick the dog away and hobble to his car, and he had to catch Satan. You couldn't have a fucking pit bull loose in the street.

He managed to grab Satan's collar as the dog ran past him but had to punch it in the head to stop it from writhing and twisting to bite him. He dragged it back to the passageway, slipping when he aimed a kick at the Pakistani as the man stumbled away clutching his bleeding face. But it was only a glancing blow.

What with holding the dog 'n' that.

Mark pulled shut the iron gate and ran to the over-revving car as it struggled out of its parking space. He put a nice dent in the passenger door, stood side-on to the window, and shattered it with his elbow before the driver bumped past the car in front and accelerated away.

Almost ran over me fookin' foot.

He waited until the lights had disappeared and silence had returned to the street, and looked around at the windows of the neighbouring houses. If anyone had been watching from behind their curtains . . . well, he'd just been defending himself.

Innit.

His elbow was hurting now and he couldn't straighten his arm easily. His right hand had started to swell, too. Mark dried his hand on his trousers, took a can from the fridge and went into the darkened sitting room. He took a long drink of beer and managed to roll a loose cigarette with his swelling hand. He pulled the curtain to one side and peered into the street. Those two wouldn't come back in a hurry. They'd be in A&E for hours. He'd bring a couple of dogs into the house later, just in case. They'd keep him company if he spent the night down here, and wake him up if someone came to the door. Pete's Fiat Punto was outside and he still had Dave's number in Burntwood. It would be risky going over there, but if he left it till dawn there'd be less Old Bill on the roads. He could park outside the chop shop and wait at the café for Dave to bring him the money for the motor.

He'd be back in Wolves by ten o'clock.

What would he tell Beauty? Wouldn't she want to know why he was in a hurry to move? Would she come with him?

Mark was glad she hadn't woken up. She didn't need to know.

*

At midnight he tapped on her door. He'd noticed the light on when he went to the toilet, but no noise had come from her room all evening. He knocked again. Mark turned the handle, pushed the door open a few inches and went in.

Beauty lay on the bed fully dressed, her arms thrown wide. The care had passed from her brow, her forehead was free of lines, her lips slightly parted and smiling.

Beauty opened her eyes and looked at the man standing at the foot of her bed.

It felt right for him to be there, near her. The pain and heaviness in her head was gone.

Mark let himself be looked at.

'What happened to your hand?' she asked him.

'Nothing . . . one of the dogs had a giw at me.'

Mark picked up the mini hi-fi he'd found that morning and sat by the window to keep an eye on the street. The stereo had no power cable, but he reckoned he could fix it. He decided not to mention moving house until he got back from selling the car. It wouldn't be any bother to pinch. He'd disabled the alarm the first day he had met Peter.

Beauty sat on the sofa with her feet tucked under her, sipping from the mug of tea he had made. She watched him open the back of the stereo and pick out the small screws with his large fingers. It felt comfortable being with him, as if she could say anything she wanted to him. And she liked watching him fix his machines.

'Where did you learn to do them stuff?' she asked.

Mark looked at Beauty as his fingers felt their way past circuit boards inside the stereo. 'Dunno, just picked it up, I guess.'

'Did your dad teach you?'

'Me old man? He waar there!' He cut a piece of gaffer tape with his teeth. 'I'll teach my kids though,' he said. 'A girl 'n' all. It's useful stuff. People chuck all sorts of things out cuz they caar fix 'em – computers, the lot, man.'

He gestured around the room at the various pieces of equipment wired together. His integrated computer-stereo-TV-DVD components had all come from the re-cyke or people's front gardens.

'You gonna have kids one day?' she asked.

They exchanged glances and Beauty looked away.

'Hope so,' he said.

Mark wanted to tell her. He'd never talked to anyone about it before, not even his ex. That slag.

'Me girlfriend lost a babby when I were nineteen. I'd've loved that kid to bits, man, and stayed outta jail 'n' all, I reckon.'

A screw dropped to the floor and Mark was glad to look down and fumble for it.

Beauty didn't speak. She didn't want to ask what had happened. If he wanted to tell her, he would.

'Had a miscarriage, dey she?'

Mark pushed a plug into the socket of an extension lead at his feet and switched on the stereo. The standby light came on and he smiled at Beauty with satisfaction.

'Found that this morning. There ay much wrong with it,' he said. 'Just the CD drive to sort out.'

Beauty smiled back. He was a good man. She'd had to trust him from the moment he'd saved her in the street.

Mark prised off the front of the stereo.

'What about you?' he asked without looking up. 'You planning on having lots of kids?'

Beauty remembered the baby she had dreamed of inside her and the faces of her family around her.

Leave her alone now.

She's going to be a mother.

Insh'allah.

'If God gives them to me,' she said.

Mark nodded as he placed the drawer of the CD player on the windowsill. He pulled back a corner of the net curtain. The street was quiet in the dull street light.

His hand trembled as he put down the clips to the sliding door of the stereo.

Fook it, giw for it.

'Does it have to be with a Muslim bloke?' he asked.

He tried to make the question sound casual . . . her being from a different culture. But he felt his face turn red as he stared into the stereo, waiting for her to answer.

Beauty watched him. She'd never been able to picture a husband's face. But she was free to choose now. She had everything she needed: work and somewhere to live; she'd begun to read; she could do what she wanted. And he was the best man she'd ever met. She wouldn't meet another like him. He would be a good husband and father and make her happy. She'd cook for him and clean the house while he repaired things in the sitting room. He'd work hard, they would have everything they needed in a small house and she'd be safe with him.

'He has to be an honest man, who works hard and looks after his parents,' Beauty said.

Mark had no idea where his father was, he told her. There was just his mam, who didn't seem that bothered about seeing him at the minute. Not that Mark could blame her. He'd let her down too many times.

'I ay gonna do that again.'

Beauty rested her head on the arm of the sofa.

*

Mark plugged in the soldering iron and waited for it to heat up.

'Can I ask you summing?' he said.

Beauty wasn't embarrassed any more in front of him.

'Will you take your headscarf off?'

She sat up and pulled the edge of her scarf over the tips of her ears. 'My hair's a mess. That's why I wear it,' she said.

Mark dripped solder onto a piece of card and held the tips of the copper wires in a spot of the silvery liquid.

'Do' matter. It's more natural,' he said, looking round.

Beauty wanted him to see her.

Her chest and neck flushed as she slipped the scarf from her head.

45

The morning was grey over the roofs of the terraces opposite, the dark slates polished by the rain.

Beauty put the lady's envelope with the train ticket and the address of the refuge in her breast pocket. She closed the front door behind her, slipped her arms through the straps of her rucksack and looked up at his window.

Mark Aston heard the front door close and pulled back the curtain in his bedroom. She looked up, raised her hand and smiled. He watched until her rucksack disappeared at the end of the street, and let the curtain fall back.

At the end of Prole Street Beauty headed towards the mosque on the corner of Stafford Road. The rain spotted her face but she didn't mind. The shops in Graiseley were closed, their metal shutters pulled to the floor. Paper stuck to the wet road and pavement.

It was too early for the white people walking their dogs.

Mark sat on the edge of the bed and looked at his pale, thin legs against the mauve carpet. The dump valve on the black bloke's car from down the road sneezed as it changed gear passing the house.

She'd gone.

She had his phone number if she ever needed anything. It was all he could say when she told him she was leaving. He understood why.

He'd call her from time to time to check she was doing all right, he said.

And who knew . . . perhaps he would see her again?

Mark was glad he hadn't stolen the car. If he'd been pulled over driving to Burntwood he'd be heading straight back to jail. His mam wouldn't have spoken to him again. At least if the Pakistanis came back, Beauty wouldn't be there. He could look after himself.

His mam.

Should he go and see her?

Nah, he'd get a job first – show her he was working and invite her to the house, now that it was clean. If Poles and Kurds could work fourteen hours a day on minimum wage, so could he. He'd be better off than getting dole and he wouldn't need the housing benefit any more. He could use the money to build decent kennels out the back, start the breeding as a sideline and save up for a mechanic's van while he waited for his ban to expire. In a few months he could be up and running, could even think about appealing his driving ban . . . and trying to make his mam proud of him.

Would he see Beauty again?

At the bend in Dunstall Avenue Beauty saw figures crossing the road towards the mosque. Old men in long shirts and skullcaps passed through the high gates, and young men in Pakistani clothes and trainers, with beards and shaved upper lips.

Did that make them holy?

But they didn't scare her any more. Not now that she was free.

Mark had read Kate's note aloud to her. They were expecting her at the refuge in Derby. She just had to give them a ring before she left. The address was written on a scrap of paper attached to the train ticket and a fifty-pound note. She'd have all the peace and quiet she needed, a long way from this city, far away from her brothers. She'd stroke the horses she had seen in the photos, hold the chickens in her arms and plant things in the vegetable garden. She'd go for long walks in the fields around the house. But better than anything else, she'd have time to think about herself, to find out what she wanted to do with her life.

Beauty thanked the white lady in her heart. She hoped the lady would be forgiven for the wicked things she'd said about her own mother. If her mother didn't, neither would God.

At the Stafford Road roundabout she turned away from the train station, into Fox's Lane, towards home.

Was it too soon to go back? Beauty counted the days since she had left.

Ten.

Would they give up the wedding talk?

Or was it too late? Would they take her back? Would her brother lose it and kick her out again?

Bonemill Street was quiet. The road twisted under railway bridges and ran alongside the canal. She looked at the broken windows and smokeless chimneys of the factories around her, at the rubble and rusting iron gates and forecourts overgrown with weeds.

Beauty's chest and throat tightened. She took in deep breaths to calm her heartbeat.

They gonna turn their backs on me?

No. Her older brother loved his family. He'd do anything to get her back. Wouldn't he?

At the bridge on Cannock Road, she stopped to look down at the dark water of the canal.

What if the old man aynt given up?

He can't force me. They know that . . . I'll leave again.

But was it really her destiny to live alone and not look after her parents as they grew old?

Better not to live.

Toba, toba, astaghfirullah.

The rain came down hard at the end of Grimstone Street. She looked around for shelter and ran to a telephone box.

It was the same one from the night she'd left home. The handset had been repaired and the dial tone purred in her ear. She replaced the receiver on its cradle, rested her head against the window and watched the rain run down the glass. That night she had cried to God for help. He had listened to her and sent Mark, Allah give him a good life.

But she still needed His help.

They gonna give up? They gonna try and take me back to Bangladesh?

No, that wouldn't happen now. She'd tell them she had a job, that she would be expected at work, that she had friends who would phone if they didn't hear from her. They couldn't lock her in a room.

But she didn't want to threaten anyone. She'd *salaam* the old man, touch his feet and beg his forgiveness. It wasn't his fault. He'd been poisoned by the mullah's pervert brother's lies that she was flirting with men.

Anyway, *Bhai-sahb* would make the decision.

Dulal aynt gonna tell me to marry no one.

He'd agree to keep her there. She was still young. She could stay unmarried until she was twenty-five before she was considered old.

They want me back.

And they aynt gonna hit me no more.
They aynt gonna swear at me neither.
Had she given them an excuse by acting loony? Had
she flirted with boys to wind them up? They said she did
it, so she did it. It wasn't her mum's fault either. How
many mothers like hers were there, sitting in kitchens
complaining of aches and pains, old in their fifties? She
hadn't had the strength to fight for her daughter.
'You'll never see your children's eyes.'
She didn't mean it. They told her to say them things.
But could everyone pretend nothing had happened?
It didn't matter, as long as they let her look after her
parents. Asian girls didn't want to do it these days. Not
the ones born in this country. How long before there
were care homes for old Asians, too? Did they exist
already? She shivered at the thought of old Bengalis
sitting in a line of armchairs. She'd heard her cousin-
brothers' wives and how they talked about their mothers-
in-law. How could she trust anyone else to do *her* job
properly?

The rain had stopped. She pushed open the door of the
phone box and headed towards the squat block of flats
on the grassy mound.
The shop next to the Chick King Burger Bar was open.
Beauty wanted a cigarette before she went up to the flat.
Last one. She'd throw the rest away. A girl shouldn't
smoke.
The Jamaican guy with the long-eared hat and padded
jacket stood at the counter paying for a can of Kestrel
Super.
'Yo, sister!'
She stood next to him in front of the chocolate bars.
'Hi.'
He looked at her from headscarf to sandals.

'Whe' ya bin?'

'Staying at a friend's.'

'Ah well, welcome home.'

Beauty stood at the bottom of the concrete stairwell and lit the cigarette.

Al-lāh help me, whatever happens. Give them Rahmut. Let them understand.

Would He still help her?

Yes.

She was making her future, like the white bloke said. She *was* free. Before she wasn't, and now she was. How?

Take your fucking hands off her!

That's what the lady said.

You do not have to put up with this.

She'd said that, too.

Al-lāh, let me look after my parents.

Don't let me come back down these steps with nothing.

She dropped the cigarette on the damp-stained paving and stepped on it. A boy ran down the stairs past her, his face hidden by the peak of his cap.

Beauty stopped at the foot of the last flight. Her legs shook. She gripped the cold handrail and pulled herself up the first step.

Wouldn't it be better if she stayed away? The little ones would get used to it. They'd forget her. She didn't have to go back home.

She closed the front door behind her quietly. The hall was empty. She breathed in the smell of home – last night's cooking and her father's cigarettes. Voices came from behind the closed kitchen door. She looked up the stairs. Her mother would still be asleep, but she hoped Dulal hadn't gone to bed yet.

Beauty walked along the corridor and stopped at the door. She could make out the low voice of her brother and the blur of shapes through the ribbed glass.

'*Asalaam alaikum.*'

Beauty Begum stood in the open doorway and looked at her brothers and sister: Dulal in his vest and pyjamas, his cheeks unshaven, Faisal's gelled, spiky hair and straight nose, the milk on his soft moustache, and Sharifa's thick hair, her eyes shining with contained excitement. The old man looked away.

Her younger brother closed his mouth. 'Sis,' he said.

Dulal kicked him under the table. 'What do you want?' he asked her.

Beauty's heart seemed to stop. Was he telling her to get out?

'I wanna look after Mum and Dad,' she said. And make sure Sharifa went to college and married a good man her own age. And everything else: the cooking and cleaning, until she went to sleep exhausted on the sofa. That was her job, wasn't it? A daughter's job.

Dulal looked at his sister, at the bag on her shoulders and the mobile phone in her hand. Her thumb hovered over the call button.

'You gonna get your *gora* to set his dogs on me, too?'

'What are you talking about?'

'You didn't see what he done last night?'

Beauty remembered the bruises on Mark's hand. What had happened?

'He aynt *my* white bloke,' she said.

Dulal Miah told the kids to go to the sitting room. Faisal looked disappointed, but followed his younger sister. The door closed behind them.

'You stayin'?' he asked her.

Beauty didn't move.

'That depends.'

She saw her brother's jaws clench. It wasn't good talking to him this way.

'I've got to go to work later,' she said.

Her brother snorted. *'Kun zagat?'*

'In a care home for white people. And in a place for Asian women.'

She saw him look again at the mobile phone in her hand. Good. Let him think she had arranged for someone to call her if she didn't turn up at work. Someone who would go to the police if she didn't answer the phone. Beauty thanked God again for having sent that other lady, too. *Take your fucking hands off her!*

'I aynt dumb no more, *Bhai-sahb*,' Beauty said. 'I learnt to read.'

Dulal grunted and sipped his tea. 'Go to work. No one's gonna stop you,' he said.

The old man mumbled something. Beauty wondered why he didn't speak. Had there been a fight?

'What about the mullah?' she asked.

Beauty stood in front of her father and brother and waited for an answer.

Her brother picked at the crumbs of toast on the table and rubbed them from his fingers onto the plate.

'I don't have to get married yet, *Bhai-sahb*. Tell Habib Choudhury's family you tried. Tell 'em I'm going to college to study something.'

She saw her brother smile. Or was he sneering at her?

You do not have to put up with this.

You're entitled to a life.

'Otherwise . . . I aynt stayin'.'

She could survive on her own now, she had a job, she

could read and work, she had somewhere to live and people to be with.

Dulal Miah stood up and stretched.

'We'll talk later,' he said.

He passed her on his way back to bed without looking at her. Her father got to his feet and shuffled to the fridge. Why didn't he say anything? Did Dulal make the decisions now?

Beauty slipped the rucksack from her shoulders as the children came back into the kitchen. She took the pot from the table and went to fill the kettle. The old man would want more tea.

Beauty asked Sharifa if she had prayed.

'Yes, sis.'

What would happen when Sharifa started looking at boys? Would her parents find her good husbands to choose from, or let her meet a boy at college and marry him?

'I prayed too,' Faisal said.

Beauty nodded her approval.

Why was he being sweet? Was the bullying and swearing over? What would Dulal say later? If he was going to kick her out he would have done it by now. But why would he do that? It was better to have her at home unmarried than not here at all.

'Eat,' Beauty said to the little ones. Sharifa ate her toast. Later, she would want to know everything Beauty had seen and heard, where she had been, and what white people's homes were like inside.

The old man shuffled out of the kitchen.

After the children had gone to school, she took more tea to him in the sitting room and put two pounds on the arm of his chair for cigarettes.

*

Later, Beauty watched from the window as he appeared from the stairwell below her and headed towards the shops in the rain. Her eyes ran along the doorways of the block of flats opposite, looking for signs of life. It was no longer a strange world. She'd been out there and was free now. No one could force her to do anything. She would look after her parents and make sure her sister married a good man one day.

She thought of Mark. She knew he understood. She'd left the money from the dole office on the pillow in the bedroom and wished she could have done more for him. He was a good man. The best.

She'd pray for him every day.

Outside, the sky was low and grey over the tower blocks. Beauty turned away from the window and went to make breakfast for her mother.

About the Author

© Stefano Luigi Moro

RAPHAEL SELBOURNE was born in Oxford in 1968. He lived in Italy for many years, where he worked variously as a teacher and translator before moving to the West Midlands in 2004.

Acknowledgements

My thanks to Tindal Street Press for publishing *Beauty*, and to DB for her help with all things Bengali.